Turn to th[e]
special Cass[ie]

Praise for the novels of
Cassie Edwards

"Excellent . . . an endearing story filled with heartwarming characters."
—*Under the Covers*

"Cassie Edwards pens simply satisfying Indian romances. . . . High adventure and a surprise season this Indian romance."
—*Affaire de Coeur*

"A fine writer . . . accurate. . . . Indian history and language keep readers interested."
—*Greeley Tribune* (CO)

"Edwards moves readers with love and compassion."
—*Bell, Book and Candle*

"Captivating . . . heartwarming, beautiful . . . a winner."
—*Rendezvous*

"Edwards consistently gives the reader a strong love story, rich in Indian lore, filled with passion and memorable characters. . . . Wonderful, unforgettable."
—*Romantic Times*

ALSO BY CASSIE EDWARDS

Midnight Falcon

Winter Raven

Sun Hawk

Thunder Heart

Silver Wing

Lone Eagle

Bold Wolf

Flaming Arrow

White Fire

Rolling Thunder

Wild Whispers

Wild Thunder

Wild Bliss

Wild Abandon

Wild Desire

Wild Splendor

Wild Embrace

Wild Rapture

Wild Ecstasy

FIRE CLOUD

Cassie Edwards

A SIGNET BOOK

SIGNET
Published by New American Library, a division of
Penguin Putnam Inc., 375 Hudson Street,
New York, New York 10014, U.S.A.
Penguin Books Ltd, 80 Strand,
London WC2R ORL, England
Penguin Books Australia Ltd, Ringwood,
Victoria, Australia
Penguin Books Canada Ltd, 10 Alcorn Avenue,
Toronto, Ontario, Canada M4V 3B2
Penguin Books (N.Z.) Ltd, 182–190 Wairau Road,
Auckland 10, New Zealand

Penguin Books Ltd, Registered Offices:
Harmondsworth, Middlesex, England

First published by Signet, an imprint of New American Library,
a division of Penguin Putnam Inc.

First Printing, November 2001
10 9 8 7 6 5 4 3 2 1

Copyright © Cassie Edwards, 2001
All rights reserved

REGISTERED TRADEMARK—MARCA REGISTRADA

Printed in the United States of America

Without limiting the rights under copyright reserved above, no part of
this publication may be reproduced, stored in or introduced into a
retrieval system, or transmitted, in any form, or by any means
(electronic, mechanical, photocopying, recording, or otherwise),
without the prior written permission of both the copyright owner and
the above publisher of this book.

PUBLISHER'S NOTE
This is a work of fiction. Names, characters, places, and incidents either
are the product of the author's imagination or are used fictitiously,
and any resemblance to actual persons, living or dead, business
establishments, events, or locales is entirely coincidental.

BOOKS ARE AVAILABLE AT QUANTITY DISCOUNTS WHEN USED TO PROMOTE
PRODUCTS OR SERVICES. FOR INFORMATION PLEASE WRITE TO PREMIUM
MARKETING DIVISION, PENGUIN PUTNAM INC., 375 HUDSON STREET, NEW YORK,
NEW YORK 10014.

If you purchased this book without a cover you should be aware that
this book is stolen property. It was reported as "unsold and
destroyed" to the publisher and neither the author nor the publisher
has received any payment for this "stripped book."

I lovingly dedicate *Fire Cloud* to my
beloved mother, Dorothy June Decker,
who has been gone from my life for so long now,
but who is always with me inside my heart
and in my precious memories of her
soft laughter and sweet smile.

—Cassie

Proud and Free

There was a people proud and free,
They stood beneath the sky,
They danced and sang upon the wind,
They watched their spirits fly.
Mother earth did give them life,
They dwelt on her with care,
Taking, always giving back,
To cherish what was fair.
Standing tall, strong, and brave,
They walked in harmony,
With nature and her boundless gifts,
A people proud and free.

—Elizabeth Henderson

Chapter 1

Minnesota—May 1853—"Moon When the Flowers Bloom"

As day waned along the Mississippi River, Fire Cloud, a ten-year-old Chippewa brave, knelt beside his campfire and added more wood.

Fire Cloud was fresh from a bath in the river and wore a breechclout, fringed and beaded leggings, and moccasins, all fashioned of tanned buckskin. His waist-length, coal-black hair was held back with a beaded band, and his copper face already showed signs of the intelligent man he would become.

Fire Cloud looked with longing toward a fresh mound of rocks beneath a weeping willow tree not far from where he had chosen to make camp, hoping that someone would come along and rescue him.

Beneath those river rocks that he had placed there himself lay his beloved mother, Rose Blossom.

Sadness filled his heart as he thought back to the day his mother had been banished from her Saint Croix band of Chippewa. She, a married woman, had been found guilty of having an affair with Gray Wind, a warrior from another Chippewa band.

And that was not her worst crime against her husband. The child that she had been carrying for eight months was discovered to be her lover's, not her husband's.

Tears came to Fire Cloud's eyes when he remembered the day before his mother's order of banishment. Fire Cloud's father and Gray Wind had had a duel with knives. His father had died. The other warrior was wounded, but not so severely that he would die.

On that day when he had lost his *gee-dah-dah*—father—and when his *gee-mah-mah*—mother—was told to leave and never return to their village again, Fire Cloud's grandfather, Chief Sitting Fox, had not wanted him to leave as well.

But Fire Cloud loved his mother too much to see her set out all alone and pregnant. And was he not now the man of the house? His mother's protector, Fire Cloud had heroically left with her.

And now he was also his brother's protector.

"*Ay-uh*—yes—a *gee-gee-kee-wayn-zee*—brother," he whispered, looking over at the tiny, blanket-wrapped bundle that lay in a makeshift cradle.

Fire Cloud's mother had given birth early, after only two days on their lonesome, sad journey. Following his mother's instructions, Fire Cloud had helped deliver the child. But Rose Blossom had lost too much blood and knew that she would not live even another hour. Before she died, she gave her newborn son a name, calling him Moon Shadow because he was born in the shadow of a bright, full moon.

She had also told Fire Cloud how to make porridge for the baby by boiling wild rice, and then how the infant could suck the porridge from small holes punched in an animal bladder that she had brought with her.

A good *nin-gwis*—son—and a good listener, he had learned the art of survival from his doting father. Fire Cloud had known how to make temporary lodging for himself and his brother.

He had cut bulrushes that he had found growing near the edge of a nearby lake, because his father had taught him that the bulrushes in the smaller lakes were the choicest since they were the least brittle.

He had made a wigwam of these bent saplings and covered them with hemlock boughs that he had fastened with bark ties so that the rain would not leak in.

Fire Cloud had lined the shelter with animal skins, and dug a firepit outside the tiny lodge for cooking and for keeping animals away. The floor of the wigwam he had covered with bark and the woven cattail mats that he found on the travois . . . the very travois that his mother had always dragged when she accompanied her husband on his long hunts.

Fire Cloud frowned when he recalled something else his mother had taught him. She had told him that a child who talked early was considered intelligent, and so to develop the baby's speech Fire Cloud should feed his brother the raw brains of small birds.

Even while stranded, he could not kill innocent birds and instead he had fed his brother nourishing liquid that he had taken from their eggs by poking small holes at each end.

Fire Cloud felt tears stinging his eyes, remembering his mother's final words. Just before she took her last breath, she had told Fire Cloud that if his baby brother lived, he should hang the placenta in a tree, or burn it.

He had placed it in the hollow of the very willow tree that overlooked his mother's grave so that, in a sense, her child would be with her forever. Fire Cloud had buried his mother close to where he made camp so that when he got too lonely he could sit and talk with her.

Sighing, Fire Cloud looked at the rabbit cooking slowly on a spit. He was thankful that his father had taught him how to survive on his own. Having claimed his father's bow and arrow as his, Fire Cloud knew that he and his brother would never go hungry.

His father had also taught him about his people's spirituality. He had told Fire Cloud that if he was ever alone and cried out for help, his prayers would be answered. It might be by the eagles or the bears, but whatever animal answered his prayers, Fire Cloud must listen well. It would be the spirit of a loved one speaking through the animal.

Fire Cloud *had* prayed, and when, soon after, he saw an eagle flying low overhead, he knew that he had just been visited by his father's spirit.

The eagle was now perched on a high branch of the willow tree as though it were there to give him comfort.

Fire Cloud felt that something was about to happen by the way the eagle kept looking downriver. It

FIRE CLOUD

was as though the majestic bird was watching for something—or someone.

At that very moment, Fire Cloud heard the sound of paddles dipping in the waters of the Mississippi.

A part of him was eager to be rescued, yet the young brave, who now had a brother to protect, also felt apprehensive. The river was the passageway for many sorts of men—white voyagers who carried their prime pelts to trading posts, enemy tribes, and white hunters who too often killed the red man, perhaps even a red child, for the sheer pleasure of doing so.

Afraid of the hunters most of all, Fire Cloud hurried to his feet and swept up his brother's cradle.

His heart pounding, he took his brother, who was thankfully sleeping, into the wigwam and hid him far behind his mother's precious belongings. He drew back a corner of his brother's blanket to provide him a passage for breathing. He knew that Moon Shadow would be warm enough in the blankets and his clothes made from rabbit and weasel skins.

Feeling confident that his brother was safe for as long as it might take the strangers to make their way past his campsite, Fire Cloud secured his father's sheathed hunting knife at his side and grabbed his prized bow.

Dragging a heavy quiver of arrows behind him, Fire Cloud crawled from the lodge and looked cautiously up into the willow tree for the eagle.

The bird had flown away.

Fire Cloud heard paddles splashing close now. He

knew that there was no way those who passed by today would not see his temporary home.

He looked heavenward and said a silent prayer that those who came today would save him and his brother from spending another night beside the Mississippi, where wolves howled, loons sang their eerie songs, and all sorts of creatures could be heard in the brush. Fire Cloud had been almost too afraid to sleep.

Fire Cloud's heart leapt as he looked back at the bright glow of the campfire. He could even smell the tantalizing aroma of the rabbit as it hung over the flames. If that scent did not attract the attention of passersby, nothing would!

"*Kitchi-Manitou*, please let them be friendly," Fire Cloud again prayed. He hoped that his father's spirit was near, protecting him and his brother.

When he saw the front of one canoe slide into view at the bend in the river, Fire Cloud still did not feel relief. The passengers had the same skin color as his, but that did not prove they were friends.

It did give him hope, though, that they would rescue him once they knew he was from the Saint Croix band of Chippewa, for his people were not known to be of a warring nature and had even kept a measure of peace recently with their natural enemy, the Lakota.

And Fire Cloud did not know of any other tribes that made their residence in northern Minnesota.

Hunkered low behind tall stalks of cane, Fire Cloud watched as not only one canoe, but many others, swept around the bend. It was a convoy.

His eyebrows rose when he saw many women, children, and elderly people in the canoes.

More than one canoe carried piles of belongings. That had to mean that these travelers had been uprooted and were on their way to a new home, possibly a new land.

He had to wonder, why? His band of Chippewa had no plans to move elsewhere. Why would others . . . unless they had been forced out.

But who would do that?

His jaw tightened when he recalled his father talking about the United States government and their sneaky ways of taking so much from other tribes.

Thus far, the Chippewa bands that Fire Cloud knew about had not been taken advantage of in such a way.

Did that mean that these were Lakota?

He did not have time to think further, for the lead canoe was already ashore, and the others waited in the river.

Fire Cloud's heart almost stopped when he saw a man who seemed to be the chief of this group take his knife from his sheath. The warriors with him already had their bows notched with arrows. Their eyes stopped on the wigwam.

Remembering his brother, Fire Cloud leapt from behind the reeds and stood with his chest puffed out and his chin held high in an effort to hide his fear.

He clutched the bow at his side. He knew that he would not have time to load it, yet he felt brave standing there holding it, for it was his father's. With it in his hand, he felt his father's presence.

"Young brave, what are you doing alone? Where are your parents?" a tall, thin warrior asked, his widened eyes showing his surprise. He looked slowly around the camp, then into the darker depths of the forest.

The warrior, dressed in only a breechclout and moccasins, saw the rabbit cooking over the fire. "Your food?" he asked, gesturing toward the rabbit. "It is small. It will not feed many."

"It was not meant to feed more than one person," Fire Cloud finally found the courage to say. "It is for Fire Cloud's belly only."

"You are Fire Cloud?" the tall warrior asked.

Fire Cloud nodded warily.

"Since the meat that you are cooking is only for you, does that mean that you are camping alone?" the warrior prodded.

Fire Cloud caught himself just before looking toward the wigwam. He instead gazed steadily into the warrior's eyes, again unable to speak. Could he trust this man?

"My arrival has frightened you," the warrior said, then nodded to the others to lower their bows and arrows.

He knelt before Fire Cloud and reached out to his bare shoulder. Fire Cloud tensed beneath the pressure of his hand, but did not pull away. He was catapulted back to those times when his father had knelt before him in such a way, placing a comforting hand on his shoulder as he explained one or another thing to him.

At this moment he missed his father more than ever.

But when the eagle swept down over his head, then perched on the limb of a tree a short distance away, Fire Cloud realized that his father was there again, in spirit.

"Who are you?" Fire Cloud blurted out. "Why are you and so many of your people in canoes? Where are you traveling?"

The warrior smiled gently, and Fire Cloud suddenly knew he was in the presence of someone he could trust.

He could almost taste food cooked by someone besides himself, and hoped that his brother would have milk by night's fall, instead of the dreadful porridge that Fire Cloud had been feeding him.

"I am Chief Black Eagle," the man said. He lowered his hand to his side and rested it on the handle of his knife. "I am Lakota. I am *mita-koda*—friend. You asked why you see so many of my people in canoes? It is because the white man wants the Lakota all penned up in little islands. They want to make the red man like *wasichos*—whites. My people are now on their way to a land that the government has assigned them in Missouri, along a river called the Meramec."

"You are Lakota," Fire Cloud echoed, fear again creeping into his heart. "And you have been forced from your homes?"

"Yes, we have always lived in the northern lake country. But now, six bands of Lakota have broken camp and scattered in all directions after signing treaties with the United States government. One of the government's interpreters lied to the Lakota, forcing them to uproot their families and move elsewhere. My band, the Eagle band, is now on our way to our home on the Meramec."

He paused and again placed a hand on Fire Cloud's shoulder. "You have yet to tell me where your parents are," he said. "You have not told me your tribe. Were you among those of my tribe who were forced to go elsewhere? Are you lost?"

Fire Cloud's eyes wavered as he searched for an answer. His mother and father had taught him the ways of the Lakota in case the knowledge was ever needed for his survival, and he could speak three languages—his own Chippewa language, Lakota, and English.

Knowing the Lakota language as well as their other customs, could he not pretend to be Lakota? he wondered.

But Fire Cloud was a proud Chippewa, who until he left the village with his mother, would have one day been chief of his Saint Croix band. If he was to grow up proud and honorable, he must tell the truth now. He was Chippewa. He would always be Chippewa!

And he could not help but notice this Lakota chief's quiet and dignified manner. How could the Lakota and Chippewa, who were so alike, hate each other so much?

"Both my father and mother are now in the heaven world," Fire Cloud finally said.

He then proceeded to tell Chief Black Eagle what

had happened to his mother. He sadly pointed to her grave. Fire Cloud explained how his father had died, and how he had chosen to leave with his mother when she was banished.

He even felt comfortable enough now to tell Chief Black Eagle about his little brother.

He told how he stayed strong by eating boiled and baked cattail roots and drinking *timsilia* soup, made of wild turnips. He also had prepared and drunk juniper tea.

He pointed to the cooked rabbit, which proved he had been a successful hunter.

"I am Chippewa, from the Saint Croix band," Fire Cloud stated at last.

Chief Black Eagle did not seem affected by Fire Cloud's confession. Instead he looked over to the lodge that Fire Cloud had erected.

He gazed at Fire Cloud again. "You built the wigwam?" he asked softly.

"*Ay-uh*—yes," Fire Cloud said, pride in his eyes.

"You are a smart young *zongh-gee-day-ay*—brave," Black Eagle said, smiling and nodding. "You have proven that you will grow into as great a warrior."

"Thank you," Fire Cloud said, touched by the chief's compliments. "But this is only true because my mother and father passed these things on to me in their teachings."

Then Fire Cloud ducked his head as he fought back the tears that always came with thinking about his father. "My father was a good hunter," he gulped out. "He was a good man. He should not have died."

Fire Cloud lifted his eyes again, holding the bow

out for Black Eagle to see. "This bow, and the quiver of arrows, were my father's," he said. "They are now mine."

"Your pride for your father is *o-nee-shee-shin*—good," Black Eagle said, again nodding. "As was your choice to stay with your mother to protect her with the weapons of your father."

Black Eagle gazed at the wigwam again. "And your *gee-gee-kee-wayn-zee*—your brother?" he said, raising an eyebrow. "He is asleep in the lodge?"

"*Ay-uh*. He is a good baby who sleeps often and, except for that first cry that gave him life, he never cries," Fire Cloud said, no longer afraid. "*Mah-bee-szhon*—come. I'll show him to you."

Black Eagle crawled into the wigwam behind Fire Cloud and waited for the boy to lift the cradle from where he had hidden it.

When Black Eagle saw the cradle, he knew that the young man had also made this, and saw Fire Cloud as more and more special.

Fire Cloud placed the cradle beside Black Eagle, then slowly drew back a corner of the blanket to proudly show off his brother.

"His name is *Dee-bee-gee-zis O-gee-chag-o-sin*—Moon Shadow," Fire Cloud said as Black Eagle looked more closely at the baby.

Chief Black Eagle saw a rosy little nose peeking out from the sleeping sack. The sack was filled with soft floss, the wrap gossamer light, yet cozy against any brisk breeze.

"The child is *mee-kah-wah-diz-ee*—beautiful," Black

Eagle said, then smiled over at Fire Cloud. "The sleeping sack—your mother made it?"

"*Gah-ween*—no—it is something else I made," Fire Cloud said. "I saw new mothers make such sleeping sacks at my village."

Black Eagle nodded as he again looked at the baby. "I cannot leave two young braves stranded, even though you are from an enemy tribe," he said. He gazed at Fire Cloud again. "You and your brother are welcome to join my people. But it must be in one of our canoes. Our horses have been taken to Missouri land by another route."

"Truly? You will allow me and my brother to travel with you?" Fire Cloud said, trying hard to hold down his excitement. Fire Cloud would not tell the Lakota chief just how relieved he was by his generosity, for he knew that if these warriors did not take pity on him and Moon Shadow today, he and his brother might not last long enough for someone else to have the chance to.

"Fire Cloud, usually children who are taken in by the Lakota, especially *gwee-wee-zance*—boys—are adopted by a family, but since you and your brother are Chippewa, you cannot have that privilege," Black Eagle said somberly. "You are invited to live among my people, but you will have to earn both your and your brother's keep."

"I will gladly do that in exchange for a home for my baby brother," Fire Cloud said.

"Take what you wish to keep of your mother's things, then come along to the canoes and I will assign you and your brother to one," Black Eagle said, already backing out of the low-roofed wigwam.

Fire Cloud nodded eagerly. He was excited to be a part of a people again, even if it was not his own.

He sorted through his mother's things, choosing to keep her main travel bag. It was made of a soft and pliable hide and beaded along two edges. The front was covered with embroidery in beads and quill. It was his mother's handiwork. It would be like having her with him.

After carrying everything else he wished to keep to the waiting canoes, he went back for his brother. He carried Moon Shadow over to the grave and said one last good-bye to their mother; then, with hope in his heart, he hurried to the canoes.

He discovered that his personal belongings, as well as his father's bow and quiver of arrows, were placed in a canoe of women and children.

"You will travel in this canoe, for there are boys your age and a mother who will share her milk with your brother," Black Eagle explained.

Almost ready to cry with relief, yet knowing that he could not let himself look like such a baby in the presence of the other children his age, Fire Cloud climbed into the canoe.

A beautiful lady whose name was White Lily and who looked almost the same age as his mother, was already wrapping Moon Shadow in warm buffalo calfskin. She placed a soft cap of calfskin on his head, and then put Moon Shadow to her breast.

Fire Cloud gave a silent prayer of thanks to the heavens and looked over his shoulder at the land they were leaving behind. He hated leaving Minnesota, with its beautiful lakes, rugged, scenic shores, and many moose and wolf.

Most of all he hated leaving the grave of his mother, for he knew that he would never see it again. But he would never forget her. He would carry her within his heart forever!

"My Chippewa people," Fire Cloud whispered, vowing that some day he would find his way home again.

But for now his home was with the Lakota. And he would make sure that Chief Black Eagle would never regret having helped two young braves in distress, even though they were Chippewa.

Fire Cloud sat proud and alert as the convoy of canoes swept onward through the calm waters. A noise overhead drew his attention. He smiled when he saw the eagle as it dipped low, and then rose into the clouds again, for he knew that his father's spirit would always be there to look after him.

Chapter 2

Missouri — August — "Moon When Cherries Turn Black"

A small canoe carrying a lone traveler sliced gently through the Meramec River. It was Fire Cloud's, made by his own hands. He wanted it this size so that he could travel alone to explore this new land where the Lakota had settled, several miles south of a city named after some sort of white man's saint—Saint Louis.

As he drew his paddle through the water, he could see fish flashing just beneath the surface and smiled. He was happy in his new life. It was not at all like being penned in as Chief Black Eagle had thought. It was a lovely place . . . a place where Fire Cloud could find a different adventure every day if he wished to.

Ay-uh, he had adjusted well enough to the Lakota's customs and beliefs.

He even looked forward to the tepees that they were just erecting for the winter months at their village. Now, during the warmer temperatures, their bark-covered lodges were almost the same as the wigwams that the Chippewa used year-round.

Fire Cloud was also content with his status among the Lakota. As he knew that he must, he performed chores for his and his infant brother's keep; not only for Sky Woman, the elderly widow who had taken them in, but also for others who needed assistance in one thing or another.

White Lily, the same woman who had offered her milk to Fire Cloud's brother that first day, still fed him when he was hungry.

But Fire Cloud was free to come and go from the village as often as he pleased, for the Lakota knew his love of adventure and exploring.

Today he had traveled much farther down the Meramec River than he usually did. He found the land that surrounded the river too beautiful and fascinating not to. Fire Cloud had been told that the river was a tributary of the much larger Mississippi River, the name Meramec having been derived from the red man's word for catfish. He loved the tall, white bluffs that in places lined both sides of the river. He was also intrigued by the limestone caverns in the area, one especially, named Meramec Cavern, that was much larger and deeper than the others.

He thrilled at the sight of bear, deer, wolf, coyote, fox, and many other animals that he had seen while on his adventures. And the blowing sea of grass was so endlessly abundant that he felt it was a treasure greater than gold.

The land was thickly carpeted in trees as well. Scattered among evergreens were colorful poplar, tall oak, maple, wild fruit trees, and birch trees which were used by the red man in many ways. His canoe had been made from birch.

Fire Cloud's eyes watched the water again, and he

saw numerous catfish darting out of the way of his canoe. He had caught many of those fish for Sky Woman.

Ay-uh, in this land of timber-lined valleys and open prairie ridges, he was in awe of something new each time he ventured out.

Suddenly he saw something that made his eyes widen. He stopped paddling to take a good look at a huge, four-story brick building that sat back from the river on a rise of land.

Who lived in such a vast, tall lodge? he wondered.

It was an impressive home to a young brave of ten winters who had never lived in anything but wigwams and tepees.

He could not imagine how it would feel to enter such a place, or even to stand in its shadow!

The white people often amazed him with their large lodges, made with materials that he now knew were called bricks.

Fire Cloud was not aware of his canoe idly drifting toward shore until he saw that he was only a few paddle strokes away from a black-robed person fishing on the riverbank.

Intrigued, Fire Cloud could not help but hurry onward. After beaching his canoe, he turned to find the man scrutinizing him, the fishing pole now lying at his side on the rocky shore.

Smiling awkwardly, his heart pounding, Fire Cloud approached the man.

When he got a better look at the face, which was surrounded by a strange head apparatus, Fire Cloud took a shaky step backward, stunned to see that it was not a man at all. It was a woman!

"Hello there, young brave," the woman said as she pushed herself up from the ground. "And what might your name be?"

The kindness of the woman's voice and the soft smile on her lips made Fire Cloud relax. He returned her smile. "I am called Fire Cloud," he said in English, proudly lifting his chin. "And what is your name?"

"Sister Mary Ann," she answered with a smile that seemed to be filled with sunshine.

She glanced past him at his canoe. "Are you Lakota?" she asked. "I know of a newly established Lakota village upriver a piece."

"I live among the Lakota, but I am, by birth, Chippewa," Fire Cloud was not hesitant to say, for he never wanted to forget his true heritage, nor did he wish for anyone to think it was otherwise.

"You wear a priest's black robe, yet you are a woman, and you wear something else that I have never seen before," Fire Cloud said, looking at her black head covering. "The garment on your head is strange to me."

Sister Mary Ann laughed softly. "I am a nun . . . a person whose life is given solely to God. And, yes, priests wear similar black robes. But I am proud to be a nun."

She reached up and touched her head covering, which began at her forehead in a square, boxed fashion, then went down to surround her facial features, falling finally past her shoulders to her waist. "And what you see on my head is called a wimple," she murmured. "Like the rest of our habit, or robe, it is worn by nuns as a humble reminder that we are women of more spiritual than natural beauty, and that it is more important for us to be attractive to God than to human beings. It is always a reminder of our full allegiance to God."

"My religion differs from yours," Fire Cloud said, looking over at the tall building. He so hungered to be offered a visit inside it, yet knew it would be too forward of him to ask.

He looked squarely at Sister Mary Ann again. "As a small child I was taught to believe in a supreme being called *Kitchi-Manitou*—the Great Spirit," he said. "Both the Chippewa and Lakota believe in spirits, both good and evil, and in an afterlife."

"Tell me about it," Sister Mary Ann said, truly interested.

"The ideal of the Lakota and Chippewa is harmony, and the most powerful sign of that is peace," Fire Cloud said, then opened up and explained to her why the Lakota were in Missouri and how the white government tricked them into trading away their precious Minnesota land.

"Sometimes shameful men do shameful things," Sister Mary Ann said, sighing. "I must ask . . . how does this land compare with the one that you were forced to leave? Are the Lakota able to adjust to the change?"

"Although the Lakota prefer the land of their ancestors, they have found some peace here," Fire Cloud said, again finding himself staring at the huge building. "As for me, I find this beautiful land endlessly interesting. I explore often, and each day there is something new to discover."

"Such as the convent?" Sister Mary Ann said, her eyes dancing. "I have seen how you keep looking at it."

Fire Cloud's eyebrows rose. "What is a convent?"

Sister Mary Ann's laughter rippled in the wind. "The building on the hillside houses women like me, who are also nuns, and a head priest. Many children also live there. You see, the convent is an orphanage as well."

"Orphanage?" Fire Cloud echoed.

"Come with me," Sister Mary Ann said, offering him a hand. "I will show you. That would be much better than trying to explain so much to you."

Fire Cloud looked at her proffered hand, then slowly up at her face and saw again how genuinely friendly she was. He returned the smile and, taking her hand, walked toward the building with her.

He was eager to know things, and his questions came tumbling out, one after another.

Sister Mary Ann answered his questions patiently, letting Fire Cloud know that he had found a friend in this woman.

He was so glad that his ventures had taken him farther down the Meramec River today!

When they reached the convent, and Fire Cloud was finally standing in its shadow, he bent his neck back to see the very upper windows and roof and nearly lost his balance.

"Careful there," Sister Mary Ann said. Laughing

kindly, she steadied Fire Cloud, then took his hand again and led him up the steep stairs to a large, broad porch that ran across the entire front of the house. Wicker rocking chairs sat in a long row, moving in the soft breeze, as though people were gently swaying in them.

Fire Cloud entered ahead of her through the heavy oak door and stepped into a stark, open space, barely lit by the candles along the tall walls.

A wide set of stairs stood at one side of the room, reaching up into darkness above.

Past the vast entry hall Fire Cloud saw a long corridor, with closed doors lining each side. A chill rode up and down Fire Cloud's spine as he imagined the orphaned children brought here for possible adoption.

The doors along the corridor began to open, and several sad-faced children peered out at him. Fire Cloud could almost feel their loneliness. He felt blessed that the Lakota had taken him in, and he had not been labeled an orphan!

Suddenly, he heard a movement to his left.

He turned with a start and saw a blanket-wrapped bundle being slid through a small door near the floor.

He looked questioningly at Sister Mary Ann.

"A baby is wrapped in those blankets. This is how some women bring their unwanted newborns to the orphanage," she said as another nun picked up the baby and carried it away in her arms. "Those women who do not wish to reveal who they are send their children through this small door. We make sure we keep those babies at least three months in case the mother changes her mind and returns for the child.

If she hasn't, then the baby can be adopted out, for babies are adopted much more quickly than older children. Each baby sent through the door has a note with an initial written on it which proves who the child belongs to in case the mother changes her mind."

"How could a mother not want a child?" Fire Cloud asked, recalling how much his mother had loved him and his brother.

In fact, all the mothers of his tribe cherished their children as the hope and promise of the future. For the Chippewa or the Lakota to give up their children would be to have given up hope in their tribe as a whole.

"Sometimes husbands desert their pregnant wives," Sister Mary Ann said, her voice drawn. "By doing this, they also desert their unborn child. When the child arrives into this world, too often the woman has no means to feed or clothe it. Those women bring their babies to our convent. They know that the infant will be provided for."

"I now feel twice blessed to have been taken in by the Lakota, for they also took in my baby brother," Fire Cloud said.

"A baby brother?" Sister Mary Ann said, her eyebrows arching. "Tell me about your brother, Fire Cloud."

"His name is Moon Shadow . . ." Fire Cloud began, but his words were stilled when he saw someone coming through the front door.

His heart skipped a beat, for the girl, who seemed only a few years younger than he, was the prettiest that Fire Cloud had ever seen. She was with a tall, well-dressed man with a thick black mustache and dark head of hair. Fire Cloud assumed he was her father.

His eyes held hers as her father led her in the opposite direction. He could not help but stare.

Fire Cloud was stunned by her looks. Her eyes were the most beautiful color of azure, and her wavy, waist-length hair was golden, the color of summer wheat.

She wore a pretty white lawn dress with a huge skirt and a froth of lacy petticoats, which peeked out at the hem.

But Fire Cloud knew that he should not be looking at her with such awe, because she was white.

The man then made a sharp turn into a room, taking the girl with him.

"Sister Mary Ann, who was that girl?" Fire Cloud blurted out, still seeing her lovely face in his mind's eye.

"Her name is Janelle," Sister Mary Ann said, having seen how Fire Cloud and Janelle had noticed each other. "Janelle Coolidge. Her father, Virgil Coolidge, is a rich man who shares his wealth with the nuns and children. Janelle generously gives her hand-me-down clothes to the girls. They have usually only been worn once or twice, so they are not really used when the orphans receive them."

Sister Mary Ann continued. "Janelle is my niece, and Virgil is my brother. I must excuse myself now, Fire Cloud. Virgil apparently didn't see me standing here in the shadows. He has gone on into my office.

I don't want to keep him waiting." She laughed. "He's quite an impatient man, my brother."

Sister Mary Ann took Fire Cloud's hand as though she was going to bring him with her to meet the pretty girl and her father.

The thought frightened Fire Cloud, especially since the tall, stern-looking man seemed the sort who would look down upon anyone with a different skin color.

He yanked his hand quickly from Sister Mary Ann's and began backing toward the door.

"I must return home," he gulped out. "My . . . my brother. I have been gone from him longer than usual. Moon Shadow, my baby brother, he . . . he might be missing me."

"If you truly must leave, I understand," she said.

"I have taken up enough of your time," Fire Cloud said. "And you need to see your family."

"Will you come again, Fire Cloud?" Sister Mary Ann asked, walking to the door and opening it for him. "I would like to show you around and introduce you to my friends, especially the children."

"I can come again?" Fire Cloud asked hesitantly.

"Any time," Sister Mary Ann affirmed, taken aback when the boy suddenly flung himself against her and gave her a long, tight hug.

Embarrassed over having shown such affection to someone he barely knew, Fire Cloud stepped away from Sister Mary Ann, smiled awkwardly up at her, then fled the building. He did not stop running until he reached his canoe, and he soon had it out in the middle of the river, heading toward home.

He looked back over his shoulder at the convent, realizing that today he had made a lasting friendship. And how could he ever forget the girl with the azure eyes?

He hoped to see her again . . . soon.

And when he did, he would not hesitate if Sister Mary Ann offered to introduce him to her.

"Janelle," he whispered beneath his breath. Would Janelle ask Sister Mary Ann about him?

That thought brought his eyes back to the windows at the front of the convent. Was Janelle there, staring back at him?

Chapter 3

Janelle's hands rested on her lap as she sat primly beside her father in her Aunt Mary Ann's office. Deep in thought, she slowly swung her legs back and forth, her small black-velvet slippers peeking from beneath her lace petticoats.

She could not stop thinking of the Indian boy. She had never been so close to an Indian before. She had been fascinated with them after first seeing them along the riverfront in Saint Louis.

On shopping trips with her mother, before her mother became too ill to go out, their black carriage often passed close enough to the riverfront to see Indians in their canoes as they came to trade their goods.

Her parents had always forbidden her to go near the riverfront, and she had been warned that she must avoid at all cost any redskin who ventured farther into the city.

Indians "had their place in the world," her mother and father told her, as did Janelle, who was from one of the most affluent families in the area. She was forbidden to speak to an Indian even if she accidentally came face-to-face with one.

And that included Indian women and girls, as well as the young braves who often traveled with their fathers to learn the art of trading with whites.

But today!

Today Janelle had been close enough to the brave to get a good look.

He couldn't have been more than ten years old—two years older than her. She had seen enough to know that he would be a handsome warrior one day.

Dressed in beaded leggings, a breechclout, and elk-skin moccasins, he was quite a sight to behold. He had even, pleasant features, pronounced cheekbones, bright brown eyes, and a slender, golden-bronze body. His luxuriant black hair hung halfway down his back.

Only moments ago, she had gone to the window just in time to see him walk away from the convent and gracefully push his canoe out into deeper water. Her heart had almost stopped when he turned suddenly to look back at the convent, almost as if he had discovered her standing there, watching him.

But as he turned back around and continued his journey, she wondered if it had only been her imagination.

She did know that when their eyes had momentarily met and held, something passed between them that seemed almost mystical.

"Janelle?"

Her father's deep, commanding voice brought Janelle out of her reverie.

She knew that he was not really angry at her, so

she gave him a smile that always stole his heart away. To him, she was a little princess!

"I'm sorry, Father," Janelle said. "I guess my mind wandered."

"Good Lord, to what?" he said, heaving an irritated sigh as he slipped one of his large hands inside his black coat and took a gold pocket watch from his vest pocket, obviously having forgotten why he was questioning her in the first place.

There was much more on his mind than his daughter's daydreaming. He had recently lost her mother to a terrible lung disease.

Since her death, he had wanted to escape Saint Louis and the memories that pained him every time he entered a room in his three-story mansion. Without his wife there to greet him, it was as though his heart had been emptied of feelings. He felt nothing but numbness.

He knew that wasn't good for Janelle, and he had decided to move elsewhere so they could recover from their loss.

A diamond stickpin glistened from the folds of his cravat as he returned his watch to its pocket.

"Mary Ann, I don't have much time," Virgil said. He took Janelle's hand and held it. "The riverboat departs soon. I don't want to chance missing it."

"Do you think this is really what you should be doing?" Sister Mary Ann asked as she scooted her chair closer to her oak desk. "You know that running away isn't always the answer."

"I don't look at it as running away," Virgil said gruffly. "I see it as a way to save my sanity. I miss

Dorothy June so much. Everywhere I go in my house I see her. I feel her. I smell her. That can't be good for me or Janelle."

Tears burned at the corners of Sister Mary Ann's eyes. "How long do you plan to be gone?" she asked. She looked from Janelle to Virgil. They were all that was left of her family. Although her duties at the convent fulfilled her and kept her busy, she would miss her brother and niece tremendously.

"For as long as it takes to get my head on straight," Virgil grumbled. "This will be good for Janelle. She can attend the finest schools in Boston and get the education I've always wanted for her."

"As you know, you don't have to go to Boston for a good education for Janelle," Sister Mary Ann said. "She—"

"My mind is made up," Virgil said, interrupting her. He rose and began slowly pacing the room.

"But you *will* return to Saint Louis, won't you?" Sister Mary Ann asked.

He stopped and stared through the window at the Meramec. "Yes. I love this land. I love that river."

He turned on a heel and looked at his sister. "That is why I didn't sell my home," he said. "One day I will feel comfortable there again. By then, I might even want the memories of my Dorothy June with me as I go from room to room. But now it is too painful. Much, much too painful."

He sat down and again took one of Janelle's hands. "I'll be sending money monthly for your needs here at the convent," he said. "As Janelle tires or grows out of her clothes, I will send them to you for the children."

"You know the children's needs almost better than I," Sister Mary Ann said softly. "Thank you, Virgil, for caring so much. The convent and the children will fill the void in my life while you and Janelle are gone."

Janelle was only barely hearing what was being said, for she was again lost in her thoughts. She was so sad about moving from Saint Louis and having to leave her friends.

And now she would not even have the chance to get to know the Indian boy better.

"Aunt Mary Ann, who was that boy you were standing with when Father and I entered the convent? Is he an orphan?" Janelle blurted out, not thinking of the possible consequences of asking about the very people her father had always warned her about.

Virgil looked quickly at Janelle. "What boy?"

Janelle suddenly felt cornered. She looked from her father to her aunt, and then to her father again.

Thankfully her aunt saw Janelle's awkwardness and intervened.

"The child she is asking about, Virgil, was standing with me when you came into the convent, but you were so lost in your thoughts you did not notice either of us," Sister Mary Ann said. "Janelle did see me, but it was Fire Cloud who seemed to have her attention."

"Fire Cloud?" Virgil went and stood over the desk,

his eyes narrowing. "Who on earth is this Fire Cloud? That name sounds Indian to me."

"That's because it is Indian," Sister Mary Ann said, looking up at her brother. Then she smiled at Janelle. "And, no, Janelle, he doesn't live here as an orphan. He has only today made my acquaintance. I was fishing when he came by in his canoe. He stopped and we talked. Then I showed him the convent."

"Where did he come from?" Virgil asked, again sitting down in the chair. "And haven't I warned you about the dangers of fishing alone on the river?"

"I can take care of myself," Sister Mary Ann said. "The boy is from the new Lakota settlement. He's a precious child. I think we made a fast friendship."

"I don't mean to sound prejudiced, Mary Ann, but be careful of whom you make such fast friendships with," Virgil said somberly. "He might bring the whole village here for handouts."

"And should he do that, I shall be here with an open heart and arms to welcome them," Sister Mary Ann said.

"Yes, I think you would," Virgil said. He checked the time again and nodded at Janelle. "Come, daughter. We've got to be on our way."

Janelle moved from the chair and took his hand.

After they were outside and riding in their carriage alongside the Meramec, Janelle's heart skipped a beat, for she saw that Fire Cloud had stopped along the riverbank. He was gathering what looked to be rocks and shells. And when he heard the horse and carriage, he looked up.

She was glad that her father was too immersed in

his thoughts to notice Fire Cloud or that she waved at him as she rode past.

But the wonder at seeing Fire Cloud again quickly changed to sadness, for she knew that there was little hope of ever meeting him again. Her life was taking her one way. His would surely take him another.

But she knew that she would never forget him!

Chapter 4

Missouri—Fifteen Years Later

The leaves of the cottonwood and willow trees rustled in the breeze. The sun was high but had lost some of its strength with the coming of autumn and chillier temperatures.

Fire Cloud knelt with Moon Shadow beside the Meramec River, searching for new rocks and shells for his brother's collection. His thoughts turned to the past fifteen years, and how things had changed.

The Lakota people were doing well. They had grown to love their new land, a place of beauty and abundance.

They did a fair trade in beaver, elk, and deer, exchanging furs with white traders for guns rather than whiskey as some tribes were guilty of doing. Fire Cloud's people wanted to keep a clear mind at all times in order not to be duped again by the *wasichos*. This logic had made the Lakota strong both in spirit and body.

They had also amassed a large number of horses, the most favored kept in pens behind their lodges. Fire Cloud owned a fine black mustang. He had even taught his blind brother how to ride!

At this reminder of his brother's lot in life, Fire

Cloud paused from sorting through the rocks and shells. At the age when Moon Shadow should have reacted to sounds and movement and had not, Fire Cloud had learned that his brother could not hear, see, or talk.

Often Fire Cloud felt responsible for these things, for he remembered how his mother had told him to feed his brother the brains of a small bird, that this would develop his speech.

He had thought that this was just another tale told by people long ago—not something that was truly done.

But now he could not help but wonder if he had done so, whether his brother might be all right now.

As it was, Fire Cloud had become Moon Shadow's eyes and ears. Moon Shadow was his life, and he was very protective of his brother.

Fire Cloud made certain that his brother was happy in his silent and dark world. By using his fingers on the palms of his brother's hands, he taught him a way of communicating and so had brought color and knowledge into his brother's life.

And the rock collection—Moon Shadow was so proud of it. To him they were living things, something he could feel and study. As he touched them, each rock and shell told him a different story. By their warmth, they told him when the sun was in the sky. By their coldness, he knew that winter was upon them. He even enjoyed feeling snow falling on the rocks, each star-shaped flake like a piece of heaven brought down from the sky just for Moon Shadow.

Fire Cloud smiled sadly as he watched his brother

sort through the rocks and shells along the riverbank, sliding them into the buckskin bag that he wore around his waist.

It was his brother's inability to speak that tore the most at Fire Cloud's heart. Moon Shadow could make only strange noises that seemed to come from deep within his soul.

Fire Cloud had accepted long ago how people might stare at his brother, how some thought his brother was ignorant, and looked past him as though he was not even there. But that had made Fire Cloud more aware of the importance of his own speech. He tried to make his thoughts clear and pointed and had taught himself to measure his sentences like the words of a song. When he spoke, everyone listened.

Above all else, Fire Cloud had become a man of honor, truthfulness, and generosity. He acted with dignity and accepted praise and honor without arrogance.

Suddenly Fire Cloud's eyes were drawn elsewhere. He was downriver from Sister Mary Ann's lodge, yet close enough to see a stately carriage pulled by two white horses roll along the dirt road that ran in front of the convent. He remembered the last time he had seen such a grand carriage.

Many visitors had come and gone from the convent since that day; still, he could not help but recall the girl who had arrived so many years ago.

That day was engraved in his heart and mind forever.

As always, he forced himself to look away from the carriage. He had tried to forget the pretty girl named Janelle. After hearing that she had moved away from the area, he never mentioned her again to the nuns, especially Sister Mary Ann.

But now, as so many times before, he recalled that day as though it were only yesterday.

Hearing the rumble of the carriage wheels growing stronger and knowing that it would soon make a sharp turn up the rocky road to the convent, Fire Cloud stood up and stepped a few feet away from his brother.

As the carriage began its turn, something in the window of the carriage made his heart skip a beat.

The shine of golden hair!

He had never forgotten it, how it was the color of sunshine and lay in deep waves down Janelle's back.

He turned away quickly and tried not to let his imagination run wild. But the way his heart was thudding erratically made Fire Cloud turn around again, and this time he stood his ground as the carriage drew up and stopped in front of the wide porch of the convent.

Even though he was some distance from the building, he could clearly see Sister Mary Ann rush from the door, lift her black skirt, and hurry down the steps to meet whoever had arrived. Fire Cloud remembered other times he had watched Sister Mary Ann greet visitors, and he had never seen her as eager and happy as now. She held out her arms for the person just stepping from the carriage, and the two women embraced.

Their embraces ended and they hurried up the steps of the convent. Sister Mary Ann put her arm affectionately around the waist of the petite woman whose golden hair lifted in the breeze. They laughed and chatted, as though they had not seen each other for an eternity. Fire Cloud's heart seemed to soar, for he could not help but believe now that Janelle *had* returned. She had just been reunited with her aunt!

It took all of Fire Cloud's willpower not to run to the convent to see if it was, in fact, Janelle.

He knew that he would look foolish if he did. And what would he say to her anyway? They had separate lives. How could he expect them to become a part of each other's lives now? He had his responsibilities just as she surely had hers.

Fire Cloud felt downhearted, an unfamiliar emotion to him, and did not want Moon Shadow to pick up on his strange mood.

In their way of communicating, he told his brother that it was time to return home. When they got there, Moon Shadow could share his new finds with his friends. Moon Shadow had many people who cared about him even if he could not socialize in the normal way. He was such a fine, caring person, who could not love him?

With the rocks secured in the buckskin bag, they were soon on the river heading for home.

But Fire Cloud couldn't get the girl off his mind. He wanted to finally ask Sister Mary Ann about Janelle, to see where she was and what she had been doing.

But he decided against it. Even though Sister Mary Ann had become like a mother to him, he would not want to risk his pride if Janelle was not interested.

And Janelle might be married by now.

Fire Cloud hadn't chosen a *gee-wee-oo*—a wife. Besides focusing so much of his life on his brother, Fire Cloud had become a leader among the Lakota, who now considered him one of them.

But he could never be chief, as he might be now if he lived among his true people.

Through the years he had ached to see his grandfather, to be among his own people, but had put off returning to them. They would resent Moon Shadow because of how he had been conceived, and by whom. Fire Cloud, too, despised Gray Wind, his father's killer, yet he could not act on his desire for vengeance. How could he when this man was Moon Shadow's father—a man whom Fire Cloud's mother had loved enough to give up everything for?

No, vengeance was not in his plan. Giving his brother the best life possible was.

Yet his need to return to his people was building as each year passed.

He thought of his chieftain grandfather. Did he miss his grandson?

Fire Cloud knew that Chief Sitting Fox must have been lonely over the years. His son's death had caused his wife to go into sudden heart failure, and then he also lost his grandson at nearly the same time.

Ay-uh, one day Fire Cloud would return, but now was not the time.

Fire Cloud paused his paddling to take one last look at the convent. The women had gone inside, but a man had left the carriage and was carrying a large box, which whites called a suitcase, toward the lodge. The yellow-haired woman had come to stay at the convent, not only visit.

Now he knew that nothing would stop him from going there to see her.

His brother's hand on his shoulder reminded him that his thoughts should be on taking them home. Fire Cloud reached up to reassure Moon Shadow that things were all right.

He saw a smile brighten his brother's face, and Fire Cloud knew that was all he needed to get him past these next hours, perhaps days, before he had the opportunity to go to the convent.

Noticing eagles soaring overhead, he was reminded of that day when one had appeared to him and he had felt his father's presence.

Fire Cloud smiled. "*Gee-dah-dah*—Father—I will be going to the convent soon to ask about that woman who has been in my thoughts for so long now," he whispered.

He could not get that golden hair out of his mind!

Chapter 5

The evening meal and the private moments with her aunt behind her, Janelle gazed out of her fourth-floor bedroom window as the setting sun splashed orange hues across the limestone bluffs and the river below.

She was lost in thought, remembering the day she had seen the young, handsome brave in his canoe. It was strange how she could not get that moment off her mind.

"Fire Cloud," she whispered as she unconsciously ran her fingers through her hair.

By now he should be a handsome warrior.

"And married?" she whispered, thinking that he must make some woman deliriously happy.

Sighing, she went to a rocking chair and sat down. Her eyes strayed to the walls of the room. It could be hers permanently, should she make the final decision to become a nun.

Compared to how she had lived all her life, the convent was devoid of opulence, especially the nuns' private rooms. Janelle's room had no curtains at the windows, no rugs on the hardwood floor, and no bedspread on the white iron bed. There was only a patchwork quilt and a lone pillow in a drab, yellowed case.

In her bedroom at home she had frills and lace everywhere. She had enjoyed them as a child, and now as a woman, too.

Could she give up everything she was used to?

This room did not even have a mirror, only a vanity where she had space enough to place her comb, brush, and a lone bottle of perfume.

All of her jewelry and fancier clothes had been left at home. Until she made her final decision, she had brought plain skirts and blouses and dresses to wear. If she chose to become a nun, she would then wear black, and her hair would be cut almost to the scalp and covered by a wimple.

"Oh, I just don't know," Janelle said at the thought of cutting her hair.

She rose and began pacing as she again tried to work things out inside her weary brain.

Janelle had met with her aunt a few days ago and confided in her how unhappy she was with her life. She wasn't fulfilled working at Coolidge College, which her father had founded a year ago when they returned to Saint Louis, to their opulent mansion overlooking the Mississippi River.

Her father wanted to see his daughter excel in learning. Having her do things only sons usually did made her a son in his eyes. So, Janelle had been sent to college, although it was a rarity for women to go so far as to become even an instructor, as Janelle was. Like her father, Janelle had studied archaeology. Her father was also the curator of the Museum of Natural History in Saint Louis.

But none of that had made her happy. She could not share the love of the things that guided her father's life. She was bored. She needed something else.

While she was in Boston, Janelle had kept up a correspondence with her Aunt Mary Ann. Recently, joining her at the convent seemed perhaps the answer to her restlessness.

But she had put off making vast changes in her life because her father had a weak heart. Janelle always treated him gently. She was all that he had, but she was beginning to feel smothered by her responsibility to him.

Worst of all, she regretted agreeing to marry Jonathan Drake, her father's friend and associate. Although her father was kind-hearted, he also liked to control her life.

She had found herself agreeing to marry Jonathan Drake only to please him. Now she was engaged to a man old enough to be her father.

Both her teaching and Jonathan had been pushed on her by her father. She knew that she must search for something for herself. Becoming a nun was the first thing to come to her mind because her aunt had always been so content at it.

And even though she felt she was betraying her father by becoming a nun, she knew that if she didn't do it now, she never would.

Becoming a nun seemed to be her only way out . . . her only way of keeping her sanity.

So, Janelle had come to spend a few days at the

convent to observe the nuns' daily activities and decide if this was what she truly wanted for herself.

Her aunt had told her not to rush into anything. While she was in God's house, God would give her the answers she was seeking.

But as she had expected, her father was upset over Janelle's visit to the convent. And her fiancé was fit to be tied.

She prayed that her father and Jonathan would not come and make a scene. This had to be her decision alone!

She needed something that made her feel alive. Standing before a classroom had not done that for her, and neither had Jonathan, especially not romantically.

No matter what she decided at the convent, she would never marry Jonathan. And she would not stand before a classroom again either.

Again she went to the window.

An Indian warrior was paddling a canoe down the river.

She thought again of that young brave. She had hoped that when she returned to Saint Louis, she might somehow come face-to-face with him. She knew that it was foolish to ask her aunt about him, for surely she would not remember.

And how could Janelle explain her young girl's infatuation with an Indian brave after only one quick meeting?

Yes, it was best left unsaid.

But she was alert to discussions of Indians, hoping to hear the name Fire Cloud. She had even considered riding her horse close to the Lakota village.

But she had thought better of it, for she did not have the nerve to ask someone about the little boy's face that she could not let go of.

Weary of feeling so torn, Janelle walked to the bed and drew the quilt back.

Tomorrow.

Yes, tomorrow she would decide the rest of her life.

If she chose to become a nun, though, it was forever.

And if she then found Fire Cloud, there could be no future between them.

Hers would already be mapped out.

Chapter 6

Fire Cloud sat on the floor with Moon Shadow in the center of a roomful of orphans. He tried to keep his focus on why he and his brother were there, rather than on the woman who had arrived yesterday.

It was hard not to go to Sister Mary Ann and ask her if it *was* Janelle who had come for a visit.

Instead, he went through his weekly routine at the orphanage. The children looked forward to their visit because Moon Shadow always brought his collection of rocks and shells to share with them.

The children scooted more closely now as Moon Shadow began taking rocks from his bag, each one different from the last, their colors and shapes varied and beautiful.

Forcing himself to place his brother and the children first in his mind today, Fire Cloud waited for his brother to choose the first rock.

Once the treasure lay on his brother's outstretched palm, Fire Cloud began telling the children where Moon Shadow had found it and how he felt about it.

Fire Cloud had already taught these children that the deaf and blind could still feel as loved and useful as those who could hear or see. His brother was proof of that.

After the most important rocks had been taken from the bag and talked about, the children took turns letting Moon Shadow feel their faces with his fingers.

Fire Cloud was proud of how his brother had memorized each one of these children through their facial features. Having touched their faces many times, Moon Shadow knew each child by their name, which Fire Cloud had told him in their way of talking.

After the children filed from the room, Fire Cloud and Moon Shadow always shared a delicious meal with the children and the nuns in the huge dining hall. He could already smell the tantalizing aromas wafting from the kitchen.

The very first time he sat with Sister Mary Ann in the dining hall, Fire Cloud had discovered that eating with white people was very different than eating with the Lakota and Chippewa.

At the convent, everyone sat around long, huge tables. Food was served on plates the nuns had said came from a country called China, and it was eaten with utensils known as forks and spoons. Glass drinking vessels always held a sweetened, delicious drink called tea.

Fire Cloud was in awe the first time he saw butter spread with a shiny sort of knife. It was nothing like the knives worn in sheaths at Lakota warriors' waists.

Now all of this came naturally, for he had joined the nuns and children for meals many times since he met Sister Mary Ann fifteen years ago.

He had taken two days to find the nerve to accept her first offer to come again for a visit. Those visits had continued over weeks, then months, and now years.

And it had been wonderful to bring Moon Shadow when he grew old enough to go places with him.

Today Fire Cloud was particularly eager to enter that dining room. He had to believe that the golden-haired woman would join everyone to eat.

Surely he could not be wrong about her still being there, because she had brought a travel bag with her. That had to mean that she planned to stay a while.

Then a thought came to him that made his heart skip a beat. Were not most women who came to the convent nuns? Was Janelle here to dress in black, and to hide her cropped hair beneath a wimple?

He hated to believe that she would take scissors to her lovely hair for any reason.

It was as beautiful as a morning sunrise!

His brother's hand on his drew Fire Cloud from his thoughts. He realized that all the children had left; he and Moon Shadow were standing there alone.

Then Sister Mary Ann hurried into the room, smiling widely.

"Come now, Fire Cloud and Moon Shadow," she said, picking the bag of rocks and shells up from the floor. "I shall keep your bag in my office until you are ready to return home. You go on to the dining hall. I'll be there shortly."

Fire Cloud opened his mouth to finally ask Sister Mary Ann the question that had been plaguing him since yesterday. But Sister Mary Ann was too quick for him and had already left the room with the bag.

Fire Cloud sighed.

But realizing that surely he would come face-to-face with the golden-haired woman in the dining hall, he placed a gentle hand on his brother's elbow and led him from the room.

As they walked down a shadowy corridor, Fire Cloud watched the others move toward the dining hall.

The nuns were subdued as they swept down the stairs in their long, black garments. He watched for a face that just might be that of the lovely girl from his past. He tried to see if any of the nuns showed tiny tendrils of golden hair at the edge of her wimple, but they all kept their heads slightly bowed. He saw no one who could be Janelle.

The children were more lively than the nuns. Some laughed and skipped. But others walked more slowly and too often alone, their sadness showing in their eyes.

His brother still dutifully following beside him, Fire Cloud suddenly wondered about their attire today, whether or not the scantiness of their breechclouts would shock this new lady at the convent.

Though everyone else there was used to their clothing, some had at first been surprised by how so much of their bronze bodies was revealed.

But once the nuns learned that a breechclout was the usual attire of the red man on the warmer days of spring, summer, and autumn, they no longer stared or whispered.

But today?

Would he and Moon Shadow be accepted by this newcomer to the convent? Would she blush when she saw their bare chests and legs?

All women with red skin looked at him with admiration. Even some warriors envied him, for Fire Cloud's daily regimen gave him the muscular physique required for grueling hunts for food and for protecting his people should whites decide to chase the Lakota from their land.

All of those thoughts were swept aside when Sister Mary Ann caught up with Fire Cloud and Moon Shadow, chatting like a magpie as they approached the door of the dining hall.

Fire Cloud only half heard what she was saying, for his thoughts were on the visitor he might see at any moment. If it *was* Janelle, would he even recognize her?

Would she recall that one brief glance they had shared so long ago?

If he discovered that the woman was not Janelle, he would make himself stop this foolishness.

He gave Sister Mary Ann a quick look, ready to finally ask his question.

But then a nun rushed to Sister Mary Ann with a problem about a child, and again she was gone from Fire Cloud's side.

Anxious, Fire Cloud paused momentarily before entering the dining hall. He was suddenly almost afraid to meet the lovely woman, for he would be so disappointed if it was not Janelle.

Moon Shadow took Fire Cloud's free hand and, stretching it out palm side up, asked him why his body had stiffened. Moon Shadow could tell they were at the dining hall by the smells of food and wondered why they did not go in. Fire Cloud knew that he must take control of the situation and go on as though nothing at all were different.

He reassured his brother that everything was all right, that they would go now and take a seat. He remarked with gestures to Moon Shadow that the smells were those of baked turkey, were they not?

He was glad to see Moon Shadow smile and nod. His brother enjoyed the way the convent's cooks prepared the turkey more than the way it was cooked at the Lakota village. It had a wonderful tasting food called "dressing" stuffed inside.

At the thought of that delicious dish, Fire Cloud finally entered the room. He and his brother took their usual seats to the side of Sister Mary Ann's chair, which was still vacant. So were two chairs on her other side.

He wondered if one was reserved for the special visitor.

Fire Cloud tried to control his pounding heart, but still watched each person who came inside to sit at the long tables.

All around him women and children talked as they waited for Sister Mary Ann.

A fire roared in a huge stone fireplace at the far end of the room. Although the colder weather of autumn had not yet arrived, the rooms of the convent were cold. With their tall ceilings and stone walls, they had to be warmed to fight off the dampness, which threatened the children's health.

Fire Cloud's eyes finally left the door when aproned women began carrying large platters of food from the kitchen and placing them in the center of the tables.

He could tell that his brother was enjoying the smells of browned turkey and dressing, dumplings, mashed potatoes, and steaming gravy.

Fire Cloud was always amazed by the food and clothes paid for by Janelle's father. Sister Mary Ann had told him long ago of the generosity of her rich brother, who saw to all of the needs of the orphanage.

Fire Cloud reasoned that anyone this generous was surely kind, too.

He hoped to test that theory one day if he saw Janelle again.

If they ever did have the opportunity to meet and know each other, Fire Cloud would cast aside thoughts of what was forbidden by the white community—that a red man should court a white woman.

Fire Cloud sighed as he caught himself thinking such foolish thoughts again. He was glad when Sister Mary Ann finally sat down beside him. He hoped that she would soon say the prayers, for then he could enjoy the food, talk with Sister Mary Ann, and at last leave and take his brother home. He would never allow himself to think of Janelle again!

Today proved how infatuated he was with her. It

was an impossible dream, and he would finally put it behind him.

Yes, soon he would begin looking for that perfect woman with skin color that matched his own. They would marry and have children. It was time to begin the rest of his life and to stop living in a dream.

Those promises were abandoned as he looked at the door. Everything else in the room disappeared—there was only the golden-haired woman standing there, her eyes searching for her aunt. It was Janelle!

Chapter 7

Fire Cloud waited anxiously for Janelle to sit beside Sister Mary Ann. But when two other nuns filled the empty chairs, Fire Cloud's heart sank.

If the beautiful woman was Sister Mary Ann's niece, wouldn't they sit together while eating?

He recalled how they had so fondly embraced when the woman arrived at the convent. That alone had made him believe that Janelle had returned to the area and had even come to stay a while.

And now they acted as though they were strangers?

No, it did not make sense. Surely white families sat together during meals as the Lakota and Chippewa did.

The beautiful woman sat down at another table and broke into conversation with nuns on each side of her. It seemed proof enough that Fire Cloud was wrong about who she was.

But knowing that did not make him less intrigued by this woman's loveliness. Her blue eyes now and then strayed and held his, just as the young girl's had those many autumns ago.

It was strange how she seemed to somehow know him.

FIRE CLOUD

She gave him a slow, sweet smile, then looked away quickly as though too shy to allow the moment to linger.

Her blond hair and azure eyes did send him back in time. But much was different about her, too. This golden-haired beauty had the body of a woman. When she had been standing in the doorway, he noticed her petiteness. Yet although gracefully small, she had a figure that would make any man take a second look.

Ay-uh, the more he looked at her, the more he knew that this was Janelle. There must be a logical reason why she would sit away from her aunt.

Fire Cloud turned quickly to Sister Mary Ann to ask her before she stood to say the prayer that came before each meal in the convent.

"Sister Mary Ann?"

She faced him with her usual gracious smile. "Yes?" she asked, lowering her cup of tea to the white-linen-covered table.

Her smile faded when she saw Fire Cloud's serious expression. "Fire Cloud, what is bothering you?" she murmured. "I can tell that—"

"Sister Mary Ann, I could not help but notice the woman who came into the room a few moments ago," Fire Cloud said, interrupting her. "Yesterday, when Moon Shadow and I were gathering shells and rocks, I saw her arrive. You looked so happy to see her. Sister Mary Ann, who might she be?"

"Why, Fire Cloud, she is my niece," Sister Mary Ann said. "That is Janelle Coolidge, all grown up. As I recall, you noticed her many years ago when she came with my brother, her father, to say goodbye before leaving for Boston. Do you remember her?"

She took another sip of tea as she looked over at Janelle, who was just now gazing at Fire Cloud as though she might also be recalling that brief encounter. Sister Mary Ann would never forget Janelle's interest in the young Indian brave, and how her brother had tried to stifle it.

Virgil had discouraged Mary Ann's acquaintance with Indians as well—advice she had always ignored.

She was glad that she had not listened to him. She cherished her relationship with the Lakota, especially Fire Cloud and Moon Shadow.

Fire Cloud's heart pounded as he returned Janelle's gaze.

It was hard to believe that it was her, that they had been given a chance to meet again, even though it had taken many years for this moment to arrive.

He could tell that she did have feelings for him, which meant that she must have thought about him through the years, as he had thought about her.

And it made him glad to see appreciation and acceptance in her eyes. He could tell that she was not disappointed by how that little brave had grown up.

Ay-uh, he could not believe that he had the chance to know her after having thought of her so often. It was a wonderful miracle that their paths had crossed again.

"If you like, I shall introduce you after the meal," Sister Mary Ann said, as though she had read his thoughts and knew that he wished for nothing but that!

"*Ay-uh.* Yes, I would like that," Fire Cloud said, aware now that Janelle was looking at Moon Shadow. He was eager to introduce them and to see Moon Shadow's reaction as he studied her beautiful face with his fingers.

Although his brother had never actually seen beauty, Fire Cloud knew that he could feel it.

"Janelle and her father moved back to Saint Louis a year ago," Sister Mary Ann said, smiling at Fire Cloud. She proceeded to tell him about Coolidge College and about Janelle—how she seemed lost in life and had decided to try to find her true place in the world there at the convent.

She didn't tell Fire Cloud about her engagement to Jonathan because Janelle had told her that she was going to return the engagement ring the next time she saw him.

Fire Cloud was awed by Janelle's life. She was wealthy, had attended expensive schools, and was educated enough to be a teacher. Fire Cloud wondered how the beautiful girl had grown into an unhappy lady.

Their eyes met again, and she smiled at him, as though she knew that he had asked her aunt about her and was pleased that he would.

Fire Cloud returned Janelle's sweet smile and was touched to see a blush rush to her cheeks. Her eyes lowered, almost timidly, a surprising reaction since she was obviously a woman of the world.

Yet although she was educated and had lived a life of privilege, she seemed unspoiled and unprejudiced.

And now he knew about her sadness, that she had come to the convent to seek answers. He realized that fate had brought them together today, for it was Fire Cloud who would introduce Janelle into a different sort of life—one that did not include her being a nun. He wanted this woman as he had never wanted anything else!

Sister Mary Ann rose from her chair and reached both her hands heavenward. "Let us pray," she said, then began a prayer of thanksgiving for all their blessings. Fire Cloud whispered his own prayer of thanks to *Kitchi-Manitou*.

Now he had to make Janelle want him as much as he desired her.

Chapter 8

Janelle was stunned by her reaction to the Indian, yet knew that she should not be so surprised. All of those years ago, had she not been intrigued by an Indian boy?

But this was now.

She was shocked by how this warrior's handsomeness had affected her. She had never felt anything near infatuation for a man before.

Why now, when she had finally found a direction in her life . . . when she had all but told her aunt that she would be a nun?

She regretted now choosing to sit at a different table than her aunt. She had not wanted to look as though she sought privileges because Sister Mary Ann was the Mother Superior, but she would have loved to be next to her now, so close to the handsome Indian.

The way her aunt was talking with the warrior proved they had a special bond. Yet she had not mentioned a friendship with any particular Indian.

Janelle knew that her aunt had made friends with the Lakota who lived nearby.

Yes, this man could be one of them. It did not

necessarily mean that this warrior was the young boy who had come to the convent. Yet she could not help but compare this man with the young brave and see similarities. As she added years to the boy's face in her imagination, she wondered if this man could be Fire Cloud!

Janelle waited until her aunt was through with her prayer. Then, unable to hold back her curiosity any longer, she leaned closer to the nun seated to her right.

"Sister Jane, who is the brave sitting with my aunt?" she asked softly.

"Which one?" Sister Jane asked, taking a bowl of mashed potatoes from Janelle. "There are two Indians at Sister Mary Ann's table today."

"I would like to know about them both," Janelle said. She was most curious about the one who sat closest to her aunt, but did not want to show more interest in one than the other. She wasn't sure it was wise to talk too openly about one certain man, especially since she was there to consider being a nun.

"The warrior sitting closest to your aunt is Fire Cloud," Sister Jane said, too busy spooning green beans out of a bowl to notice Janelle's quick blush of excitement. "The other brave is Fire Cloud's younger brother, Moon Shadow. He is special to us all. He was born without the ability to hear, speak, or see. They both live in the nearby Lakota village, but are, in truth, Chippewa."

Janelle was so excited she could hardly catch her breath. She stared more openly at Fire Cloud now, her eyes no longer wavering. She was actually in the same room with the man she had fantasized about all of her life!

In her dreams she had seen him as he was now. It was as though God had planted in her mind a seed of knowledge of this man's life and it grew as he grew.

It seemed a miracle that he was there now, in person.

When Janelle had returned to Missouri she had tried her best to forget Fire Cloud, plunging into her work at her father's college.

But now she wanted only to pursue knowing him, and learning everything she could about Fire Cloud and his brother.

"Tell me more about Moon Shadow," she blurted out, still not having lifted a fork of food to her mouth. She ignored Sister Jane's raised eyebrow.

"Fire Cloud is very devoted to Moon Shadow," Sister Jane said. "He is his voice, his eyes, his hearing. It is a wonder to watch how much these brothers care about each other."

Janelle was touched by Fire Cloud's loyalty to his brother and wanted to meet him even more.

She decided right then and there that she would make their acquaintance, and she would not let Fire Cloud get away again!

He was what she wanted . . . not the life of a nun!

Chapter 9

The sun was lowering in the sky as a breeze swayed the leaves of the trees, leaving dancing shadows across the shaded yard of the convent.

Disappointed, Fire Cloud walked with his brother down the slope from the convent toward his canoe. He had not been able to meet Janelle. Sister Mary Ann had been called away on an emergency before the evening meal had ended, and Janelle seemed to have disappeared into thin air as everyone began filing out of the dining hall.

He walked with his eyes mostly on the ground after leaving the building, the usual confidence in his steps momentarily gone. Finally, his brother signaled that he was allowing his disappointment to affect him much too deeply.

Moon Shadow, being alert to his brother's feelings, took both of Fire Cloud's hands and stopped him.

With his fingers, Moon Shadow asked why he was not happy and if something had happened to him at the convent. If so, what?

Fire Cloud was angry at himself for letting his feelings show, especially about a woman who might never want to know him, who might have been only momentarily infatuated. After all, he was probably different from any other man she knew.

Fire Cloud now felt foolish for thinking that Janelle's lingering eye contact and sweet smiles meant something.

He did not wish to share his thoughts with anyone now. Yet he had always been truthful with Moon Shadow. Every moment of his day and night, Moon Shadow occupied a dark world not of his own choosing. It was unfair of Fire Cloud to keep anything from him. Moon Shadow was not only a beloved brother, he was Fire Cloud's good friend and confidante.

But Fire Cloud had not shared his feelings about this one thing with his brother, keeping them closed inside his heart through the years. Now this woman had materialized again as though he had magically wished her there.

Still, Fire Cloud did not wish to bring her into his brother's life, for surely there would not be more than mere talk between them. Anything else was more than he could ever hope for. If Janelle had wanted to know him, would she not have lingered in the corridor and introduced herself? Her aunt was not needed for such a simple thing as that.

Again his brother asked him about his mood since Fire Cloud had not yet responded.

Fire Cloud heaved a sigh, then began telling his brother about a young girl who was now a woman and was there, today, at the convent.

He had not explained everything before a ray of lingering, late sunshine caught his attention. It seemed to shine directly on his canoe, which was beached on the shore.

Suddenly someone stepped out of the shadow of the thick forsythia bushes stretching from the lawn to the river.

"Janelle," he whispered.

She slowly walked around the canoe, studying it. It was apparent that she had not yet seen Fire Cloud and Moon Shadow standing beneath the oak tree. The soft rays of the evening sun faded as the approaching night seemed to swallow the remaining light.

Stunned and almost afraid to think of why she was there with his canoe, Fire Cloud scarcely breathed as he continued to watch her.

He was not even aware of lowering his hands from his brother's, or how Moon Shadow now stood alone, amazed at his brother's strange behavior.

All that Fire Cloud could do was gaze at this beautiful woman.

She was such a sight to behold. Her golden hair, worn long and wavy to her waist, picked up the last light, making it glow like a beacon to Fire Cloud.

His gaze moved slowly over her, the plain white blouse and dark skirt not taking away from her petite, lovely curves.

She seemed to sense that she was no longer alone, and looked in Fire Cloud's direction. His heart skipped several beats when she finally did see him and Moon Shadow.

Moon Shadow took one of Fire Cloud's hands and spoke to him again, asking him to please explain

FIRE CLOUD

what was happening, that he was beginning to feel frightened.

Fire Cloud was torn between wanting to go to the woman of his dreams, and his brother, who seemed desperate now to enter his brother's suddenly private world.

Deciding to try to meet Janelle and still explain things to his brother, Fire Cloud placed a hand on Moon Shadow's elbow and began walking him toward the river, telling him at the same time about this woman and how, in his mind, she had been a part of his life since she was a girl of eight and he a boy of ten.

Moon Shadow's lips moved into a soft, wondrous smile, and he clasped Fire Cloud's hand. He understood and accepted this change in Fire Cloud's life, which Moon Shadow knew would also be a part of his.

Moon Shadow was eager to meet the woman as well, for he knew that any woman who caused such passion in his brother was worth Fire Cloud's infatuation.

Moon Shadow hoped that he would soon have a new friend and that his brother would finally allow himself to bring a woman into his life.

Moon Shadow had always wanted to be an uncle!

He laughed to himself, realizing how far he had mapped his brother's future. But a woman who had intrigued his brother for this long must be very special!

Janelle smiled and began walking toward them, and Fire Cloud's knees seemed to grow weak from anticipation. A warrior allowing himself to become this disturbed by a woman—one he had wished for for as long as he could remember? He could feel nothing but awe at this moment.

Finally face-to-face, and even heart-to-heart, Fire Cloud and Janelle stood quietly looking at each other. He was very aware of how her eyes moved downward and stopped momentarily on his breechclout, a piece of clothing that had caused many white people's eyebrows to rise.

He could not help but watch for her reaction, and was glad when she did not seem affected one way or the other by the scarcity of his clothing.

He did notice how she lingered more on the muscles of his bare chest and shoulders, making him unconsciously square his shoulders to make the muscles more pronounced.

Finally, she looked again into his eyes, her hand shaking as she held it out to him in a gesture of friendship.

Janelle hated how hard it was to keep herself from trembling with elation. She willed her hand to stay steady as she reached out for Fire Cloud's.

When he took her hand, the warmth of his flesh enclosed hers, and seemed to take a quick path directly to her heart. Janelle tried hard to wish away the blush she knew was rushing to her cheeks.

Yet nothing would stop this heat that rushed through her. She was finally with Fire Cloud, and he was more handsome than she had ever imagined.

And his eyes!

Those magnetic brown eyes!

She breathed in a sigh of delight, then forced herself to find the words to finally speak to him. Her eyes quickly took in Moon Shadow and Fire Cloud's other hand on his elbow.

Such devotion only made her admiration grow. She wanted to get to know Moon Shadow as well.

But first she had to make certain Fire Cloud wanted to know *her* better. She had waited a lifetime for him. It would devastate her if she had been wrong to keep him so close to her heart. It had been special, this secret love she had shared with no one.

"I'm Janelle," she finally hurried to say. "Janelle Coolidge."

And before he had a chance to respond, she continued, "And I know you. I remember you from that time long ago when I came to the convent with my father. I asked my aunt about you. She told me your name." She slid a smile over to Moon Shadow even though the younger warrior was not able to see it. "I now also know Moon Shadow's."

Fire Cloud found it hard to respond immediately. He was stunned to know that she had been as infatuated with him as he had been with her. And it touched him that she knew about Moon Shadow's afflictions and still looked at him with smiling eyes.

And her hand lingering in his made it even more difficult to think clearly, for never in his life had anyone's touch been so wondrous.

"My Aunt Mary Ann would have introduced us after supper, but she was called away on business," Janelle said further, surprised to find it so easy to talk to this man. She would have thought that she would be too awestruck to say anything to him.

"*Ay-uh*, I know," Fire Cloud said, then saw her smile waver at his use of Chippewa.

"I said the word 'yes' in Chippewa," he was quick to explain.

Janelle smiled again. "Aunt Mary Ann told me that you are Chippewa by birth, but you live among the Lakota. She also told me why," she murmured. "I'm so glad that although you and your brother were orphaned, the Lakota took you in and cared for you."

"We have a good life with the Lakota," Fire Cloud said, nodding. Although he regretted having to let her go, he slid his hand free of hers. They walked toward the canoe, with Fire Cloud explaining to his brother in their special language what was happening.

"Do you ever think of the people you were forced to leave behind?" Janelle asked.

She was so glad they were finding it easy to communicate, for she wanted much more than this.

She wanted to know everything about him.

She wanted a life with him.

Yet she was afraid that might be going too far. She must be careful not to frighten him away by being too forward.

It was new, this forwardness with a man.

Although she had taught young men in her classroom at Coolidge College who were not much younger than she, she was not one to mix and speak easily with men.

She was shy, sometimes to a fault!

FIRE CLOUD

But today?

Today, thankfully, conversation was coming easily for her. This man's personality made it so.

"*Ay-uh*, I think of my true people, the Chippewa," Fire Cloud then said. "And I long to see them. But now my life is my brother. I am my brother's keeper. When I brought him into this world, I vowed then to protect him forever."

"You say that you brought your brother into the world." Janelle stopped next to the canoe. The moon had now replaced the sun in the sky. The heavens were dark and flecked with glistening stars. "What do you mean?"

He explained to her about his brother's birth and his mother's death, then said, "My father taught me that a man's heart should always hold a place for courage. I prayed for that courage on the day I was given a brother and lost my mother."

"You must have been frightened to be so alone," Janelle murmured. "Your mother and father could never have been as proud of you as then."

"To keep my brother safe I prayed to *Kitchi-Manitou*, the great spirit who watches over my people," Fire Cloud said. "You see, I never really felt alone. Spirits are always around us."

He waved both his hands around him. "Spirits are found in water, rocks, trees, and stars," he said softly. "My father's spirit comes to me as an eagle."

He stood again beside his brother and told him about the conversation.

Janelle found it hard to speak as a breeze swept his hair back from his sculpted face. He seemed to have found the secret to happiness for both himself and his brother, yet she knew that much had been taken from all red men.

Recently, fascinated by the nearby Indian village, she had taken the time to study several treaties between the Chippewa, the Lakota, and the United States government. The Indian people had not been treated fairly.

The Lakota had signed a treaty with the government in 1851. One of the government's interpreters had told them that it was as fair as fair could be. They soon discovered that the interpreter had lied, for the treaty forced them from their homeland so that immigrants could settle where they pleased.

She would never forget reading one Indian's opinion: "The white man's words are like a whisper on the mourning winds. The red man was deceived again by hearts that could only hate . . . a hate born of greed."

She knew, though, that thus far the Chippewa had not been duped like the Lakota.

"Do you plan to return to Minnesota some day?" she asked.

"My heart does ache to be with my people again, especially my grandfather, who is chief of our Saint Croix band," Fire Cloud said. "But if I never have the opportunity to go back, I carry my grandfather with me here at all times. My grandmother died just before I left with my mother."

He doubled a fist and gently tapped his chest above his heart.

"*Ay-uh*, my grandfather, my cousins, my aunts and uncles, are always with me," he said, smiling.

He lowered his hand to his side, but noticed her questioning gaze.

"You see the scar on my wrist?" he said, raising his hand again so that she could see it more clearly. "I now carry blood of both the Lakota and Chippewa because I have exchanged blood with Tall Night."

"Who is Tall Night?" Janelle asked. She had read about blood brothers, and how the ritual was done.

"Tall Night is the son of the Lakota chief, Chief Black Eagle, and my closest friend," Fire Cloud said.

"I admire you for being a teacher," he blurted out. "Wisdom is everything."

She knew now that he had asked about her!

"Can I meet your brother?" she asked, quickly changing the subject. "I would like him to know me."

Fire Cloud was touched by her request. He so badly wanted to tell her that she had the light of stars in her eyes, that her laughter was like the morning sun, that both would warm the soul of any man, but his especially. He was not sure how it happened, he only knew that he was in love with this woman for eternity.

Her voice was low and musical. And her laugh was so sweet, it melted his heart.

"My brother also wants to know you," Fire Cloud assured her. "It is done in this way."

He reached for her hand and placed it on his brother's face, and then put his brother's hand on her face.

His brother studied Janelle's facial features. In his own way, Moon Shadow told Fire Cloud that he could see her beauty with his fingers as much as Fire Cloud saw it with his eyes.

Moon Shadow told him that he approved of this woman for his brother.

Fire Cloud knew that his brother's fingers saw the woman as she truly was—entrancingly beautiful, and just as sweet and sincere. They both could trust everything about her.

Janelle was almost moved to tears as she watched the brothers communicate. She was touched by the younger man's innocence and hoped to find some way to help him. Yet he seemed so content in his world the way it was.

She knew that Fire Cloud was responsible for his brother's happiness, and that fact alone spoke of this man's inner self—he was good, through and through.

"Sister Mary Ann told me why you are at the convent," Fire Cloud said, daring to bring up such a private part of her life. But becoming a nun did not seem to fit the person she was while with him and Moon Shadow.

Or had he read too much into her behavior?

Nuns never married. They were friends with men, nothing more.

He was suddenly afraid he *had* interpreted her behavior wrongly . . . that she only wished to be a friend.

He just could not see them only having occasional talks. In his heart, he wanted much more than that from her.

For the first time in his life he desired more than what he had.

His body was telling him that he wanted her as a man wanted a woman.

It would be a tragedy if she clothed the womanly side of herself in the black attire of a nun!

Janelle glanced away. She was not disturbed by his question, but tried to find a way to answer it, that would not put her in an awkward position if he only wanted a friendship with her. She took a step toward the river.

As the waves splashed their foam along the shore, she searched for the right words to say. She now knew that she had fallen in love with this man back when she was just a girl and did not know what it meant.

In the years since, envisioning Fire Cloud as a grown man, she had learned how it felt to love a man—this man.

But now? Should she reveal her feelings?

And how did she do this without looking like a bungling idiot?

"Janelle?" Fire Cloud stepped away from Moon Shadow, who was starting toward the canoe.

Hearing him speaking her name with such meaning, Janelle felt a passion she had never known before.

Slowly she turned to him.

Their eyes met and held in the moonlight.

"No, it was never my aspiration to become a nun," she finally found the words to say. "I only recently decided that it might give my life more meaning. My aunt has always been serenely happy in her life. I . . . I hate teaching so much, and I . . ."

She stopped short of revealing too much about the man she had wrongly become engaged to, and how she had felt so empty . . . until now.

She dared not tell him that seeing him had changed her whole world, that suddenly hiding away as a nun was the last thing she wanted to do.

She surely knew better than to tell him about the delicious stirrings he had caused inside her.

"I must go," Janelle said, suddenly afraid of her feelings.

"Must you?" Fire Cloud asked, puzzled by the panic he heard in her voice.

At that moment, his brother gasped in a way that meant he had found something exciting.

Fire Cloud turned quickly and smiled when he saw his brother along the riverbank, his fingers having discovered a new rock.

He was holding a piece of limestone with one hand, while studying it carefully with his other.

"He seems so fascinated," Janelle said, also watching Moon Shadow. She was glad for the distraction from their awkward moment.

"Rocks and shells are his hobby," Fire Cloud said, going to see Moon Shadow's rock for himself.

Janelle knelt on the other side of Moon Shadow and watched his fingers slowly study the formation.

Then she began talking about things that made no sense to Fire Cloud, things that only she, as highly educated as she was, would know to say. Fire Cloud

FIRE CLOUD

listened just because he liked to hear her voice. It was so soft and sweet, like a melody.

"This stone is from the Meramician Series, a division of sedimentary rocks that occurs in the Meramec River," she said, unaware of having gone on one of her tangents that came with being a teacher. "They are frequently used as building stones. Many of the limestone formations have—"

"Janelle! Janelle, darling, where are you?"

Sister Mary Ann's voice quickly stilled Janelle's words.

She was suddenly embarrassed at rattling on about things that surely were of interest only to Moon Shadow, who could not hear her anyway.

Sister Mary Ann arrived at the river. "There you are," she said to Janelle. "I became worried when you stayed away so long. Had I known you were with Fire Cloud, I would not have worried one minute."

Sister Mary Ann saw how Janelle and Fire Cloud looked at each other. Janelle had just found a meaningful direction in her life, she thought, but it had nothing to do with being a nun.

Sister Mary Ann was all right with that, for she loved Fire Cloud as though he were her very own son, and Janelle just as much. She saw those two as a perfect match.

Both were genuine, caring people.

She hoped together they would make the world a better place.

"My brother and I must leave now," Fire Cloud

said, realizing Janelle might feel awkward having been discovered alone with a man.

Of course he hoped that Sister Mary Ann did not see him as just any man, since they had such a special bond. But all the same, he thought it best to take his brother and leave.

At least for now.

But nothing would stop him from returning, for their relationship finally had a chance to begin.

"I enjoyed talking with you," Janelle said, then smiled at his brother. "Also Moon Shadow."

Sister Mary Ann took Janelle by a hand. "Come again soon with Moon Shadow," she said to Fire Cloud with a wink. He could only interpret that as a good sign!

He returned only a smile to Sister Mary Ann, gave Janelle a smile and nod, then watched them walk away into the darkness.

When Fire Cloud and his brother arrived at the village, Fire Cloud still felt as though he was floating on clouds. After his brother was asleep at home in his bed of pelts, he took out his father's bow and quiver of arrows.

He sat on a white deerskin by his lodge fire and prayed over his father's things.

He thanked *Kitchi-Manitou* for the wonders of the day, and then went so far as to pray that the woman would be his.

"I have waited a lifetime for her, have I not?" he found himself saying aloud, his voice lifted on the night air along with the smoke that wafted up from his lodge fire.

In his mind's eye he saw a young eagle spreading its strong wings as it soared above Fire Cloud's lodge. Even in the darkness, the moon made a path for it to follow. Again, his father was near and had heard him!

Chapter 10

No matter how hard he tried, Fire Cloud could not relax enough to fall asleep. Janelle was still on his mind. He was eager to be with her again, to really begin to know her.

But he might not have much time to make their acquaintance work as he wished it to, as a man and woman in love. For the fact remained that she was at the convent to become a nun.

Although she had confessed to not considering the convent until recently, she was there, perhaps even now cutting her lovely hair.

Aware that he was grumbling to himself as though daft, Fire Cloud busied himself working on a new, stronger bow. The wood of his father's bow had weakened. He wanted to set that bow aside now, to keep only as a remembrance of his father.

He shook his head to keep the dark thoughts of his father's death from creeping into his mind again tonight. They were too painful, and caused a bitterness and resentment that he did not want to experience again.

Especially this night, with the lovely woman and her beguiling smile so fresh in his memory.

It had been wondrous to see how she had treated Moon Shadow with such gentleness and respect. Her luminous eyes had said all that was needed as she allowed Moon Shadow's hand to feel her face.

Fire Cloud glanced at the lowered buckskin entrance flap and smiled. Outside, only a few footsteps away, stood his brother's own tepee. He kept his treasured rocks and shells on display along one side of the lodge. When the children of the village wanted to see them, Moon Shadow proudly allowed them into his home.

Glad that his brother was at peace with how he had been born, Fire Cloud felt peaceful as well, knowing he had done everything he could to make Moon Shadow happy.

He slid the bow across his lap and began the final stages of readying it for use. With his sharp knife, he continued carving the handle of his bow. He had already carved the likenesses of deer and bear.

Tonight he was finishing an eagle that he had begun only yesterday. He made certain that the eyes were lifelike, alert, and filled with intelligence.

The eagle looked back at him with its newly carved eyes, and he smiled. Having this animal on his bow would be almost the same as having his father with him on the hunt, for it was the eagle that had claimed his father's spirit.

An eagle had perched on a high limb of a cottonwood tree the very day Fire Cloud had carefully chosen and downed a strong, pliable young oak tree to make his bow with.

It patiently watched as Fire Cloud cut what he

needed for making his bow and followed him to where he sat planing the wood with a stone scraper. He had smoothed his wood with sandpaper that he had made by pouring sturgeon glue over tanned moose hide, and then dusting this with a very fine sand. After drying in the sun for several hours, it was ready for use as sandpaper.

His bow was as long as he was tall, which was two inches above six feet. He had gathered sinew and fish glue to finish his bow. The sinew had been removed from the spine of a deer, placed on a flat surface, and allowed to dry. It had then been smoked to make it moth- and fly-proof. Nine lengths of sinew would be used to string his bow.

Soon it would be ready, but he was proficient not only with a bow and arrow—he also owned a prized firearm. He had given twelve finely dressed robes for his first breech-loading rifle, which could be loaded while riding a running horse.

At the thought of his horse, Fire Cloud stopped his work to gaze up through the smoke hole at the aperture of his tepee. He suddenly ached to ride his steed. It might help him relax more than working on this bow.

Ay-uh, he would ride a while, and then if he still could not find comfort within his blankets tonight, he would go and see if his friend Tall Night was still awake. They had spent many midnight hours together comparing dreams and sharing stories. Tall Night took the place of Moon Shadow in actual conversation. It was good to have someone else as close to him as a brother.

After stopping to look in on his brother, Fire Cloud went to his private horse corral at the back of his and his brother's lodges. He took Midnight, his prized black stallion, from the others, secured the reins, then swung himself onto the steed.

How he loved the excitement of riding bareback. After starting off at a gallop, Fire Cloud's horse stretched out in a dead run from the village, his pounding hooves like thunder in the silent hour. Midnight whinnied happily as Fire Cloud was carried almost motionless on his straining back. The horse plunged down steep hillsides, rode hard across flat stretches of prairie, and then wound its way through the shadows of the forest.

Not wanting his damp horse to catch a chill in the cool night, Fire Cloud slowed Midnight's pace to a slow lope and headed back toward home.

When he arrived there and had dried Midnight with a handful of straw, Fire Cloud still felt a strange uneasiness. He gave his steed a hug around its powerful neck, then left the corral and started back toward his lodge.

He noticed a fire glowing through the buckskin covering of Tall Night's lodge and knew by its size that wood had just been added to it. Tall Night had not yet retired to his blankets for the night.

Needing his friend's companionship tonight, Fire Cloud hurried on to Tall Night's lodge.

Fire Cloud spoke Tall Night's name outside the entrance, and his friend soon came and held the flap aside for him.

"*Nee-gee*—friend—what brings you to my lodge

this hour of night?" Tall Night asked. He gestured toward several mats spread out beside his fire. "*Mah-bee-szhon*—come. Sit. Tell me what is keeping you from your sleep blankets."

Fire Cloud sat down opposite the fire from Tall Night. He was curious about why his friend also could not find solace in sleep tonight, yet he did not ask the reason. If Tall Night needed to talk about things that were bothering him, he would not need prodding. They were very open with each other. Each knew the other's emotions as though they were an extension of his own.

"I am restless," Fire Cloud said, sighing heavily. He folded his legs before him and rested the palms of his hands on his bare knees.

"And what is it that makes you restless?" Tall Night asked.

"I went today with my brother to visit the nuns and children at the convent," Fire Cloud said, again picturing Janelle. He could not stop thinking about her bright eyes, and how she was not only beautiful, but dignified, as one would expect of a Chippewa princess.

He could almost feel the softness of her cheeks. . . .

"*Ay-uh*, I knew that was your plan," Tall Night said, drawing Fire Cloud quickly from his thoughts. He slid a piece of wood into his fire. "But Fire Cloud, you usually come away from there feeling *o-nee-shee-shin*—good—about things, not restless. What was different about today?"

Fire Cloud frowned and eluded his friend's steady gaze, for he was not sure if he should reveal his feelings about Janelle. In the end, if she turned her back on his interest in her, he would forever look foolish in his best friend's eyes!

Yet how could Fire Cloud *not* share these feelings with his friend? He needed so badly to talk about her tonight, for if he did not, he thought he might explode!

"There was this *ee-quay*—woman . . ." Fire Cloud began guardedly. At the mention of a woman, his friend seemed to flinch strangely, as though someone had slapped him.

They usually discussed women without hesitation. So why was it different tonight for Tall Night, a man who was not yet wed himself?

"A woman makes you so restless?" Tall Night finally said. He seemed to Fire Cloud to be trying hard not to show his uneasiness. "A nun? That is why you visited the convent today?"

"*Gah-ween*—no—she is not *yet* a nun, but she is there at the convent for that purpose," Fire Cloud said. "But I hope she may change her mind after our time together tonight."

"Why would you even care what she is, or is not?" Tall Night asked, raising an eyebrow. He had not seen Fire Cloud show any special interest in a woman before even though he could have his pick.

Of course Tall Night knew that Fire Cloud had taken women to his blankets, but thus far, had not chosen any for a wife.

And now?

Had Fire Cloud met someone whom he could not have?

Tall Night knew that nuns did not marry. Tall Night also knew that nuns were *washicho*—white!

When Fire Cloud finally did open up to Tall Night about Janelle, he could not tell if Tall Night approved or disapproved of his infatuation with a white woman. Tall Night seemed more withdrawn now than earlier.

In fact, now that Fire Cloud thought about it, he could recall noticing changes in his friend's behavior for several weeks.

No. He realized that Tall Night's strange behavior had started some months ago.

Ay-uh, Fire Cloud had realized that something was bothering Tall Night, but when he had tried to get him to talk about it, his friend had grown quiet.

Because of Tall Night's determination not to discuss whatever was bothering him, Fire Cloud had stopped inquiring about it.

And it had been hard for Fire Cloud, for they had always been open and eager to share their lives.

They were like brothers.

"Her name is Janelle, and she would make any man take notice of what she does or does not do," Fire Cloud responded. "Like I said, she has intrigued me since I first saw her many years ago. I truly believe that the reason I have never chosen a wife was because I knew, somehow, that Janelle would return to me. She is the only woman I have ever really desired."

Fire Cloud's eyes narrowed as he looked more intently at Tall Night. "And, yes, Tall Night, she is white," he said, having guessed what his friend had concluded.

FIRE CLOUD

"And that does not concern you one way or another?" Tall Night asked. "Can you truly allow yourself to love a white woman after the whites have taken so much from our people?"

"Our lives have been altered because of whites, but that was not the work of this woman. She shows not one ounce of prejudice in her eyes or heart," Fire Cloud said. He folded his arms across his chest and straightened his back. "She is white, yet she thinks with the compassion of someone whose skin matches ours."

"You can allow yourself to think this much about her, even though she is at the convent to be a nun?" Tall Night asked.

"If you were there, and saw how she reacted to me, then you would understand why I can hope that she turns her back on the idea of being a nun and, instead, wants to be my *gee-wee-oo*—wife!" Fire Cloud boldly announced.

"You go this far in your desire?" Tall Night gasped. "You trust her this much?"

"Honesty and trust come in many shapes and forms, my friend," Fire Cloud said. "And I know that this woman would never be dishonest with anyone, especially a man who has deep feelings for her."

"Some women know well the art of deceit," Tall Night said, his voice breaking.

"You speak as though you know a specific woman," Fire Cloud said, arching an eyebrow. "Do I also know her?"

When he saw a guarded look on his friend's usually happy face, Fire Cloud knew that he had touched a nerve. This was a subject his friend no longer wished to pursue.

Tall Night still did not respond to his question, and Fire Cloud at last decided that it was time to leave his friend with his troubled thoughts. If Tall Night did not wish to share his concerns with him tonight, perhaps he would tomorrow.

He found this realization that both he and Tall Night kept secrets from each other so peculiar. As friends, as blood brothers, hardly anything stayed secret between them.

But this concerned women. And it seemed that many secrets—and deceits—occurred in the name of love. His beloved mother had proved that to him long ago.

"I must go now," Fire Cloud said, rising to his feet. "I am suddenly weary enough, I believe, to finally sleep."

Tall Night rose as well and went outside with Fire Cloud. He suddenly hugged Fire Cloud, a hug that seemed filled with desperation.

Yet Fire Cloud still did not press Tall Night for answers. It was each man's choice whether and when to seek comfort from a friend.

Tall Night stepped away from Fire Cloud. "It is not your normal time to go to the convent tomorrow; will you go anyway?" he asked softly.

Fire Cloud smiled and nodded that, yes, that was his plan. Then he walked back toward his lodge, counting the hours before he would see Janelle again!

Chapter 11

Janelle stood at her bedroom window, looking out at the forest that stretched out on three sides around the convent, the river on the fourth.

She was used to living closer to the city, where one could not hear at night the howling of gray wolves and coyotes, the voices of the owls, or the eerie cries of loons over water.

Yet she could not help but smile, for out there, not far upriver, was the Lakota village.

She wondered if Fire Cloud was hearing the same noises.

Was he kept awake by them? Or was he used to all sounds of nature and sleeping now in his bed?

She laughed to herself, knowing that it was not only the night sounds that were keeping her awake. It was her constant thoughts of Fire Cloud!

For so long she thought of the moment when she would get to be with him, so close she could touch him, so close she could have kissed him if she had the nerve.

And what of his brother?

Her smile faded as she remembered how cruel life

had been to Moon Shadow. Someone out there practicing medicine must know how to help him.

Saint Louis had many skilled doctors. If there was just one who could help Moon Shadow, she would find him!

"Aunt Mary Ann," she whispered.

She turned on a bare heel toward the closed door.

She glanced down at her gown and bare feet, then at the door again.

Yes. She would go to her aunt and see if she was still awake. If so, Janelle would ask if she knew a doctor Janelle could tell Fire Cloud about. Surely if Fire Cloud saw a chance to help his brother, he would.

"Yes, I shall go and see," she said, sliding her feet into her soft house slippers.

Soon she found herself in the corridor just outside her aunt's room, knocking on the door.

Sister Mary Ann, in her own night robe and slippers, opened it.

"Child, are you feeling homesick?" Sister Mary Ann asked, quickly drawing Janelle into her arms.

"No, that's not what brings me here so late," Janelle said, following her aunt into her room. Janelle then rushed to tell her aunt about how she would like to find a doctor for Moon Shadow.

Sister Mary Ann nodded. "Yes, I believe I do know someone who might be able to look into this for you," she murmured. She sat in a leather chair, and Janelle sat opposite her, her eyes anxious.

"I only recently heard about this specialist," Sister Mary Ann said. A candle in a golden holder flickered in the soft light of the room. "He recently established an office in Saint Louis. I was going to tell Fire Cloud about him the next time I saw him. Today too many other things interrupted our usual time together."

"Oh, Auntie, let's tell Fire Cloud soon," Janelle said. "Wouldn't it be wonderful if something could be done for Moon Shadow? Imagine how it would be for him to see, hear, and talk. If this doctor could help him with even one of those things it would bring so much more pleasure into his life."

"There is only one thing," Sister Mary Ann said, her voice drawn.

"What is that?" Janelle asked. She noticed that her aunt's voice was not as hopeful as moments before.

"The Lakota and Chippewa beliefs are very different than white people's," Sister Mary Ann said. "Especially when it comes to medicine. I'm not sure Fire Cloud would take his brother to a white doctor."

"Surely he would, if he saw that there was even a chance that Moon Shadow might be helped," Janelle said softly.

"All we can do is ask," Aunt Mary Ann said.

She ushered Janelle from the room. "But for now, sweet niece, we both need to get some rest," she said affectionately.

Janelle smiled. "If I can."

Back in her room, Janelle stood at the window again. "Fire Cloud, I hope you will be as excited about this as I am," she whispered.

But she knew that Fire Cloud might not even consider taking his brother to a white doctor when the Lakota had their own ways of healing their people.

He must give this doctor a try, Janelle thought to herself. And surely he would, if there was the slightest chance that Moon Shadow's future could be changed for the better.

Chapter 12

It did not seem real to Janelle that she was actually alone with Fire Cloud, walking beside the river with him. When he had arrived at the convent a short while ago asking to see her, she had known then why she had not slept almost the entire night. Something within her knew that Fire Cloud would come today.

This was not his usual day to come to the convent, so when Aunt Mary Ann had seen him arriving in his canoe, she knew whom he would ask to see.

She had rushed up to Janelle's room and told her that he had just beached his canoe even before Fire Cloud could ask for her.

As Janelle descended the stairs and saw him gazing up at her, it was as though time stood still and there were only the two of them.

And now, the longer she was with him, the more she knew that she could never take vows as a nun. This feeling she had for Fire Cloud was far deeper than any she would have as a nun.

"I'd love to take a ride in your canoe," Janelle blurted out as they passed by it. "Strange as it must seem living beside a river, I have never been in one."

"That is because white people use other means to travel the Meramec," Fire Cloud said. He stopped and turned back toward the canoe. "The canoe is not usually adequate for carrying the white man's many large belongings. The red man has learned to make do with the river craft of their ancestors. It can hold many pelts, which we trade at your people's posts. It also holds much wild rice during the harvest season."

"I have never heard of wild rice season," Janelle said, watching as Fire Cloud slid the canoe into the water.

Then he swept her into his arms as though he had done this countless times before, carried her through the knee-deep water, and placed her on the seat at the back of the canoe.

"The Chippewa make their home in wooded areas near rivers and lakes," he said. "From the forest comes everything the Chippewa own, and from the lakes comes their wild rice.

"Wild rice is a staple of the Chippewa," Fire Cloud said, paddling the vessel into deeper water. "I miss the harvest, especially now, for autumn is when my people in Minnesota gather the rice and prepare it for use during the long months of winter."

"When you speak of your homeland, there is melancholy in your voice," Janelle said.

The damp air grew cool as the canoe traveled faster. She tried to ignore the goosebumps on her arms where her three-quarter-length sleeves did not cover enough of her skin to keep it warm.

She hugged herself and watched Fire Cloud's

golden-bronze back and broad, muscled shoulders. His long, slender body was clothed only in a breechclout.

She wondered if he was as cold in his breechclout as she was in her own clothes. His only other attire was his beaded moccasins and a headband that held his thick black hair back from his face. She loved how his hair, as lustrous as a raven's wing, fell loosely down his back.

She was very aware of how his arms rippled with bands of muscles. Her pulse raced, and things happened in the pit of her stomach that were new to her.

She knew these strange feelings were passion, for she ached to be held in Fire Cloud's muscled arms and kissed by his beautifully shaped lips.

She hoped these things happened soon, for if not, she just might explode with her need to be with him.

"Dishes made from wild rice were my mother's favorite," Fire Cloud said, purposely not commenting on Janelle's reference to him sounding melancholy. He knew she was right, for he felt a deep sadness whenever he thought of the past and those he loved and missed.

But just speaking of his mother made her close, at least for that moment.

He enjoyed talking with Janelle about his mother. In time, he wanted her to know all about his Chippewa people.

When he returned to his homeland of Minnesota, he hoped to have Janelle with him to meet all those he had left behind. He could imagine his grandfather's eyes lighting up when he saw Janelle that first time. He, a man who found beauty in all things, especially women, would look past Janelle's white skin to her sweet nature and gentle kindness, her luminous eyes, her beautiful face, and her lovely petiteness.

Fire Cloud knew almost without a doubt that his grandfather would accept Janelle into his family. If his grandson had chosen her over all other women, then she must be worthy of becoming one of their people.

Fire Cloud also wanted Janelle to meet the Lakota, who had become his family in the absence of his own. He had now lived more years with the Lakota than he had with the Chippewa.

"My mother had many favorite dishes also," Janelle said, missing her mother, too.

Fire Cloud turned and looked at Janelle over his shoulder. "Did your mother teach you how to cook these dishes?" he asked, finding it easy to imagine Janelle in his lodge beside the fire, preparing food for their meals.

He could see, and even feel, her body next to his in his blankets.

Their shared passion would be sweet, yet steamy.

He felt the heat in his loins just imagining making love with her. He fought off such thoughts, for he would never show anything less than respect for this woman he wished to be his wife.

He was brought from his sensual thoughts when she began explaining why she had hesitated in answering his question.

"Mother had many favorite dishes, but she did not

cook them herself," Janelle shyly confessed. "Nor did I ever learn how. You see, my family is quite wealthy. Cooks were hired to prepare the meals, as they are at the convent."

Fire Cloud was stunned that she did not know how to cook at her age. Cooking was one of the primary daily activities for the women of his village, who learned how as early as age six. Fire Cloud was momentarily at a loss for words.

Janelle saw his astonishment at her confession. "Does that matter to you, that . . . that I do not know how to cook?" she asked. "I'm a fast learner. I am sure I can learn quite quickly how to make those rice dishes if someone took the time to teach me."

Seeing that he had made her feel embarrassed and ashamed over not knowing how to cook, Fire Cloud hurriedly tried to correct his error. He smiled at her. "Everyone has to learn how to do different things at one time or another," he said. "Cooking will come to you as easily as releasing an arrow from a bowstring came to me."

"I am sure that I can learn how. I even want to," Janelle told him. "I have been so unhappy with my life. Doing something different excites me."

"Tell me what else excites you," Fire Cloud asked softly, his eyes devouring her, his arms eager to hold her.

"Fire Cloud, I find it so easy to talk with you," Janelle said, her pulse racing. "I feel comfortable enough to tell you that for so long now, nothing has truly excited me."

She smiled shyly and then added, "Not until recently, that is."

"And what happened recently that made you feel differently?" Fire Cloud asked, although he thought he already knew the answer.

But could she say the words?

Was she ready to make such a commitment, which would not be as easy to back away from as becoming a nun?

Janelle did want to tell Fire Cloud exactly how she felt about him, but it was hard. She had never talked openly with a man like this before. And she had never felt passion for a man either.

Yet she knew that if she did not tell Fire Cloud now, he might not see her as someone who could share her true feelings with the man she had loved since they first met.

"Fire Cloud, I do have much to say to you, yet I would rather not say it in the canoe," Janelle finally found the courage to say. She could feel the heat rush to her cheeks, and he seemed to know why she blushed.

"I will take you to shore and find a place where we can both share the things that have been waiting an eternity to be said," Fire Cloud told her.

He turned on the seat so that they were facing each other, and he reached both hands to her face. His eyes slowly took in her features. And then one of his hands went to her hair, and his fingers ran sensually through the thick, wavy tresses.

"I wonder if you can possibly know how beautiful you are," he said, his voice now husky with longing.

"No, I do not know," Janelle said, trembling with emotion. "Please tell me?"

"You are as beautiful as a butterfly's wings," Fire Cloud said.

His hands slid down and gently gripped her shoulders.

He moved to his knees before her, slid his hands back up to her face and, framing it between them, drew her lips to his.

Their breaths caught with passion at the first warm press of their lips.

Fire Cloud's tongue delved between her lips.

Their kiss deepened, their moans of pleasure mingling.

Carried away with passion, they did not notice the canoe rocking and swaying in the water.

Fire Cloud came out of the rapturous kiss just in time to stop both himself and Janelle from being tossed into the Meramec.

Laughing, Janelle clung to the sides of the canoe while Fire Cloud steadied it, their eyes speaking volumes to each other, their hearts now entwined as one, forever.

"I will get us to shore before we find ourselves joining the catfish in the river," Fire Cloud said, his voice filled with joy and excitement as he resumed his place on the middle seat.

They were both quiet as he beached the canoe. From the floor of the canoe he grabbed a blanket that he kept for the cooler days of travel.

Hand in hand, they walked to a place that would

be private enough for them to be together in whatever way they chose.

Janelle was amazed at how her body had reacted to Fire Cloud's kiss and his hands on her breasts. It was as though she had suddenly come alive, making her wonder if until now, she had only been pretending to be.

The wondrous throbbing warmth between her thighs was still there, and she unashamedly ached for him to touch her heated flesh. She had saved herself for him, had she not? She was ready to give herself to him entirely, to finally experience the bliss that men and women in love felt.

No, she did not, *would* not, feel ashamed for what she was thinking, for anticipating being nude with Fire Cloud and seeing the rest of his body. She did not even feel brazen over wanting to touch that part of his anatomy hidden beneath the breechclout.

Fire Cloud was lost in his own thoughts of how she had reacted to the kiss. Their shared passion was beautiful, and soon he hoped to take her to new heights. Although she had returned his kiss with abandon, and even leaned into his hands as he caressed her breasts, he knew that she was not practiced in such things. That she had participated so willingly only proved how she felt about him. They were meant for each other. It was their destiny to be together. It was only right that soon he would fill her with his heat, and that she would open herself to him. She would be as in awe of how he could make her feel, as he was in awe of her.

"It's so beautiful this time of year," Janelle said,

needing to say something to fill these now awkward moments.

Was she only minutes away from making love to a man whose very nearness took away all her inhibitions?

If he did ask that of her, she would willingly go there with him.

"*Ay-uh*, autumn and its colors cannot be matched," Fire Cloud said, moving past a stand of goldenrod shimmering beneath the sun. Autumn had unfolded beneath this warm sun, and trees from horizon to horizon showed leaves of red, copper, and burnished gold.

Fire Cloud led Janelle beneath a towering canopy of giant yellow tulip poplars, scarlet maples, and russet hickories.

Long-fronded ferns dangled from sandstone cliffs, and mossy boulders rose from the forest floor. Fire Cloud and Janelle walked next to a brook that barely trickled on the gravel bottom of a deep ravine. Pines and hemlocks stood close by in a cool hollow, their roots extending like slender, bony fingers.

He led her along a steep, curving path that continued into a deep gorge where scarlet spice bushes sprouted jaunty tassels, and where papaw trees, their leaves resembling a beagle's ears, grew in great clusters.

He took her past a recess cave, which was a shallow hollow found in sandstone cliffs.

Janelle tried not to show her apprehension as the path drew unnervingly close to the sheer cliffs.

At last, the trail grew more tame, then wound alongside a smaller stream.

There they stopped. Fire Cloud spread the blanket and held Janelle's hand as she sat down.

"How do you know this place?" Janelle asked, amazed at how confidently he had led her there. She did not like to think that he brought other women to this place for private trysts.

"My brother enjoys exploring while he searches for a special rock or shell," Fire Cloud explained. "We have been here often. It is a paradise, don't you think? Listen to the forest sounds. They fill my soul with peace."

She gazed at the languid willows bending toward the water, as if admiring their fall reflection. Beyond, in the forest, she recognized a fleet-footed coyote, and then the bold, dark eyes of a white-tailed deer as it came to see who had invaded the forest's privacy.

She thrilled at the sound of a meadowlark somewhere behind her.

Fire Cloud also heard the song. He smiled at Janelle. "The meadowlark's song is supposed to be *Hinenta Tceitaksa*, which translates as, 'a person is crawling toward me,'" he told her. "Lakota and Chippewa children sometimes imitate this song, even though their parents forbid them to. Its song is thought to be evil, or obscene."

Janelle gasped. "How could something so beautiful be seen as evil or obscene?" she asked, her eyes wide.

"It is just a myth, nothing more," Fire Cloud said, laughing. He stretched out on his back and gazed through the canopy of trees cloaked, like royalty, in crimson and gold.

Caught up in the wonder of not just being there with Fire Cloud, but hearing him talk about things that were new to her, Janelle stretched out on her stomach beside him and propped her chin in her hands.

"Tell me more," she said excitedly. She heard a slight noise at her side and turned to see what had caused it.

Several squirrels scampered by, their beautiful thick tails twitching. She laughed and pointed them out to Fire Cloud as he leaned up on an elbow to see.

"Ah, the squirrel," he said. "Did you know that the ground squirrel got his stripes because he said that a good man was his arch enemy? Because of that, man and other animals scratched his back in anger, and made the dark stripe."

"How interesting," Janelle said. Then, wanting to impress him with her own knowledge of nature, she pointed out a cluster of sweet birch trees to him. "Do you see the birches?"

Fire Cloud nodded. "*Ay-uh*, I am very familiar with birches," he said. "They are used for many things by my people."

Her smile faded, for surely if this tree was so important to him and his people, she would not be telling him anything new about it.

But she decided to at least show him that she knew about such things.

"I see these particular types of birches as 'scratch-

and-sniff trees,'" she said, her eyes dancing when she saw his eyebrow rise.

"And why are they called that?" he asked, confirming that he did not know this particular secret.

"Why?" she echoed teasingly.

She moved to her knees and crawled closer to him, thrilling when he sat up and placed his hands at her waist and lifted her upon his lap, facing him.

"Yes, why?" Fire Cloud said, his eyes gazing into hers.

She thought there might be some devil in his smile, as though he was teasing her after all.

She lowered her eyes. "You already know, don't you?" she said softly.

Seeing that she did seem to need to show him something about nature that he did not already know, Fire Cloud felt guilty.

In truth, he did believe he knew almost everything about birches, for he had been taught all of this by his father.

"No, I do not know," he said, feeling that this white lie was necessary to bring her eyes back up to his. "Please share with me what you know."

Janelle realized that he was saying this to please her and was thrilled that he would. Smiling, she looked into his eyes. She so badly wanted to fling herself into his arms and kiss him instead of just talking.

"It is a 'scratch-and-sniff tree' because its young branches smell beautiful, like wintergreen," she said hurriedly.

Then, unable to hold back her passion, she brazenly wrapped her arms around his neck and drew his lips toward hers.

"Please kiss me?" she whispered.

She did not have to ask him twice. She shuddered with bliss as his lips pressed into hers, and his arms clutched her hard against his chest.

She could feel the pounding of his heart through the cotton fabric of her dress.

She sucked in a breath of ecstasy when he slid his hand between them and gently kneaded her breast. His hand felt warm through her clothing.

"I want to make love with you," he whispered against her lips as he momentarily stopped his kiss. "But I do not want to rush you into anything. With you having thought of being a nun, is it not difficult to even consider something like this?"

Janelle admired him for not hurrying her into making love.

And, yes, she knew that he was right to question it.

Because he had, he might think less of her if she proceeded with lovemaking at this time.

She untwined her arms from around his neck and leaned away from him so that their eyes could meet.

She reached a hand to his cheek, trembling because she wanted him so much, yet certain now that they must wait until later.

"My body, my heart, aches for you. But yes, perhaps we should not go further than this just yet," Janelle said, hating herself for making this sudden decision. "What we have found together is beautiful. Another day, even another week of waiting, will not take away from the beauty of it. In fact, I believe it will enhance it."

She leaned closer and brushed a gentle kiss across his lips, then pulled back again and looked into his eyes. "Don't you think it's best we wait?" she asked. She laughed softly. "I know that it will be hard for me. Will it for you?"

"I have waited a lifetime for you. Having you here is all that matters," Fire Cloud said. "I do have you, do I not? You feel the same love for me that I feel for you?"

"Yes, I feel the same," Janelle murmured. "I love you so much. I know that we are meant to be together."

She had never felt so at peace with herself as now, for she realized that finally she had found the true purpose to her life.

She was destined to love Fire Cloud!

But she wasn't sure how to tell her aunt. Janelle knew that Sister Mary Ann had wanted her to join her at the convent.

And Janelle would love to work with the children, especially the newborn babies that came to the orphanage, so unloved, so in need of comforting arms and reassurance that life wasn't all that bad, that there were those who loved them.

But she knew that she didn't have to be a nun to help at the convent and orphanage. Even after she was married, she could be there often.

"You are deep in thought," Fire Cloud said. He placed a finger beneath her chin and lifted it so that their eyes could meet again.

"I'm thinking about my aunt, how my decision not to be a nun will disappoint her," Janelle told him.

"No, it will not disappoint her, for she will see that you are finally getting out of life what *you* want from it," Fire Cloud said. He was glad when her eyes lit up, and that she agreed with him.

"Yes, I'm sure you are right," Janelle said, recalling how her aunt had eagerly come for her when Fire Cloud arrived at the convent. "Yes, surely my aunt will be happy for both of us."

Then she reached a hand to his face again and gently touched his cheek. "But I doubt that I will be as accepted by *your* people, either the Lakota or the Chippewa," she said, her voice breaking.

"Yes, your being white will make some frown, but those both you and I will ignore," he said.

He looked up to where the sun had moved in the sky and knew that he should be returning Janelle to the convent. And he should get home to his brother. He was never away from Moon Shadow for very long.

Even when Fire Cloud was married, he would always keep his brother's welfare in mind.

"We have been gone long enough, don't you think?" he asked.

Janelle nodded.

They held hands as they walked back to the canoe. Riding back, Janelle thought of a chore that still lay ahead of her.

Jonathan!

She had a ring to return to that dreadful man.

But she would not give him the true reason why. He would learn that in time, as would her father.

She did want to keep one secret from Fire Cloud—that she had a man's engagement ring hidden amidst her undergarments in a drawer at the convent. She would not tell him, for soon it would no longer be a part of her life.

If he ever found out, she hoped that he would not see her as deceitful for not telling him.

Fire Cloud suddenly stopped paddling and turned to Janelle. "You will be my wife soon?" he asked, his eyes searching hers. "Our love is forever, is it not? Shouldn't we share that love as man and wife?"

Having heard about love at first sight, Janelle was certain that it had happened between herself and Fire Cloud. He loved her so much that he had just asked her to marry him!

She could not see her life any differently now. She had to marry this wonderful man, or forever feel incomplete.

"Yes, I will be your wife," she said, her voice breaking. "As soon as you wish to marry me, my love."

He turned fully on the seat and reached out for her.

She moved onto his lap. As she clung to him, their kiss, their bliss, consumed them.

Fire Cloud was not aware of an eagle dipping low in the sky overhead, nor how the majestic bird seemed to watch over them.

Chapter 13

Janelle had made plans to talk at length with her Aunt Mary Ann about Fire Cloud and her feelings for him. She decided to go to her room to read until her aunt found time to come and sit with her.

Walking up the stairs, she thought about Moon Shadow.

Yes, she was glad now that she had forgotten to tell Fire Cloud about the doctor in Saint Louis who might be able to give Moon Shadow a new start in life.

She would go to Saint Louis early tomorrow, alone, and speak with the doctor first. If he felt that he could do nothing for Moon Shadow, she would not have raised Fire Cloud's or Moon Shadow's hopes only to then have them dashed.

Yes, she would go to that doctor tomorrow, and perhaps from there to the village with wonderful news.

She could not help but have some apprehension about entering the Lakota village alone. She doubted that many white women went to their village, for would not most of them be afraid to?

It was no secret that many white women saw Indians as savages. They considered it forbidden to speak to, much less love, a warrior.

"I have much to teach white people. Not as a teacher in a classroom," she whispered to herself, "but as the wife of a noble warrior!"

She hoped that her marriage to Fire Cloud might help people see Indians in a different light. If so, it would be perhaps the best lesson she had ever taught.

She would be setting an example, one that would surely show the white community just how wrong they were to shun, and even hate, the red man.

She would be proud to say that it was wrong to forbid a white woman and a red man from being together.

Yes, if anyone could send a message to a larger number of people, *she* could. She was well known in Saint Louis, so would she not be the right one to set such an example?

News of her marriage to Fire Cloud would spread at all social functions.

That thought made her falter, for she had not yet taken the time to consider her father's feelings about her decision.

Oh, Lord, he would have a tizzy of a fit!

He already had to accept her leaving her position at the college, and even her *home*, to consider joining the convent.

When she told him that she had changed her mind—not to return home, but instead to marry a Chippewa warrior—she hoped the news would not send her father into an immediate heart attack.

How could she have forgotten the very reason she had stayed with him for so long, honoring his wishes, even getting engaged to that horrible Jonathan?

She firmed her jaw and continued up the stairs, for she could not let concerns for her father rule her life any longer.

She did have a life.

She would live it.

She had let herself get to the age when an unmarried woman would be called a spinster, or worse yet, an old maid.

She would just pray that her father was reasonable enough to accept that he had no more control over his daughter's life.

"Janelle!"

A loud, angry voice from the foot of the stairs caused Janelle to stop instantly.

Then her eyes narrowed angrily that Jonathan Drake had the nerve to come to the convent to confront her, and then shout at her in such a way.

She was aware that all activity had stopped down below her. The nuns and the children who had been in the entry hall were shocked into silence over the man who had arrived showing such disrespect to a woman they all loved and admired as well as lack of consideration for the peace of the convent.

Everyone at the convent knew that Janelle did not deserve such embarrassing treatment from any man.

Especially Jonathan Drake.

Her hands doubled into tight fists at her sides, Janelle made a quick turn on the step and glared down at Jonathan, who stood in his expensive dark suit and spanking white shirt with its sparkling diamond in the ascot. He stood with one foot on the first step, his hands on his hips.

She hated his beady eyes as they glared at her through thick-lensed glasses.

She hated the slicked-down red hair that framed a ruddy, pockmarked face.

She despised the thin line of lips and that long, crooked nose.

She did not see now how on earth she could ever have agreed to share vows with him.

She knew when he had given her the ring that she could never marry him. But he had asked her in the presence of her father, whose eyes had filled with pride.

Her father had never recovered from the loss of his wife. It was shortly after her burial that the pains had started in his heart.

From that point on her father had become Janelle's life, and she pampered him to a fault. She had done everything within her power to bring happiness back into his sad eyes and to keep him from having a heart attack.

"Janelle, what in the hell are you doing in this . . . this place?" Jonathan shouted. "You have caused your father much pain. He is more distraught than I have ever seen him. That's going to change, Janelle. I'm taking you home tonight. Get your things packed. I shall come up and carry your luggage to the carriage for you."

When he started up the stairs, Janelle put both hands out before her. "Stop right there, Jonathan," she said stiffly. "You are *not* invited to my room, and you are *not* going to dictate to me what I will or will not do. I do not like doing anything that causes my father stress, but I have given my life to him for too long already. I have my own life now, and I will live it as I choose."

"But as a *nun*?" Jonathan said, taking a step backward onto the first-floor landing. "Janelle, what of me?"

Seeing that Jonathan wasn't about to budge, Janelle saw no choice but to go downstairs and try to reason with him in private. She had been afraid of something like this happening, yet after one full night and two days without him coming to the convent, she thought that he had accepted her decision, as had her father.

Her father had seen how disheartened she had become with her life, especially over her career and Jonathan. She had talked at length with him about it and thought that she had convinced him when he gave her his blessing.

Now she knew that it was something he had done in haste and had regretted ever since she left.

Janelle went down the stairs.

Sister Mary Ann came to her and took one of her hands. "Do you want me to have him escorted from the convent?" she asked, her eyes revealing an anger rare for someone as gentle as she.

"No, I will talk to him," Janelle said, frowning at Jonathan.

"Go to my office," Sister Mary Ann said, stepping away from Janelle. "You will be assured privacy there."

She cast Jonathan an angry look. "But should he cause you uncomfortable moments, come and tell me. I shall see that he is removed from the premises."

"Thank you, Auntie," Janelle said, hugging her.

Then with a flip of her skirt, she started toward her aunt's office. "Come with me, Jonathan," she said over her shoulder. "We've much to settle between us."

He hurried to her side once they reached the office. A stately desk, the most prominent piece of furniture, sat in the middle of the room, with chairs flanking it. The walls were lined with volume after volume of books. Janelle closed the door and nodded toward a chair, which Jonathan quickly took.

Janelle sat down opposite him instead of at the desk. She folded her hands on her lap and glared at him. He sat hunched over in his chair, his eyes steadily watching her.

"Janelle, what on earth possessed you to come to this place?" Jonathan finally said more calmly. "Why do you feel the need to be a nun? I'm a rich man. I can give you everything a woman should ever want and need just as your father has. And what about your career? Does it mean so little to you? And your father? Don't you realize that he hasn't come to the convent because of his heart? He is afraid he might discover that you have made a decision that will eliminate him from your life forever. His heart couldn't take the pain of losing you. Your father depends on you. He needs you."

Until now, Janelle had thought that her father might be behind Jonathan's visit, that he might have told Jonathan to come and do the dirty work that he could not.

She was convinced otherwise now. Jonathan was using her father to further his own plans. And they did not only include marrying her. He wanted the money. Jonathan had hoped that eventually he would have her father's money to add to his own wealth.

If she felt guilty for abandoning her father, she would return home to be with him, and in turn, go ahead and marry Jonathan. After all, Jonathan had already been asked to live in the mansion with Janelle and her father after they were married.

And not only that. Janelle knew that Jonathan planned to further his career. By marrying her, he could take over everything at the college when her father died.

He had just lied about her father being so terribly distraught. In fact, when she left, he had embraced her and wished her well. He had promised not to come to the convent until she made her final decision about being a nun, for he did not want to influence her decision one way or the other.

She loathed Jonathan even more now, for stooping so low as to lie about her father's welfare.

"You are nothing but a weak, conniving man whom I have never had any feelings for," she told him bluntly. "I absolutely refuse to allow you to manipulate me. My father has always spoken for himself. And so would he now if he thought that he should come for me. I shall mail your ring to you, for I never want to see you again. Do you hear, Jonathan? And if Father is smart, he'll see through your schemes as well, and have nothing else to do with you."

Jonathan rose from his chair so quickly that it fell over backward and crashed on the wooden floor. He waved his fist as though he might use it on her. Janelle eased from her chair and backed away from him.

"You bitch," he hissed. "You'll be sorry for what you've done to me. No one humiliates Jonathan Drake and gets away with it!"

Suddenly very afraid of this man, Janelle covered her gasp of shock behind a hand as she took another slow step away from him.

Janelle was glad when Sister Mary Ann rushed into the room with two burly men who worked at the convent.

"Janelle, darling, I heard the commotion. Are you all right?" Sister Mary Ann gasped as she looked at the overturned chair, and then at the flashing anger in Jonathan's eyes.

She hurried to Janelle and wrapped her in a protective hug.

"I'm fine, but please get him out of here," Janelle said, fighting off the urge to cry.

Sister Mary Ann looked over her shoulder at the two men and nodded at them. "Remove him," she said flatly. "Make sure he leaves immediately and watch him until he is far down the road on his horse."

"Like I said, wench, you'll pay!" Jonathan shouted

over his shoulder as the two men grabbed him roughly by his arms and began dragging him away.

Not wanting to see the fury in his eyes, Janelle closed her own until he was gone and she could no longer hear his shouts.

She sighed with relief and went limp in her aunt's arms when she heard the hard gallop of Jonathan's horse.

"What was your father thinking, expecting you to marry a man like that?" Sister Mary Ann said, as she led Janelle to a chair.

Sister Mary Ann righted the other chair and scooted it closer to Janelle. She sat down and took both of Janelle's hands in hers. "Now, now," she said soothingly. "Things are going to be all right."

"I'm so embarrassed," Janelle said, choking back another sob. "How could he have come here like that? Has he no pride?"

Sister Mary Ann giggled. "It is men like him who made me decide to become a nun," she said, then grew serious again.

"Now, Janelle, let's have that talk that circumstances forced me to delay," she said. "My time is now yours for as long as you want. I love you, sweet niece. I want only what you want."

"Thank you, Auntie, for everything," Janelle said, finally able to relax after being verbally assaulted by a half-crazed man. She was glad to have something to talk about that would make her forget these past moments.

She had Fire Cloud to discuss!

"Auntie, I wanted to talk about Fire Cloud," Janelle said, feeling a sweet bliss even speaking his name.

"Then I am here to listen," Sister Mary Ann said, smiling.

"I have made a final decision about something," Janelle said softly. "I can't become a nun. I feel something in my heart that is deliciously sweet, but it has nothing to do with taking my vows. These feelings are because of Fire Cloud. I probably fell in love those many years ago when I was eight and he was ten. When I saw him again—a man, handsome, kindhearted, and loving to his brother—how could I not fall head over heels in love with him again?"

"Yes, how could you not?" Sister Mary Ann said, gently smiling. "Were I many years younger and not a nun, I would set my sights on that young man myself. There is something about him that makes everyone love him. The children here at the convent adore both Fire Cloud and Moon Shadow."

"Yes, I know," Janelle said, remembering the children crowding around both men.

"I have always been uncomfortable with my father's riches, especially after seeing so many orphaned, poor children here at the convent," she continued. "And through the years I felt a need for something I did not understand, something mysterious to me. I only recently thought that being a nun might be that mysterious something, since I have always felt so happy with you and the others."

"But now you know what caused those torn feelings," Sister Mary Ann said. "A man came into your

FIRE CLOUD

life long ago and has stayed locked within your heart."

"Yes, it was because of a man," Janelle said. "It was because of Fire Cloud." She smiled timidly. "And, Auntie, both Fire Cloud and I know our feelings well enough to agree that we are ready for marriage."

She paused, then smiled broadly. "To each other, Auntie," she said dreamily. "To each other."

Sister Mary Ann rose from the chair and embraced Janelle, then sat behind her desk in her plush leather chair. "I knew your feelings for each other after that first time you came face-to-face as adults, but I said nothing about it," she said. "I knew that it was something that you and Fire Cloud had to discover yourselves, and work out in your own way. I wish you well, darling. I will pray for you, for I do believe you will need many prayers once you tell your father. He has groomed you for life in the white world, not the red. He won't tolerate thinking of you living in a tepee, labeled a 'savage squaw.'"

"Yes, I know. I should go talk with him now, but I can't, especially after what I have just gone through with Jonathan," Janelle said, shuddering. "Tomorrow I plan to go into town and meet with Doctor Edwards about Moon Shadow. Hopefully I can get the courage to go to Father then for a talk. But if not, I will soon. I must."

"Well, for now, do not feel as though you have to rush into telling him your plans with Fire Cloud," Sister Mary Ann said. "If you feel so uncomfortable about it, I can do it for you. I've always had a way with my brother, you know. He would be less apt to explode if I told him. Would you rather I do it for you, Janelle?"

"I'll think about it, and thank you, Auntie, for being so understanding," Janelle said. She rose from her chair and went around the desk to hug her aunt. Then she left the room.

Janelle went to the front door of the convent and opened it, which gave her a full view of the river.

She smiled when she thought of her time today with Fire Cloud.

But the smile faded when she recalled Jonathan and his heated words. She had never seen such hate in a man's eyes. She could not help but wonder what he might be capable of.

Chapter 14

When Fire Cloud heard the sound of an approaching horse and buggy outside his tepee, his eyebrows lifted. It was unusual for whites to arrive unannounced. When a white person did make plans for council, the whole village was alerted ahead of time, for there were not many who came these days for such meetings.

Except for the nuns at the convent, and the men at the trading posts, there were no others who had reason to come.

"But there is Janelle," he whispered, his eyes lighting up with the thought.

The thought of seeing her again so soon made him leave the tepee immediately.

As he closed his entrance flap behind him, Janelle drew up next to him.

Janelle had found her courage had waned upon first entering the village. All of the people outside their lodges had stopped to watch her.

She had expected a warrior to step before her horse at any moment and demand to know why she was there.

But since she did look as though she knew what

she was doing, no one had ventured to stop or question her.

Not knowing where Fire Cloud's lodge was, she had prayed that he would hear her horse and buggy and leave his tepee. She was not sure if she could be brave enough to ask any of the Indians, for she did feel scrutinized like a "pale invader."

Whites had been labeled the "pale invader" from the time they encroached on Indian land and began claiming it as theirs.

Knowing this, she wondered if those people who stared at her suspiciously could accept her relationship with Fire Cloud and Moon Shadow.

Today she had decided to test their feelings, for she had already been to Saint Louis and made an appointment for Moon Shadow for one o'clock that afternoon.

She hoped that she had done the right thing and that the doctor could do something for Moon Shadow.

But there were other hurdles to get past before knowing that answer. She was already past the first—coming into the village alone.

The next was to convince Fire Cloud to allow a white doctor to examine his brother.

And finally she had to get Moon Shadow to agree!

She smiled with relief at Fire Cloud when she saw him standing outside his tepee. She hoped to hurry inside, forcing the eyes of the village to look elsewhere.

In time, she wanted to be able to come to the village without anyone looking at her in any way except welcomingly.

She wanted to be accepted as Fire Cloud's wife!

"It is good to see you," Fire Cloud said as he helped Janelle down from the buggy. "I did not expect you." His smile broadened. "Come inside. My lodge fire is also yours."

"It will feel good, thank you," Janelle said. The shawl draped around her shoulders had not kept her warm on this cool day.

As he stepped ahead of her and lifted the entrance flap, she paused to look over her shoulder at the people who still stood quietly watching.

Past them a semicircle of cone-shaped tepees dotted the land near a tree-fringed stream.

She smelled roasting meat and the smoke from lodge fires and long-stemmed pipes, which she had seen elderly gentlemen smoking in a circle around a huge outdoor fire.

And suddenly, as though someone had given a signal, everyone resumed the daily activities that they were performing before Janelle's unexpected appearance in their village.

She could see several women carrying packs of wood on their backs with straps. Some women came from the stream with jugs of water. Others sat just outside their lodges scraping stretched-out pelts from deer, moose, or elk, turning them into finely tanned hides.

The children had resumed their play, their laughter and the barking of dogs filling the air with merriment.

"Is not it a peaceful scene?" Fire Cloud asked as he watched Janelle take everything in. "The Lakota are happy because they no longer feel threatened by the government. No one has come for many moons with new treaties to sign which would remove us from the land we have grown to love. There is no indication that this will happen anytime soon, either. It is a place I will be proud to share with a wife."

The word "wife" drew Janelle's eyes quickly to his. She smiled shyly, then walked past him into his tepee.

The fire's glow, and the sunshine pouring down from the smoke hole overhead, gave off enough light for Janelle to see how spacious, clean, and neat the tepee was.

Fire Cloud gently ushered her over to the plush white pelts beside his lodge fire in the center of the tepee. She could envision herself sharing this home with Fire Cloud, even though it was vastly different from the way she had lived all of her life.

She had eagerly left her old life when she went to the convent. Now, with her decision to be with Fire Cloud, she would have to leave that life behind her as well.

As Fire Cloud sat down beside her and leaned over to place another log on the fire, Janelle noticed bags made of soft, pliable hides along one section of the wall. Surely used for keeping and transporting clothes and similar articles, they were beautifully beaded along two edges and covered in front with embroidery in beads or quills.

Luxurious rabbit-fur blankets woven from long

strips of cottontail pelts seemed to serve as bedding. She realized that she was sitting upon the same sort of pelts, so white they resembled newly fallen snow.

She saw a cache of weapons along another section of the curved inner wall, among them a rifle, two bows, and a quiver of arrows.

"What has brought you to my village?" Fire Cloud asked. "I planned to come soon to the convent."

Janelle looked quickly over at him. "Do you mind that I came?" she asked, hoping that he was not uneasy at her having come uninvited.

"How could you think that I would?" Fire Cloud said, reaching over to take her hands.

"I hope that you will think my news is good," Janelle said, searching his eyes.

"You are doubtful over my reaction?" Fire Cloud said, raising an eyebrow.

"It has to do with Moon Shadow," Janelle said.

"Moon Shadow?" Fire Cloud said, dropping his hands away from hers. "What about my *gee-gee-kee-wayn-zee*—my brother? What news have you brought to me about Moon Shadow?"

"My Aunt Mary Ann told me about a new doctor in Saint Louis," she rushed out, too excited not to hurry on with what she had found out at the doctor's office. He did want to see Moon Shadow and examine him. He even seemed eager to.

"This doctor says that he might be able to help Moon Shadow talk, hear, and especially to see," Janelle said quickly. "He has attended schools in Paris and London to learn how to treat the ailments that plague your brother."

She grabbed his hands, her eyes anxious. "Can we take him there?" she asked. "Can we see if Doctor Edwards can perform a miracle on your brother?"

"No miracles have worked yet," Fire Cloud said, frowning. He again eased his hands from hers.

"Perhaps this time one might," Janelle softly encouraged him. "He is a specialist in such things. Oh, please don't say no to this opportunity. Please go to Moon Shadow and see if he is interested in this."

"My people do not believe in the white doctor's way of healing," Fire Cloud said, looking away from her when he saw disappointment in her eyes. "My people have their own healing ways . . . their own shaman."

Not ready to give up on this so soon, Janelle reached over and gently touched his face. "At least go and talk with Moon Shadow?" she murmured. "It's his life. Please let him be the one to make such a decision."

Fire Cloud reached up and removed her hand, then rose to his feet.

When he left the tepee, she could not help hoping that he had gone for Moon Shadow to ask his decision.

Wondering if he had gone into Moon Shadow's lodge and was speaking with him, Janelle moved to her feet and shoved the entrance flap aside.

She found Fire Cloud still standing there, just outside of his lodge, his gaze on Moon Shadow's tepee. She was disappointed that he had to think this hard about a decision that could change his brother's life forever.

When he felt her presence, Fire Cloud turned to Janelle. He held a hand out for her. "Come with me to speak with my brother?" he asked.

Touched deeply, Janelle smiled and took his hand.

They entered Moon Shadow's tepee, and Janelle saw him sitting beside his lodge fire shining a newly found pinkish-colored rock. Then she saw his full collection laid out on one side of his tepee and gasped in wonder, for they all looked different from each other. They were sparkling clean, and some were so shiny, she could see her reflection in them.

Moon Shadow reached for his brother's hand and spoke to him in their special way, saying, "Fire Cloud, I know it is you by your familiar smell, but I smell something else, like a flower?"

Moon Shadow smiled, then pressed something else into his brother's hand. "No. It is not a flower," he said. "I recognized the perfume of the white woman. Janelle? Is she here with you?"

Fire Cloud responded to his brother's question, then told Janelle what Moon Shadow had said.

Stunned that Moon Shadow was so alert about things, Janelle looked at him for a moment, then sat down on a plush bearskin mat at his side when he patted it and motioned for her to sit there.

Fire Cloud sat down on his brother's other side.

"Tell him now, please?" Janelle urged, anxious to know Moon Shadow's response.

Fire Cloud nodded, then took his brother's hand and told him that Janelle had come to their village, and now his lodge, for a purpose other than a social visit.

Moon Shadow gently laid his rock aside and asked Fire Cloud why she *was* there.

Fire Cloud proceeded to explain about Doctor Edwards, and his belief that there might be a way to help Moon Shadow.

Moon Shadow was scarcely breathing as his brother went into detail, and when he was through, contemplated what Janelle had come to offer him.

Then Moon Shadow asked Fire Cloud what his feelings were about this.

Fire Cloud told him that he saw Janelle as wonderfully generous for having gone to the trouble of meeting with the white doctor, then coming here to offer help, but that he could not say what Moon Shadow should do, that it was up to him. Whatever Moon Shadow wanted, they would do.

Moon Shadow nodded. Then, turning toward Janelle, yet still holding his brother's hand, he said that always their people used the services of their own shamans. He did not think that a white doctor could know more than their shaman.

Fire Cloud relayed this message out loud to Janelle.

"Tell him that this white doctor has attended many professional schools to become a specialist in these matters," Janelle replied. "Ask him if it wouldn't be wonderful to at least take a chance with a white doctor, especially if something could be done for him? If there is some physical cause for his lack of seeing, hearing, and speaking, and it can be fixed, wouldn't that open up an entirely new world for him?"

Fire Cloud explained all of this to his brother; then

Moon Shadow responded that, yes, he would like to give it a try. It would be wonderful to truly see his rocks and shells, not only feel them!

Excited and relieved, Janelle stood up and waited for Moon Shadow to prepare himself for the visit to town, praying that she was right to give this young man such encouragement. She prayed that she was not getting his hopes up for nothing!

She did not want to be responsible for doing harm instead of good!

Chapter 15

Janelle stood at the window in the doctor's office as she waited for Fire Cloud and Moon Shadow to come from the examining room. She had chosen not to go in with them, since it might look as though they could not be alone with a white doctor without her. She did not want to do anything that would take away from Fire Cloud's masculinity. Having a woman escort him and his brother into the doctor's examining room might do just that.

As she saw it, Fire Cloud was a man of much intelligence. He had learned from life's experiences, instead of schools. She believed that had he ever had the chance to get an education, he would have excelled in everything and performed better than his white classmates.

He most certainly did not need her to talk for him in Doctor Edwards's office.

Hopefully, though, his brother would come away from this experience with the senses that nature had thus far denied him.

Sometimes she could not help but wonder if Moon Shadow was paying for his mother's sins. It was tragic, whatever the cause, for, except for Fire Cloud, she had never met a finer young man than Moon Shadow.

Alone in the wood-paneled waiting room with its plush leather chairs, she still chose to stand at the window and watch the activity outside on the street. When she was in Boston, she had sorely missed Saint Louis. As a girl, she had loved to go to the millinery shops and giggle with her mother as they took turns trying on hats.

One day Janelle had accidentally stuck herself in the head with a hatpin, and let out a squeal of pain. At first her mother had been horrified.

But when Janelle had seen the humor in what she had done, and had set off in a fit of giggles, her mother soon joined her. They left the shop that day with four hat boxes containing the fanciest hats they could find among the many.

Memories like that made her miss her mother very much, and she understood how her father could still mourn her. Janelle again felt guilty over her decision, since her father had now in a sense lost not only a wife, but also a daughter.

But Janelle reminded herself that had she not changed things now, she might have never been able to. Her father had become far too dependent on her.

She hoped that by changing her life, she might force him to change his. He needed to find a woman to take the place of the one he no longer had. It was not healthy to think that a daughter could fill the void left in his life when his wife died.

And had she not decided to go to the convent when she did, she might not have met Fire Cloud again, for had not a full year passed since her return to Saint Louis, during which she had not seen a trace of him?

Their chance meeting at the convent the other day had to be the work of fate, for he had been her destiny from the day she took her first breath of life.

Suddenly her knees grew weak as she saw the familiar face of a man walking down the sidewalk across the street in a fine, dark suit.

"Father . . ." she gasped.

It *was* her father, and today he was walking with the aid of his cane instead of just carrying it to show off its fanciness, having only purchased it for the wolf head on the handle and the sleek ebony of the cane itself.

She scarcely breathed as she watched him moving down the sidewalk at a slower pace than usual, leaning hard on the cane, with his shoulders somewhat slumped. To her it was the look of a beaten man.

She could not help but feel she had let him down, yet she would not change things now for the world.

She had her own purpose in life now.

Fire Cloud!

She could not give him up, not for anything, or anyone.

Suddenly her father looked in Janelle's direction.

She glanced at the horse and buggy secured at a hitching rail just outside the doctor's office. Her father might recognize them. Just after they had returned to Saint Louis and he had established his stable of horses again, he had brought this horse to

Sister Mary Ann. He had given her the buggy before they had left for Boston.

If he recognized them, would he wonder who was making a call on Doctor Edwards and go across the street to see?

She breathed a deep sigh of relief when he turned his head away and continued on down the sidewalk at his slow pace. Janelle concluded that the afternoon sun must have blinded him so that he could not recognize either the horse or the buggy.

For now Janelle had a reprieve from confronting the questions she still was not ready to answer. She *would* go to him when she felt certain that he could not find a way to end her relationship with Fire Cloud.

She might not even feel safe to tell her father about Fire Cloud until she was already his wife.

Then her father could do nothing but accept his daughter's love for the handsome, wonderful Chippewa warrior.

She did know that Jonathan had not gone to him yet with the news of their broken engagement, or her father would have made a prompt visit to the convent to plead his friend's case.

Her father had not thought that Janelle would truly accept the life of a nun once she observed what he would call its drabness. He believed that she would return home instead and go on with her marriage to Jonathan.

At least she could thank Jonathan for not ranting and raving to her father over what had happened at the convent.

The drone of voices coming down a long corridor caused Janelle to spin around just in time to see Fire Cloud enter with his brother and Doctor Edwards. The doctor was talking intensely with Fire Cloud about something as he led Moon Shadow into the waiting room.

Fire Cloud glanced over at Janelle with a wide, pleased grin, then turned his attention to the doctor.

"I have done several tests today on your brother," Doctor Edwards said, smiling over at Moon Shadow, who stood dutifully at his brother's side. "I do see promise in them." He again looked at Fire Cloud. "Return in two days. I should be able to give you the results of those tests then."

Janelle went quickly to Fire Cloud's side. "So, Doctor Edwards, you do think there is a chance for Moon Shadow to be well?" she asked eagerly. This man was her father's age, yet his hair had gone completely white.

"As I just said, I do see promise in his reactions to some of the tests," the physician replied, sliding his hands into the pockets of his white jacket.

His thick-lensed glasses reminded Janelle too much of Jonathan, but as quickly as she saw the resemblance, she pushed it from her mind.

"What did you do to make—" Janelle began, but was interrupted by the doctor.

"Just let us wait, Miss Coolidge, before we talk more about it," Doctor Edwards said. He clasped his hands together behind him. "Come in two days. Hopefully I will give you all good news then."

That word "hopefully" discouraged Janelle somewhat.

And she did not like the way the doctor's eyes had wavered when he interrupted her, as though he no longer wanted to talk about this. Had she been wrong about him? Did he not enjoy working on behalf of Indians?

Perhaps he had only pretended to, to get the money she would pay him for his services?

"Just go on now, and when you see your father, tell him I've missed having coffee with him," Doctor Edwards said, taking Janelle by an elbow and ushering her toward the door.

Janelle stopped suddenly and turned to the doctor. "Coffee?" Janelle asked guardedly. "You know my father?"

"Yes, we met by chance one day in the coffee shop next door," Doctor Edwards said, smiling broadly. "We became acquainted and have met often since. He has spoken of you. I have been too busy lately to meet with him, but I shall soon. Tell him that I'll send word to him at the college when I am free enough to see him. Better yet, tell him that I will take him to dinner at the new Grand Hotel's dining hall."

Janelle's stomach tightened. If the doctor took her father to dinner soon, he would see nothing wrong with telling him about Janelle's visit to his office with the Indians.

She wanted to urge him to say nothing, but that would only prompt more questions from the doctor that, at this moment, she did not wish to answer.

"Yes, when I see him, I shall give him your message," Janelle said, she knew much too blandly.

She was glad to get outside and into the buggy. Purposely avoiding her father, she took side streets until they finally reached the forest road, and she could ride beneath the colorful canopy of trees.

"Your conversation with the doctor seemed strained," Fire Cloud said, finally breaking the silence.

He knew that Janelle had been uncomfortable when the doctor mentioned her father. He had not brought it up right away, giving her time to sort through her thoughts. But he had seen the difference in her attitude when her father's name came into the conversation.

He knew that she was torn about her father, and worried about disappointing him with her choices in life, which now included not only being with Fire Cloud, but helping his brother.

"Only because I'm afraid that he might reveal too much to my father that I wish to tell him myself, but only when I am ready," Janelle said, smiling weakly at Fire Cloud. "You see, I have been the center of his life for too long. He is missing me and having trouble with my dislike for teaching, especially after spending so much time and money sending me to the best schools and colleges in Boston. I hate disappointing him, but I want my life back to do with as I please."

"And that is only right," Fire Cloud said. "No one should depend on someone else so much."

He gazed over at his brother. "Except when there is no other way," he said. "My brother has not really had a life of his own. In a sense, it has only been what I have allowed it to be."

"But you have been so considerate of his feelings. Surely he knows that you do not resent his dependency on you," Janelle murmured.

"I want him to get well for his sake, not mine," Fire Cloud said. "It would be so wonderful to see him experience all that you and I do. If this Doctor Edwards does this for my brother, I shall forever be grateful."

"And if he doesn't?" Janelle forced herself to say.

"Then I shall still be there for my brother until we are both old and gray," Fire Cloud said.

"As will I," Janelle said, reaching over to take one of Fire Cloud's hands while her other held steadily onto the reins.

The trail's path narrowed, and it became more difficult to lead her horse through the low-hanging tree branches. She was relieved to see an opening ahead and the outskirts of the village. She could hear children's laughter and smell the smoke of the cook fires.

This time she did not feel uncomfortable entering the village, for she was not alone. But she did recall how the entire village had earlier watched her leave in the buggy with Fire Cloud and Moon Shadow.

She had seen not only intense curiosity in many of the people's eyes, but also a dark resentment.

She knew that Fire Cloud would meet in council soon to tell the warriors of today's experience, and hoped to meet again with them to tell them good news about the doctor's final findings!

She rode into the village and did not look to either

side this time. She continued on to Fire Cloud's lodge. After Fire Cloud had his brother settled in his own private tepee to rest, Janelle was finally alone with Fire Cloud in his lodge with the entrance flap tied closed.

The shawl fell from around Janelle's shoulders when Fire Cloud placed his hands at her waist and drew her against his muscled body, clothed today in full buckskin since he had been in a town of white people who would gawk at his breechclout. His brother had been fully clothed today, as well.

"My woman," Fire Cloud said, his dark eyes gazing into hers. "How can I ever thank you for what you have done for my brother? And for what you have brought into my life? I have never felt more alive than I have these past several days. You do this to me, you know."

He reached for one of her hands and placed it over his heart. "Do you feel it?" he said huskily. "Do you feel my heartbeats? They are for you. I love you so much."

"As I love you," Janelle murmured.

She sighed when he wound his fingers through her thick, golden hair and brought her lips to his in a deep kiss, which led them down onto a thick bed of white rabbit pelts beside his lodge fire.

Fire Cloud had hoped that Janelle would come inside with him. He had purposely prepared this special bed of pelts for that wonderful moment they had both hungered for.

Making love.

He did not think that he could wait much longer, nor could she.

Such a love as theirs came only once in a lifetime. It was hard not to fulfill all of their longings now, to wait until vows were exchanged between them.

"We did not make love when we last wanted to," Fire Cloud whispered against Janelle's lips as his hands slowly caressed her breasts through her blouse. "Should we still wait? Or do your hungers need to be fed now, as mine do?"

Janelle reached up and gently pushed his hair back from his face. "Now, my love . . . oh, now, please make love to me," she said in a near whisper. "Make it all real, not just a fantasy."

Again he kissed her.

Their bodies moved together.

His hands roamed over her, feeling the shape of her thighs through her skirt.

He placed the palm of his hand over where her womanhood lay beneath the fabric of her skirt.

He touched her lightly, enough that she would feel the pressure and awaken into wanting him even more. When she pressed herself against his hand, he knew that she was responding.

He massaged his hand against her over and over until she moaned.

She slid her hand between them and pressed her fingers around the bulge in his buckskin breeches.

Fire Cloud groaned with pleasure as she stroked him. She felt a strange sort of wetness through the buckskin fabric.

"Enough . . . enough . . ." Fire Cloud whispered huskily as he slid his mouth from her lips.

"I shall never have enough of you," Janelle murmured, thrilled to be saying such a thing and discovering so much pleasure with a man. They had not even made love yet, and her body tingled with rapture. She ached now to experience it all.

Fire Cloud took her hands and helped her stand before him.

He stepped back from her.

"Undress as I undress," he said, his hands already at the fringed hem of his shirt and slowly raising it upward. "My woman, this moment with you will live inside my heart forever. It will sustain me when I am on the hunt far from our bed of blankets. It will be with me even when I am in council tending to business. You will never be far from me."

He tossed his shirt aside, then placed a hand over his heart. "You are here now," he said. "Forever."

He held his breath as Janelle slipped her bodice completely off and revealed her round, firm breasts, her nipples pink and swollen.

She tossed the rest of her clothes aside, her silken body nude and beautiful before his feasting eyes.

"I had imagined how beautiful your body would be, but imagination is no comparison to the reality," he said, reaching out to slowly run his hand over her breasts.

Janelle trembled as his hands moved lower, his fingers sweeping over her.

She closed her eyes in sheer ecstasy and leaned into his hands when he placed it over the golden

FIRE CLOUD

hair between her thighs. Then, with his fingers, he caressed her where her longing seemed to center.

The more he caressed her, the more mindless with bliss she became.

And when he slowly began sliding his finger into her, Janelle's eyes flew open.

No hands had ever touched her there before. She felt alive with wondrous pleasure. She knew that soon another part of him would be inside her.

She closed her eyes and threw her head back and concentrated to keep from crying out.

And then she felt his hands leave her body.

She opened her eyes and scarcely breathed as she watched him place his thumbs inside his waistband and slowly lower his fringed breeches.

When he revealed himself to her, and she saw his readiness, she took a deep breath and slowly looked up into his eyes.

He wrapped his arms around her waist, drawing her up against him.

He bent lower so that he could feel his manhood against her where she now ached and throbbed so urgently. She welcomed his lips as he kissed her hard and deep.

She was barely aware of him leading her with his body down onto the pelts until she was pressed into their softness.

His kiss still fueling the fires of her passion, she gave in to it as he moved her legs apart and eased his throbbing member into the folds of her womanhood.

Knowing that virgins often felt pain the first time they were with a man, Fire Cloud entered her as gently as he could. When he broke through her barrier, she flinched and looked at him with surprise. He stroked her face and stopped moving inside her.

"What you just experienced is natural," he said. "Nature gives all women a barrier that is broken the first time a man fully enters her. The pain is always brief, and then the woman is introduced to pleasure far beyond her wildest dreams. Are you ready to find pleasure with me?"

"Need you ask?" Janelle said, smiling shyly at him and placing her arms around his neck. When she arched her hips up toward him, that was answer enough.

He wrapped his arms around her, kissed her again, and began his rhythmic strokes within her, his mind spinning with an ecstasy he had not felt with any other woman.

He held her close to his heart as he continued loving her.

He smiled when she seemed to know that the lovemaking would be enhanced if she wrapped her legs around his waist, for she did this now, her body moving with his, her moans of pleasure mingling with his as the passion swept them higher and higher.

"My love, my life," Fire Cloud whispered against her lips. He cried out in rapture when he finally reached that highest place of pleasure and knew that she had, too, as her body shivered sensually against his.

Later, when they lay side by side next to his slowly burning lodge fire, Janelle did not feel any shame for having made love before speaking the marriage

FIRE CLOUD

vows. Nothing they shared could ever be wrong, for they loved totally and had waited an eternity for each other.

"Let us do something special tomorrow," Fire Cloud said, turning to face Janelle. He placed a hand on her cheek.

"Nothing could ever be more special than now," Janelle said, leaning into his hand contentedly. "But what are you thinking of? What do you want to do tomorrow?"

"Something not new to me, but I think it might be for you," Fire Cloud said softly. "And I want to include Moon Shadow."

"Tell me," Janelle said, her eyes gleaming.

"I would like to take you into Meramec Cavern and show you the wonders there," Fire Cloud said. He leaned up on an elbow. "Moon Shadow loves to go there and feel the intricate rock formations. Taking him tomorrow might relieve some of his anxiety about the results of his tests."

He laughed softly. "As would it also help relieve ours," he said.

"I would love to go," Janelle said, sitting up and folding her legs before her. She did not even feel at all timid as she sat there completely nude in a man's presence.

This was not just any man—it was the man she loved. The man she had just made endearing love with; the man she would soon call her husband.

"Then either come share the morning meal with me and my brother, or share it with Sister Mary Ann and then come for the outing," Fire Cloud said.

"I will have breakfast with my aunt, for soon I will not be there to eat with her," Janelle said. "I will be here. I will be your wife!"

"My wife," Fire Cloud said, reaching over to take her by the shoulders and gently draw her down next to him. "Let us pretend now that you already are, and make love again, and again."

Janelle laughed softly, and then her mind began swirling with renewed pleasure as once again Fire Cloud proved just how masterful he was at making love!

Chapter 16

It was like nothing she had seen before. Even her father's descriptions of his exploring treks into Meramec Cavern did not prepare her for its wonders.

The torch sent dancing shadows along the walls and ceiling of the cavern as Janelle and Fire Cloud walked on each side of Moon Shadow, leading him onward by his elbows to keep him safe from loose rock and dangerous, sheer drop-offs. His hands were free so that he could touch things whenever he chose to.

"I hope that Moon Shadow will see this underground splendor soon," Janelle said. Her voice echoed back at her from all directions as it bounced off one wall of rock, and then another.

"If *Kitchi-Manitou* and your God are willing, *ay-uh*, Moon Shadow will soon be able to do more than *touch* these miracles," Fire Cloud said.

He held the torch steady as they continued slowly through limestone passageways, carved by an underground stream. The action of the water had left fantastic formations.

"My father has studied this cavern extensively," Janelle said, her heart aching at the thought of him.

In her mind, she saw her father as he had looked yesterday, his shoulders slumped, his slow gait that of a defeated man.

Yet she still could not find the courage to go to him, for she feared that she would deepen his despair even more.

If she had decided to live as a nun, it would have disappointed him, yet he had told her that he would learn to live with her choice.

But were she to tell him that she had, instead, chosen a life with a Chippewa warrior at a village where she would be the only white person, his devastation over losing her would turn into rage. He would not accept her living with Indians when all of her life he had warned her about keeping her distance from them.

She even recalled her father's warning to Aunt Mary Ann that "redskins" had their place, and it was not among whites.

"You are lost in thought," Fire Cloud said as he looked questioningly at Janelle. "It seems the mention of your father always causes a change in your mood."

"I saw him yesterday," Janelle blurted out. "While you were in the examining room with Moon Shadow, I saw my father through the window. He . . . he looked so alone, so beaten."

"As would anyone who had lost your companionship," Fire Cloud said, his voice gentle with understanding. "One day he will see how wrong he was to stifle you. Does he not have his own life? You said that he established a college in Saint Louis that bears his name. Is he not a professor there, and an important man at the Saint Louis Museum of Natural History?"

"Yes, he does have all of that, but he always shared it with me," Janelle said, sighing. She looked away from Fire Cloud and again began studying the lovely formations. "He will have to adjust to his new life without me."

"And he will," Fire Cloud said. "As do *all* fathers whose daughters grow up and choose a man to be with. That is how it should be. Daughters are only meant to be with fathers until they grow up and find the man who will then father *their* children."

She smiled at Fire Cloud. "Children," she murmured. "I want many. I was an only child. And although my father kept me busy with schooling and social activities, I was lonely."

"You will no longer be lonely," Fire Cloud said. "You have me, Moon Shadow, and one day children."

"I love you so much, Fire Cloud," she said. "Isn't it a miracle how we've been brought back together? How quickly we recognized our love for each other? With you, I feel as though I am living a piece of heaven on earth."

"They say true love is written in the stars when the lovers are only children," Fire Cloud said. "As they look up at the heavens, in awe of the shapes and patterns of the stars, they do not realize they are seeing visions of themselves as adults in love."

"That is so beautiful," Janelle said, then laughed softly. "But everything you say is. You are very gifted with words and things that I never learned in the fancy schools my father was intent on my attending. I wish I could have been here these last fifteen years learning from you."

"I would have been a boring teacher," Fire Cloud said, suddenly aware that he was blushing for the first time. He had never met a woman who could stir such emotions in him.

"Never, never boring," Janelle said, loving the innocence of that blush from such a strong, valiant warrior.

A yank on her hand interrupted Janelle's thoughts.

Moon Shadow was now on his knees, his fingers moving over the slender, totem-like stalagmites that rose from the cave floor.

Fire Cloud moved to Janelle's side and took her hand. They watched Moon Shadow memorize what he was feeling for him to recall and think on when they returned home.

"He has no vision, yet he sees more than you or I ever could," Fire Cloud said proudly. "Every place he touches becomes a new memory. Were he able to talk, what memories he could share with us. There is more depth to his mind than we could ever imagine."

"Yes, and I wonder if that will change when he has the ability to see what today he can only feel?" Janelle said. "Do you think that he places more emphasis on remembering the things he touches than he would if he knew he could always see them tomorrow?"

"I believe my brother will be so eager to relive all of the things he knew only by touch that he will never allow himself to become lazy about exploring this world," Fire Cloud said. "He will be joyous over what has become mundane to so many—the wonder of everyday experiences."

"If Moon Shadow does receive the gifts of sight and sound, and even speech, I will come back here with him as often as he invites me," Janelle said, looking around again at what the torch's glow revealed to them.

She had never known there could be such grand underground rivers in a cavern, or blind fish that swam as easily as the fish in the Meramec. She had heard her father talk about long, hanging stalactites that took one's breath away, and the stalagmites that thrust up from the floor, in some places like prison bars.

They had gone through what looked like underground rooms, with boulders in the shape of chairs and tables. At other times, the rocks glowed a ghostly white.

She could imagine this place becoming known far and wide one day, with people coming from as far as California and New York to experience its beauty.

She smiled when she could even imagine outlaws hiding in the farthest recesses, cooking the colorless blind fish over a slow-burning fire.

Moon Shadow finally rose to his feet and told Fire Cloud that he was tired and wanted to go home, but that he would come again when his eyes could truly see the cavern.

Janelle and Fire Cloud led him from the cave into the evening air.

At the river Fire Cloud led Moon Shadow splashing to the canoe. Janelle ignored the coldness of the water as she waded knee-deep behind them.

After she was in the canoe seated beside Moon Shadow, she soon forgot the wet end of her skirt, which was cold and heavy against her legs, and welcomed Moon Shadow as he leaned against her and fell asleep.

Eight years younger than Janelle, and so innocent and sweet, he seemed almost like a younger brother to her.

She was glad that he put such trust in her, and perhaps even saw her as a sister he had never had.

Making sure she did not disturb his sleep, she carefully picked up a blanket from the floor of the canoe. Spreading it over both of them to their chins, she enjoyed this moment of bonding with her future brother-in-law.

She smiled at the thought of him being her brother soon—and at the thought of receiving good news at the doctor's office tomorrow!

She would not allow herself to doubt that something positive had come from that visit to Doctor Edwards.

Moon Shadow deserved so much more from life than he had been given!

The canoe swept past the great trees that lined each side of the Meramec, their brilliant purple, red, and orange leaves stretching over the river.

Chapter 17

The wind whistled outside the tepee, a reminder of what was soon to come as autumn changed quickly to winter.

The closed entrance flap shuddered as the wind crept around its edges. Smoke spiraling up from the firepit almost seemed to hesitate before disappearing into the chilly gray heavens.

Janelle glanced over at Fire Cloud, who sat quietly beside her, his mood somber. His eyes stayed on the fire as it consumed the stacked logs in the firepit.

Swallowing hard, Janelle looked away from Fire Cloud. The whistling of the wind seemed especially eerie today because of how things had turned out for Moon Shadow.

The air inside Fire Cloud's tepee was heavy with disappointment as they sat there, the trek into Saint Louis for the second appointment with Doctor Edwards behind them.

As the wind grew louder, Janelle looked solemnly at the closed entrance flap, yet her concern was mostly for Moon Shadow. She felt so helpless now. Except for showing her love and support for Moon

Shadow, she knew there was nothing more she could do to help him.

Sighing, she drew a blanket more snugly around her shoulders and watched Fire Cloud lift another piece of wood into the hungry flames of the fire.

She could almost feel his sadness for his brother, whom he cherished with every beat of his heart.

And she understood because it was an extension of her own, as well as Moon Shadow's.

And there was a good reason for this.

When Janelle, Fire Cloud, and Moon Shadow had arrived at the doctor's office, the news had been anything but good.

The trip back to the village had been one of silence and disappointment. Moon Shadow had gone to his tepee after explaining to Fire Cloud that he needed to be alone.

Janelle understood. She knew that Moon Shadow did not want to show his brother the full extent of his disappointment over the results. The doctor had studied the tests thoroughly and had consulted numerous medical journals before Moon Shadow's appointment, but he could find nothing physically wrong with him, which meant that nothing could be done for him.

The doctor concluded that Moon Shadow's condition was all psychological!

Janelle battled with her own emotions about the findings. It was she who had given Moon Shadow hope, a hope that he had not even considered until she had talked him into going to Doctor Edwards.

Had she not interfered, Moon Shadow would still be that smiling, happy young man she had first met.

He had been content in his world because he had known nothing else since he was born.

Had Janelle not . . .

"How can it be psychological when Moon Shadow was born that way?" Fire Cloud blurted out, bringing Janelle from her troubled thoughts. "The doctor seems almost certain that some sort of trauma has taken these normal abilities away from my brother."

Janelle brought her blanket over to him and gently placed it around his shoulders.

"Janelle, ever since my brother took his first breath I have protected him from all hurts," he said, lifting one corner of the blanket around Janelle's shoulders so they were sharing it.

"The trauma came *before* he was born," Fire Cloud said, again looking into the fire. "Is it possible that while he was in our mother's womb, he might have experienced her pain of rejection, her guilt, as well? When my grandfather banished her, do you think it caused him the same stress as her?"

"Darling Fire Cloud, no one will ever know," Janelle said, once again feeling guilty over her role in what had happened today. "And had I known that I would cause your brother, and you, this unhappiness, I would never have mentioned Doctor Edwards's name. I had just wanted so much for Moon Shadow. But to him, he already *had* a wonderful life, without the need to hear, speak, or see. I did not look far enough ahead to consider the consequences should I be wrong."

Not wanting her to labor over her guilt, Fire Cloud slid the blanket from around them, turned to her, and lifted her onto his lap, facing him.

Their eyes met, and Janelle felt better at once when she saw a measure of peace in Fire Cloud's face.

He was a man of understanding, compassion, and insight.

He was not one to linger too long over disappointments, for he knew that holding things like that inside oneself allowed them to fester, like a wound that becomes infected.

"My woman, what you did for my brother was from the very depths of your heart," he said. "I know that. Moon Shadow knows that. So never regret having tried to better my brother's life. *Ay-uh*, at this moment he feels disappointed, but that is natural for someone who loves life and would enjoy it twofold if he could experience it with all of his senses. But he was a contented boy who grew into a contented adult. Right now, if you went to his tepee, you would not see a beaten man. My brother recovers quickly and is probably even now studying his rocks and shells, happy to be able to see them in the way he knows how."

"You do truly believe he is all right then?" Janelle asked. "You don't think we should go and take a quick peek?"

"*Gah-ween*—no—that is not necessary," Fire Cloud said, smiling slowly. "His asking to be alone is not unusual. When he is alone he is lost in the world he has created for himself, and it *is* a contented world. It just got disrupted for a moment today when he discovered that the tests were negative. But nothing keeps my brother down for long. He is perhaps the happiest person I have ever encountered."

"Then I feel much better about things," Janelle said, her usual happy smile finally returned. She leaned closer to Fire Cloud and brushed a soft kiss across his lips. "Your happiness, your brother's happiness, is *my* happiness."

"Then rest assured that you are free to feel happy," Fire Cloud said. Then Janelle saw his smile wane and a frown crease his brow.

"There is something that I carry around with me day and night that I have not told you," Fire Cloud said. He stroked her cheek as he spoke. The touch of her soft skin was like an elixir, fighting off the feelings that he had never seen as healthy.

But it had been hard not to think about the cause of all these difficulties in his and his brother's lives. It had been the work of one man—his mother's lover!

"Only tell me if you feel comfortable in doing so," Janelle said, seeing how his jaw had tightened and his eyes had narrowed angrily.

"My mother's lover changed my life, and my brother's, forever," he said, again battling his deep resentment for Gray Wind. "Had he not taken my mother's love from my father, had he not slept with her, she might still be alive, as might my father. After my mother went into that man's arms that first time, nothing was ever the same."

"I know how you must feel, Fire Cloud, but there is another way to look at this," Janelle murmured, having had much experience at trying to work out her own secret ghosts, which had become a part of her life the moment her mother died.

And only until recently had she finally taken charge of her life. Although she did feel guilty over how she was affecting her father, she was also happier than she could have ever imagined.

"How do you mean?" Fire Cloud asked.

"Had your mother not been with this other man, would your brother have been born for you to love and cherish?" Janelle said softly. She took his hands and held them. "I have learned from hurts in my own life to always look for the good in things, not linger over the bad. And how can you not feel blessed when you think of Moon Shadow? How he was conceived should be put aside."

"*Ay-uh*, you are right, but it is not easy to do, not when I have lost so much because of that man's eagerness to bed another man's wife," Fire Cloud said.

"Your mother must have loved this man, and you always talk about your mother with such affection. If she loved this man, something about him must have been worthy of it," Janelle said, searching his eyes and hoping he saw the wisdom of her words.

Fire Cloud went quiet as he thought through what she had said. He could see logic in it; yet he had carried such resentment for Gray Wind for so long, it was hard to let go of it.

Smelling rain, Janelle looked up through the smoke hole and saw that the gray clouds outside were worsening. As the wind continued to sneak in around the entrance flap, she sighed.

She framed Fire Cloud's face between her hands. "I hope I have made you feel somewhat better about things," she said softly. "And I hate to go, but I must. I don't want to be caught halfway between your village and the convent in the rain."

"Your words have filled my heart with their warmth and wisdom," Fire Cloud said, truly feeling more at peace. "I shall remember them every time my mind strays to Gray Wind. Hate is not healthy, so I try hard not to let my emotions grow dark."

"I hope that Moon Shadow is all right," Janelle said, slowly rising from Fire Cloud's lap. "But I will not invade his privacy to see."

She grabbed her shawl and swung it around her shoulders.

Fire Cloud walked her outside and helped her up onto the seat of the buggy. "The Lakota hold a special dance for their people every full moon," he said, gazing up at Janelle and memorizing her loveliness, to hold close to him until she returned. "Tomorrow night the moon will be at its fullest. Will you come? Will you share the excitement with me, Moon Shadow, and the Lakota?"

"I would love to," Janelle said. "When should I arrive?"

He chuckled. "At daybreak," he said, then smiled broadly up at her. "I jest. I would like for you to arrive that early, but for me, not for the celebration. But come as day wanes. And if you can, spend the night?"

"I will first see my Aunt Mary Ann's reaction to the suggestion," Janelle said. "If she thinks that it is not wise for me to travel after dark, she will even encourage me to stay the night with you and your people."

"I shall count the seconds until you are with me again," Fire Cloud said, then stepped back and watched her drive off. Soon she would not have to leave him when rain threatened or night came upon them like a dark shroud.

She would be with him forever, as his wife!

Chapter 18

The moon was full and high in the sky.

The flames of an outdoor fire leapt heavenward.

Deerskin moccasins moved to the beat of the drums, as many of the warriors of the village, decorated in their fine feathers so that maidens could watch and admire them, danced around the fire. Everyone else sat back from them on blankets and pelts.

Janelle sat with the women, opposite the fire from those warriors and braves who were not dancing. She could not take her eyes from Fire Cloud as he moved to the rhythm of the music.

She tingled all over when he glanced her way, smiled teasingly at her, then resumed his dance, the fringe of his breechclout bouncing on his thighs, the feathers in his hair fluttering.

Young braves led the warriors' horses behind those who were sitting. The steeds were as decorated and proud as their owners, their eyes reflecting the fire and gleaming in the night.

Janelle had earlier singled out Fire Cloud's horse, Midnight. She knew how much grooming it took to make a horse's coat glisten as Midnight's did tonight.

When she first saw him, she had gasped in wonder at the beautiful feathers tied into his thick mane. She knew that Fire Cloud had spent a good portion of his day preparing his steed for the night's celebration.

She felt at peace with herself tonight. When she first had entered the village in her horse and buggy, she could see Moon Shadow with Fire Cloud rubbing down and brushing Midnight. To her, this meant that Moon Shadow had accepted the doctor's news and was not in despair as she had thought.

And as she drew up next to them, Fire Cloud told him that she had arrived. Moon Shadow's smile had filled her with happiness. It did seem that he was going to be all right after all.

He was now sitting among braves his own age as they took turns speaking with him in the language they had learned from Fire Cloud.

Yes, she did feel that Moon Shadow would be fine; either that, or he knew well the art of pretending. She hoped that was not the case and that he could continue on with the life he had accepted long ago and enjoyed.

The drums beat steadily as the warriors danced, and Janelle felt content. Tonight she had only briefly thought of her father and how she had last seen him looking so downhearted and alone.

Although it had pained her, seeing him had proved to her just how right she had been to leave him. If he depended on her that much, he would never have let her go if she had asked him.

She would have spent the most precious years of her life seeing to her father's happiness and neglecting her own. And she might have ended up hating him for it.

He had these lonely weeks to get past, and then she knew that he would again be happy in his teaching and love for his work at the museum.

Perhaps he would come to her and give her his blessing once he knew of her love for Fire Cloud. She wanted him to be there when she had children so that his grandchildren could know and love him.

"It is now your turn to dance," Fire Cloud said, jolting Janelle from her thoughts.

She looked quickly up at him and noticed a playful glint in his eyes. He was holding his hands out for her.

"My turn to dance?" she said, as his words finally sank in.

"Do you see behind me?" Fire Cloud said, casting a quick look over his shoulder. "Do you see the women moving around and choosing their partners? This dance is the squaw dance. Normally the women choose the men, but since you do not yet know how it is done, I, the man, shall choose *you*."

Janelle was hesitant, for she knew nothing about Indian dancing. Thus far it had been hauntingly beautiful to her, but she had seen the intricacy of their footwork and body language.

How could she possibly follow along without fumbling and looking awkward? She would get in the way!

"My woman, during your adult life you have been a teacher," Fire Cloud said as he realized why she hesitated. "Let Fire Cloud now teach you."

Wanting to know about his customs and make him proud when she participated in them, Janelle took his hand, smiled, and rose to her feet.

But just as she was about to move to the dance circle forming around the fire, she saw something that was not only peculiar, but frightening.

The color drained from her face upon first sight of the lethal-looking whip that some warriors were giving to the women.

Did that mean that during the dance, it would be required for the women to whip the men?

She looked quickly at Fire Cloud, questioning him with her eyes. She was glad that he had not handed *her* the whip.

"I see that you are puzzled by something," Fire Cloud said. He placed his hands at her waist and drew her around to face him. "It is in your eyes. It is in the paleness of your face. What has alarmed you this much?"

She stood on tiptoes and whispered to him as her eyes held steady with his. "The whip," she said. "Why are men giving some of the women whips?"

Now understanding, yet himself seeing humor since it was only innocence, even pride, involved in the ritual, Fire Cloud's eyes danced as his lips formed a smile.

"If the warrior chosen for this dance gives the woman a whip, he signifies that he will present her with a pony later," he said, glad to see that that explanation caused the rosy color to return to Janelle's cheeks, and her lips to quiver in a soft, slightly embarrassed, smile.

"Then I am not to be given a pony?" Janelle said teasingly, in an effort to prove to him that her mood was no longer strained.

"I do not have to play the game of whip before dancing with my woman," Fire Cloud said, drawing her more closely into his embrace. "Come and dance!"

Fire Cloud took her by a hand and swung her around to face the crowd of dancers as the drums again began beating out a steady rhythm. Janelle saw as the dance began that the women followed the men.

"*Mah-bee-szhon*—come," Fire Cloud said, pulling her with him among the dancers. "Laugh! Enjoy!"

Janelle tried not to show her apprehension at looking foolish to the Indian women. She smiled at Fire Cloud, then closely observed how the women danced—their bodies swayed, their feet shuffled, and their hands sometimes rose into the air and clapped.

As they danced they sang in their language, which she could not interpret, or mimic. But still, Janelle found herself relaxing and truly enjoying being a part of the dancing. The knowledge of their songs would come later when she was among them permanently.

She *was* glad that she had worn an ankle-length brown leather riding skirt and a matching brown vest over a long-sleeved white blouse. She had arrived in her riding boots, but had changed into fancily beaded moccasins that Fire Cloud had asked her to wear.

They were soft on her feet as she pranced upon the hard, stamped-down earth around the fire. Her wavy golden hair was long and loose down her back, and it bounced and swayed with her body.

Her eyes never left Fire Cloud as he danced in front of her, the ribbons in his hair fluttering as though they were alive.

She never grew tired of looking at his copper body, the muscles rippling now with each of his movements.

When she did glance down at his breechclout, which almost gave anyone who looked a peek at that part of his anatomy there, she could not help but remember how he had taken her to heights of passion she had never known existed.

Her face flushed as she recalled how it had felt to touch him with her bare hand, and how his manhood had seemed to come alive in her fingers. But most of all, she remembered his moans of pleasure mingling with her own.

Her thoughts came back to the present when the music suddenly stopped and the dancers began leaving the circle.

Fire Cloud turned to Janelle and led her down onto their fine white rabbit-fur robe.

She was quickly aware of the changes being made where dancers had just been. On one far side of the outdoor fire warriors were arranging several drums decorated with symbolic paint and beadwork, and covered with calf hide. Two stools were brought and placed behind each individual drum for the warriors to sit on.

"I see your eyes questioning things again," Fire Cloud said as he moved closer to Janelle. Everyone else occupied their own blankets and robes spread along the ground, except for Chief Black Eagle, who sat with his wife on a special platform decorated with wildflowers and moss.

Fire Cloud had noticed the absence of his friend Tall Night, but had not had yet gone to ask what was bothering his friend so much that he would not come and enjoy the full moon with everyone else.

Fire Cloud planned to approach Tall Night soon, though, and offer a friend's ear in hopes that he might finally reveal what was so heavy in his heart these days.

"Yes, I'm eager to know what happens next," Janelle said, her eyes still on the warriors positioning themselves behind the beautifully decorated drums. "Are these drummers more special in their talent than others? Is that why their drums are more elaborately designed?"

"This music is usually used during a dance called the Drum Dance, but tonight we will instead sit and listen and enjoy the music itself," Fire Cloud explained. "And *ay-uh*, these men behind the drums are the most talented drummers of this village. You will soon hear why."

"From what I have seen already, your people have many varied dances," Janelle said. She smiled at him. "I am enjoying everything so much, Fire Cloud. I love being here. And your people no longer look at me with resentment. It seems they have accepted my presence. Is that because you explained to them that we are soon to become man and wife?"

"I did meet in council with all the warriors and

told them how it is and will be between you and me, and I asked them to go to their women and explain, who then will explain to their children," Fire Cloud said in a low voice that did not travel farther than Janelle's ears. "You are accepted now as one with them even before our vows are exchanged, for they know that inside my heart you are already my wife."

"I am so very, very happy," Janelle murmured, fighting back tears of joy, which threatened to spill from her eyes.

"You have brought a happiness into my life that I cannot even define, it is so beautiful," Fire Cloud said.

Out of the corner of his eye he saw the last drummer take his place on a stool. He nodded toward them all and moved even closer to Janelle so that he could quickly explain the purpose of this particular event.

"Let me tell you the story of the Drum Dance so that while you listen to their music you will understand more about it," Fire Cloud said, smiling when she looked so eager to hear.

"This dance was originally based on the Omaha Grass Dance," Fire Cloud began. "The story concerned a young Lakota girl who tried to flee some Indians and white soldiers after a battle, but was trapped in a nearby lake. There she was said to have stayed for a week, hidden by lily pads, neither eating nor drinking. Finally, *Kitchi-Manitou*, praising her for her courage, took her up to the sky, where he told her about the Drum Dance. He explained how the ceremony was to be carried on and gave certain instructions. He told her that peace would occur between all Indians and whites if she induced her people to perform this ritual.

"Although she had been close to death, when she awoke she was cured. What she had been taught about the drums she took to her people, the Lakota, who then presented their knowledge to the Minnesota Chippewa who, in turn, taught it to their relatives. The teachings included peace, good moral conduct, a sense of responsibility, obedience to law, and helping one another."

He paused then, as the drums began pounding out their steady beat, the warriors who played them humming along.

Then one warrior stood up and acknowledged the help of the drum spirits tonight. He mentioned all the virtues that Fire Cloud had just told Janelle about, then sat down and joined his brothers in drumming. Everyone listened, their heads bobbing in rhythm with the music.

"During those times when dancing accompanies the drumming, each member has his own song to which he will dance when his turn comes," Fire Cloud whispered to Janelle. "When each finishes their song, he contributes something to a fellow member of his choice—perhaps a blanket, gun, or piece of clothing. The person who received the gift will, in turn, give one of his own."

Suddenly a small hand grasped Fire Cloud's shoulder.

Fire Cloud turned with a start and discovered a

young brave of ten winters standing there, his eyes filled with concern.

"Little Bear, what troubles you?" Fire Cloud asked as he turned fully to face the child.

Janelle's spine stiffened, for she could see that the child was obviously distraught about something.

She turned and listened, but the child chose to speak fully in his Lakota tongue instead of English.

She turned to Fire Cloud to watch his reaction to what was said, then knew that something was wrong when a look of alarm showed in his face.

Janelle reached a hand to Fire Cloud's arm to ask why.

Fire Cloud turned to her. "It is my brother," he said. He took her hand, urging her to her feet as quickly as he hurried to his own.

"What about Moon Shadow?" Janelle asked, very aware that the drumming had stopped and all eyes were on Fire Cloud.

She turned and looked across the crowd to where she had last seen Moon Shadow sitting among friends, seemingly content enough.

"He left some time ago, but it was not a cause for alarm. He told Little Bear that he was going to get a small bag of rocks he had gathered for Little Bear as a special gift," Fire Cloud said, holding Janelle's hand tightly as he began working his way through the crowd. People stood quickly and made space for them to move through.

"But he hasn't returned?" Janelle asked uneasily. Her sense of guilt had returned. She had thought that he was past his disappointment.

He had seemed so happy tonight!

Please let it be that something has delayed him in his tepee, she prayed to herself. *Please let us find him safe and sound there!*

But her prayer seemed to have been misplaced somewhere in the heavens, for when Fire Cloud swept aside Moon Shadow's entrance flap and found no one there, not even a lodge fire, Janelle knew that Moon Shadow had not meant to come to his lodge for rocks. If he had been there, he would have added wood to the simmering coals of his fire.

"He must have gone to the river," Fire Cloud said, no longer holding Janelle's hand as he swept past her and broke into a hard run toward the Meramec.

But the full moon's glow proved too soon that his brother was nowhere beside the river. Not even when Fire Cloud ran up one long length of it, and then down another.

Janelle stood watching, her heart aching to see Fire Cloud feeling so desperate and afraid.

She stifled a sob behind a hand when he came to her and gently placed his hands to her shoulders. The whole village, it seemed, stood behind her, silent and watching.

"My brother is *gee-mah-gah*—gone," he said, his voice breaking as their eyes met.

Then he yanked her into his embrace.

Feeling so guilty now for everything, Janelle pulled herself free and ran, sobbing and stumbling, beside the river.

Soon Fire Cloud caught up with her.

He stopped her and held her close. "Never blame

yourself for what my brother might have chosen to do," he said. "You offered hope. There is no sin in that."

"But it was such a false hope," Janelle sobbed as she clung to him, her tears wetting his bare chest.

"There is no such a thing as false hope," Fire Cloud tried to reassure her. "Hope is hope. You gave this to my brother because you loved him."

"Where do you think he's gone?" Janelle said as she eased from Fire Cloud's arms and gazed with fear at the darkness of the forest beyond.

"We shall find him," Fire Cloud said.

He turned to everyone. "Torches!" he shouted. "Light and bring many! My brother cannot be far away. We shall find him!"

Janelle hugged herself with her arms, for she knew how intelligent Moon Shadow was, and knew that if he did not want to be found, he could get lost forever.

And she still could not help but hold herself to blame!

Chapter 19

The torches cast ghostly orange shadows through the night as the search for Moon Shadow continued into the wee hours of the morning.

The only woman among the searchers, Janelle felt a deepening despair as each moment passed with no signs of Fire Cloud's brother. Although Fire Cloud told her that Moon Shadow had never been taught the art of hiding his tracks, he did seem skilled enough at keeping everyone from finding him tonight.

It was as though he had vanished into thin air.

Fire Cloud moved closer to Janelle as they kept a steady pace with the others in the shadow of a high bluff. The river close by murmured into the night.

"Moon Shadow has never wandered off alone," he said.

His drawn voice proved the depth of his concern.

Janelle noticed how his dark eyes had lost their vibrancy, as if his hope was dying.

"I don't want to think the worst, yet how can I not?" Janelle said, her voice breaking.

Janelle stopped, hung her head sadly, and lowered her torch.

Fire Cloud stopped with her and was glad when the others kept going, knowing that was what he would want of them. It had to be obvious to all of them that Janelle was having trouble with what was happening, for most knew the guilt that lay heavy in her heart.

Fire Cloud was proud of his people for not openly casting blame on Janelle, for he did know that too many privately held her responsible for Moon Shadow's disappearance. How could they not? They knew her role in Moon Shadow's visit to the white doctor, and the disappointment that came with it.

His brother had seemed to accept that his life would remain the same, and he had always said it had not been bad.

Now Fire Cloud had come up with a new reason why his brother might have wandered off alone to face danger head on in the forest. Could Moon Shadow's disappearance have to do with Fire Cloud's plans to marry Janelle?

Perhaps knowing that Fire Cloud had a woman now to occupy his time made him feel as though he was in the way, especially since there was no chance that he would ever fully fend for himself.

Did Moon Shadow believe that he would forever be a silent, sightless man, never knowing a woman's love?

Gah-ween—no! Fire Cloud would not allow himself to think these things. He might conclude that if he did find Moon Shadow, he would have to give Janelle up in order to prove to him that he was still as important as he had been the day that Fire Cloud had brought him from his mother's womb and heard that first cry....

Fire Cloud's heart momentarily stopped. His eyes widened and his free hand gripped Janelle's shoulder.

"My brother has not been voiceless forever," he said quickly. "In his first few moments of life, I recall now that he did cry! I heard him. My *gee-mah-mah* also heard my brother's soft cries. When he did not cry anymore, I thought it was only because he was content. I was so proud that I had quieted him since I was a child of only ten winters with no knowledge of how to care for a baby."

He grabbed Janelle's hand. "Come," he said, urging her into a fast walk beside him and soon catching up with the others. "Raise your torch up high. Look at every inch of the land, behind every tree and bush, behind every boulder. My brother is out here somewhere. I have to find him. He needs to be told that he did have the ability to cry out when he was a baby. From that I know that deep down inside him somewhere is that ability to talk, to laugh, to cry so that I can hear him. Hope is hope! No one should ever lose it! Especially not my brother who has everything to live for. I must tell him that he has never been a burden and never shall be, that when you and I are married, he will not only have my devotion, he will also have yours. *Gah-ween!* I cannot allow him to think that he is a burden only because I have found a woman and brought her into my life. I must convince him that you are also a part of his life."

"A burden?" Janelle gasped out. "You think that

Moon Shadow left because he feels as though he is a burden? You think that he is feeling such a thing because of me?"

"Perhaps, yet my brother has never been selfish, which he would be were he to deny my happiness," Fire Cloud said, sighing deeply. "I have to believe that he has left because of a combination of many things. When I find him, I will convince him that life does get complicated sometimes for everyone, but that most things do work themselves out in the end."

When the sky began to lighten overhead, and the moon slid away, Fire Cloud stopped again and looked from warrior to warrior.

"Warriors, I can see and hear your exhaustion," he said, his own voice scratchy from weariness. "It has been a dedicated search. I thank you all for that. But a body needs rest and food. We shall return home now and resume our search again when the sun is at its midpoint in the sky. I plan then to search the rest of the day, and a full night. If my brother is not found then, I will know that he cannot be found."

One by one the warriors went to the river and lowered their torches into the water, extinguishing their flames, and began walking back in the direction of the village, heads hung and eyes sad.

Fire Cloud and Janelle doused their own flames and walked listlessly behind the others.

Feeling as though she might not be able to take another step, Janelle was glad when she saw the outskirts of the village and knew that sleep was not far ahead.

Hopefully then she could find some solace, for although Fire Cloud preached against losing hope, she now most definitely had none of ever seeing Moon Shadow again. They had covered almost every inch of land from the village almost as far as Meramec Cavern. . . .

"Meramec Cavern," Janelle whispered, her pulse racing. They had not gone as far as that. She recalled Moon Shadow's curiosity with the cavern, and how he had enjoyed their visit there.

But the cavern was quite a distance and not normally reached by walking. They had searched the village carefully before leaving and found neither a horse nor a canoe missing along with Moon Shadow.

Janelle wondered if Moon Shadow could have found the cavern tonight on foot. Was that his destination when he left, or had he just walked endlessly onward and found himself there?

No matter how, or why, Janelle saw this as a perfect hiding place for a young man who did not want to be found.

Lost in thought, Janelle had not noticed that many of the warriors had broken into a trot as they reached the very edge of the village. Their eagerness to be home—either to sleep, or just be reunited with their loved ones—had put life into their steps again. Janelle reached over for Fire Cloud to take his hand and tell him her thoughts on Moon Shadow, but stopped when Red Dawn Wolf, one of the Lakota's most esteemed warriors, came to a halt breathlessly before them.

"My wife, Bright Smile, is not in our lodge," Red Dawn Wolf said, his eyes wild. "I have checked with the other women. No one has seen her since she retired to our tepee. She is heavy with a child due any day now, so where could she be? We passed by where the women bathe, and she was not there. She is too heavy to go for firewood. Lately, she has hardly left her bed. The village women have even supplied us with our meals, fuel, and water. Where could she be, Fire Cloud? Where?"

Tall Night stepped from his lodge to listen, his hands doubling into tight fists at his sides. He had surprised everyone by not joining the search for Moon Shadow, his mood so dark and somber even before Moon Shadow's strange disappearance that he had not attended the earlier celebration. He looked first at Fire Cloud, and then at Red Dawn Wolf as they stopped only a few feet from Tall Night's lodge.

Janelle glanced at Fire Cloud. "I have heard that some Indian women go into the forest alone when it is time for their babies to be born," she said softly. "Do you think that Bright Smile might have done this?"

"She would not do this," Red Dawn Wolf said stiffly. "She promised me that she would not have the baby away from the village."

"As you know, we did not see Bright Smile on our search for my brother," Fire Cloud said. "If she did decide to go into the forest to have the child and was in trouble out there, would she not have cried out for us if she heard us passing by?"

"This is not like Bright Smile," Red Dawn Wolf said. "She gave me her word."

"Perhaps something changed her mind," Fire Cloud said, placing a hand on the warrior's shoulder.

Red Dawn Wolf hung his head. "*Ay-uh*, something..." he said, his voice breaking.

"We have not had rest or food, so we should take time enough to at least fill our bellies with something nourishing before heading out for another hunt," Fire Cloud said. "But Red Dawn Wolf, we *will* leave again soon, and this time our eyes and ears will also be alert for signs of your wife. We will do everything in our power to find her. We have combed this land in our search for my brother, and we shall do so again for your wife. There might have been a place we forgot to look."

"The Meramec Cavern," Janelle blurted out. "We did not go as far as the cavern. I think we should this time."

"My wife's condition would not allow her to go that far," Red Dawn Wolf said.

"If she traveled by canoe, she could," Janelle said, wincing when Red Dawn Wolf gave her an angry stare. She had to believe the look was for her being there more than her suggestion.

Then, Tall Night stepped over to Fire Cloud. His eyes wavered as Fire Cloud watched him.

"Fire Cloud, by not helping in the search for Moon Shadow, I have let you, my best friend, down," he said. "But everyone else joined you. I did not think I would be missed. And ... and I have much on my mind that keeps me from doing what I normally would."

"What might that be?" Fire Cloud asked, placing both hands on his friend's slumped shoulders. "I have known you since we were both children. Lately you have been a stranger to me in all ways. When will you share with me what is causing this change in you?"

"Soon," Tall Night said, swallowing hard. He sucked in a quavering breath. "I would like to join the search now for both Moon Shadow and Bright Smile. That is, if you wish me to."

"Your help will be welcomed, my *nee-gee*—friend," Fire Cloud said. He turned to face the warriors who had made a wide circle around them after hearing of Bright Smile's absence. "I know that you are all weary from the long search. Your eyes show your need to sleep. But we must fight that need for now. Go to your lodges. Eat. Then come to the council house. We shall discuss our newest hunt and our hopes of now finding not only my brother, but also Bright Smile."

Janelle glanced over at Tall Night. She could not help but believe there was more to his change of heart than he had said.

When he found her looking at him questioningly, he turned quickly away again, his head hung. It seemed to her the behavior of a man filled with a deep guilt.

She wondered what could cause him such guilt. It could not be only from having let his friend down.

No. It was something more than that, something much deeper.

Could it have something to do with the missing woman?

Chapter 20

After combing the forest again and finding no clues to the whereabouts of Moon Shadow or Bright Smile, the searchers had boarded canoes and followed the river to Meramec Cavern.

With torches flaring, the search had gone into the darkest recesses of the cavern. Ropes attached each individual to the others and kept them from losing track of one another.

After an exhaustive search, the canoe journey back to the village was one of silent gloom and disappointment. Everyone was truly worn out this time, and now believed that neither Moon Shadow nor Bright Smile was in the cavern.

Janelle glanced over at Tall Night, who rode in the same canoe as she and Fire Cloud. She was still puzzled over his attitude. He seemed even more despondent than Red Dawn Wolf. Before boarding the canoes to return home, Janelle had seen Tall Night go to a bluff and pray.

Janelle saw Fire Cloud also watching his friend Tall Night, silently and questioningly. She knew that he, too, was confused by Tall Night's strange behavior.

It did not seem right that his sadness should be greater than Fire Cloud's or Red Dawn Wolf's.

Yet it was.

Janelle saw that Fire Cloud had not pried into his friend's private despair, for his own was all that he could handle at this time. It seemed that he had lost a brother forever.

Janelle wondered how this would affect their relationship, for surely, deep inside himself, Fire Cloud did hold her partially responsible for whatever might have happened to his brother.

She was glad when they were finally in his tepee.

And even though it was daylight and her aunt expected her home after spending her one night with the Lakota, Janelle could not leave Fire Cloud alone at a time like this.

As they entered the tepee, they discovered a large pot of stew simmering over his lodge fire. She found two wooden bowls and spoons, and a ladle. They were soon eating the stew, although far too quietly. She hated that Fire Cloud now seemed to hold so much inside him which she knew would be better discussed.

All she had to do was look into his eyes and know that he was not going to give up on his brother without a deep, agonizing struggle within himself. She only hoped that he would allow her to be there for him and would not hold her to blame for too much.

How could she lose him now that she had found him?

No. She would not allow his grief to destroy what had been wonderful between them.

She would fight for Fire Cloud every inch of the way. She would not let his guilt, or hers, stand in the way of their future, which had looked so joyous until Moon Shadow chose to take that walk out of his brother's life!

"I'm staying," Janelle blurted out, scarcely breathing as she waited for Fire Cloud's reaction.

He turned to her, set his empty bowl aside, and held his arms out for her.

"Come to me," he said, his voice breaking. "I need you. Let me hold you, for you are all that is sane for me at this moment. How could my brother have done this? Why would he? I will not blame anything for his decision, but destiny. Destiny sometimes can be so cruel. Today it could not be any crueler."

Janelle sat on his lap facing him, her legs straddling him.

She wrapped her arms about his neck and drew his lips to hers. They kissed softly and gently. Then Fire Cloud rested his head against her bosom.

"You need sleep," Janelle said, stroking his cheek. "Let's go to your bed. I will pour some water and bathe your face for you. Then I shall kiss you to sleep, my love."

Fire Cloud's lips moved into a slow smile. "You are my everything," he said, reaching to shove strands of her hair back from her face. "I am blessed to have you. If you were not here with me now, I would be in despair. As it is, your sweetness reminds me of what life can be, now that I have you with me."

"I'm so sorry about Moon Shadow," Janelle said.

"If I had one wish, I would wish him here with us right now."

"All is not lost yet," Fire Cloud said, his voice breaking. "I will not stop looking until I find my brother."

"But you must sleep first," Janelle said, slowly rising from his lap. She reached a hand out for him. "Come on. You are going to bed. I will caress your face with a cool, damp cloth. Then I'll give you those butterfly kisses."

He took her hand and rose to his feet. After removing his moccasins and the sheathed knife at his waist, he stretched out on his back on his pallet of pelts and blankets.

He closed his eyes and felt somewhat at peace after Janelle softly ran a cloth over his brow and cheeks.

"Relax," Janelle murmured. "Sleep, my love. When you awake you will be refreshed, and I will join you on another search for your brother."

"And Bright Smile," Fire Cloud said. "I do not like to think of her having the child out there all alone. I remember the day my mother had Moon Shadow. Had I not been there . . ."

Janelle placed a gentle hand over his mouth. "Shh," she murmured. "Do not think about anything right now. You must get your rest."

He opened his eyes and gently pushed her hand aside. "Come now and lie with me," he said softly. "You also need rest. You are such a courageous, strong person to have kept up with us as the search went hour after hour. You are an amazing woman.

You will be an even more amazing wife and mother."

"Do not expect too much of me," Janelle said, laughing quietly. "I do not like to disappoint."

"You could never disappoint this warrior," Fire Cloud said, glad when she stretched out beside him. He drew her fully up to his body, her breasts pressed into his bare chest. He yawned and closed his eyes. "My woman, sleep with me."

"Sleep does sound wonderful," Janelle said, yawning as well.

She cuddled closer to his chest, her cheek next to his heart, whose steady beat soon lulled her to sleep.

Much later, loud screams and shouts of wonder awakened Janelle and Fire Cloud with a start.

She looked up through the smoke hole and saw that the sky was dark. She and Fire Cloud had slept the entire day away.

Fire Cloud sat up quickly, and then saw a strange orange glow through the smoke hole, spreading brighter and brighter across the dark heavens.

"What can that be?" he said, rushing to his feet.

Janelle almost fell over as she hurried to her feet.

They ran outside together, then stopped and gasped when they saw the cause of the confusion and cries of wonder, which had now turned to horror.

A fiery ball was falling from the sky!

"A meteorite?" Janelle whispered to herself, stunned at the sight.

Chapter 21

Almost at the same moment, the fireball hit the ground near the far edge of the village with a loud boom, making a crater six feet in diameter.

Chaos ensued, for as the meteorite made contact with the ground, sparks and fiery debris scattered into the air, causing trees and some closer tepees to catch fire.

Fire Cloud hurried to help put out the fires while Janelle, almost in a trance, walked toward the glowing object. Others followed her, their eyes wide and voices now quiet as they stared at what had come to them from the heavens.

From all that she had learned during her years as a student and teacher, Janelle knew that this had to be a meteorite. She was stunned to actually see one, since they had only fallen anywhere a scant few times.

But there it was, fiery, glowing, and pulsating. The heat was too intense to get very close, and she stopped to shield her face with a hand. Perplexed, she continued to stare at this foreign object. Darkness was only now beginning to take on the slight bluish hues of early morning.

"It is an *ah-gwah-kwah-ee-gun*—sign!" someone cried out, breaking the silence. "It is a sign sent from *Kitchi-Manitou!*"

Janelle turned quickly and saw Two Bones, the Lakota's shaman, standing behind her in his long buckskin robe, the ends of his long gray hair resting on the ground behind him. He had a thin face with a very crooked nose. His eyes were fixed on the meteorite. Reaching his hands heavenward, he began chanting. Others moved closely around him, chanting as well.

Janelle did not have the chance to wonder about the shaman's theory of why the meteorite chose Lakota property to land upon, for just then she heard the clatter of wheels and the sound of horse's hooves approaching the village.

Her heart almost stopped when she turned and recognized her father's horse and buggy, with many men on horseback riding behind him. All of them stared excitedly at the glowing object.

"Father!" Janelle gasped.

Her gaze again moved past him as she saw just how many men were arriving at the Lakota village. They had surely been drawn from their beds by the fiery glow visible through their bedroom windows.

Intrigued, they had watched where it had fallen and came to investigate.

Janelle found herself backing slowly away from her father as he drew closer and closer in his buggy.

Suddenly she ran into someone.

She turned and found Fire Cloud looking questioningly down at her, for he had stepped up behind her just as she chose to back away.

"I see more in your eyes than wonder at the strange object," Fire Cloud said, scrutinizing her.

Then he, too, saw the many white people who were now dismounting.

His gaze moved to the one gentleman who had arrived by horse and buggy. He recognized him right away, even though Virgil Coolidge was much older than the last time Fire Cloud had seen him fifteen years ago.

Much about him was the same—the expensive black suit and the thick black mustache, eyebrows, and hair. Although he was thinner, he was still a big, hefty man. And Fire Cloud would never forget that pinched look on the man's face, or his piercing blue eyes, which had been so cold and unfriendly.

"It is because of your father?" Fire Cloud then asked, "At a time like this, you can only think of having to face your father?"

"It's not only that. Fire Cloud, I know my father so well, and he will not be able to just come to take a quick look at the meteorite and walk away from it," Janelle said. "He will want it, Fire Cloud, I know he will want it. It is something he has read about so often, yet did not believe he would ever get the chance to see."

She reached a hand to his cheek. "Do you know what that means?" she murmured. "He will either want to set up camp nearby to study it for several days, or he will ask to take it to the museum to study it there, and give everyone who wishes to, especially whites, an opportunity to see and study it as well."

"Meteorite?" Fire Cloud said, an eyebrow arching. "This burning thing that has fallen from the heavens has a strange name. And how do you know this?"

"In my studies I have learned much about meteorites," Janelle said, then saw that Fire Cloud had only half heard her, for he was again looking past the meteorite at her father.

Fire Cloud wanted to know everything about this strange object, and why it might choose his people's land over the whites', but his attention was drawn to someone else. Janelle's father.

Fire Cloud watched guardedly as Virgil Coolidge left his buggy and moved hurriedly to the meteorite.

Fire Cloud was at least glad that her father had not yet seen Janelle standing there, for Fire Cloud was not sure how he would react. Of course, he must know soon that his daughter planned to marry a man whose skin was bronze, not white. But Janelle would want to choose the time to tell him, and Fire Cloud was patient enough to wait until she was comfortable with the telling.

Tonight, Fire Cloud's thoughts had only been on his brother. Now, he was forced to face challenges that were almost as troubling.

Chief Black Eagle stopped beside Two Bones with his petite wife, Star Shine, standing shakily beside him, clinging to one of his arms. Her eyes showed her fear as she stared at the meteorite, then turned with her husband to look at the white intruders.

Janelle was quickly becoming aware of something

that made her insides tighten. She could see that the arrival of the white men had drawn the Lakota's eyes from the meteorite. They were now glaring at the white men. She could see that their presence was resented. They had come onto land that was not theirs, and had not asked permission or been invited.

Panic seized Janelle when she saw Chief Black Eagle walk up and stand before her father, purposely blocking her father's view of the meteorite.

Her father's eyes narrowed as he began talking with the Lakota chief, his voice growing louder with each word. Janelle could tell that her father was having a disagreement with the chief, and she knew without asking what it was about. The chief had obviously chosen her father to speak to for he was the oldest and most prominent-looking of the white men.

As the conversation heated up between them, Janelle looked desperately up at Fire Cloud.

"I know what is happening between my father and your chief," Janelle said anxiously. "My father is being asked to leave. But he doesn't want to, and I can understand why. Fire Cloud, he has waited a lifetime for an opportunity to see a meteorite up close. Can you talk with Chief Black Eagle? Can you ask him to allow my father to stay? He has spent many years studying such things. He will never be able to actually witness this firsthand again."

"Your father is not the only one who should not be here," Fire Cloud said. Even as he spoke, buggies full of white families were arriving along with more men on horseback. He nodded toward the new arrivals. "Do you not see? If the whites are not stopped, if they are not sent away, the Lakota's land will no longer be the Lakota's. It will be turned into white land again."

His jaw tightened. "It is only right that Chief Black Eagle stand firm against the interlopers who have arrived tonight," he said sternly. "No matter what has drawn them here, it is not right that they stay."

"But Fire Cloud, please see that one exception is made," Janelle begged. "Everyone knows my father's dedication to the museum and his college. They will understand if he is allowed to stay and study the meteorite and they are not. It is his place to know, so that he can take his teachings to his college and the museum, for others to learn as well."

"This is important to you that I do this for your father?" Fire Cloud asked, placing a gentle hand on her cheek.

"It is important for my father, not so much me," Janelle murmured. "He has suffered one recent disappointment. He has lost me. Please understand that he might not endure another disappointment. I do worry about how these things could affect his ailing heart."

"If I step forward to speak for him, will you be at my side, or hidden in the shadows so that he will not know that you are here?" Fire Cloud asked somberly.

"I will be at your side," Janelle said, lifting her chin.

But then her eyes wavered and her chin lowered, as did her courage. "But I will not choose this time to tell my father about us," she said, her voice breaking. "Do you understand?"

"I understand that you know what is best for yourself and your father, and I will not expect you to tell him our plans until you feel in your heart that it is right," Fire Cloud said.

Janelle wanted to fling herself into his arms and hug him for being so understanding, kind, and noble, yet she knew that time did not allow a show of affection. The longer Chief Black Eagle talked with her father, the more heated their words became.

She turned to Fire Cloud. "Thank you," she said. "You are giving me cause to love you more and more."

Fire Cloud smiled. Then they went and stood before Janelle's father and Chief Black Eagle, their backs to the meteorite.

"Janelle?" Virgil gasped, shocked at seeing her there.

Then he smiled clumsily. "Yes, you would be here, wouldn't you?" he said, reaching out and taking her hands. He drew her closer to him. "You saw the reflection of the falling meteorite from your window at the convent as I did from my window. Your curiosity, like mine, drew you here."

He slid an arm around her waist as he again turned and glared at Chief Black Eagle. "This is my daughter, Janelle," he said tightly. "She, too, has come to study the meteorite. I hope that you will reconsider and allow us both to remain. It is important that we study it so that I can take my findings back to those who would also like to know of it."

Fire Cloud intervened, stepping more closely to Chief Black Eagle. He saw the look of questioning in his chief's eyes and knew why. He and everyone else at the village knew that Janelle had been there with Fire Cloud, not at the convent, when the meteorite had appeared from the sky. Fire Cloud ignored the questioning eyes of his chief and people and spoke up in behalf of Virgil Coolidge.

Chief Black Eagle listened intently, then turned and faced Virgil again. "You can stay to study this object until the sun sits midway in the sky tomorrow, and then I will ask you to leave," he said, drawing a quick smile from both Janelle and her father.

Then Chief Black Eagle walked toward the other white people who had grouped together in a tight circle.

"As for the rest of you *wasichos*," Chief Black Eagle said, his fists on his hips, "go now. Return to your homes. This man whom you all know and admire will learn what must be learned and then will bring his knowledge to you. But go now to your homes. By treaty, this is Lakota land. Go now to your own."

Janelle scarcely breathed as she heard the white men cursing under their breaths. They stamped away toward their waiting buggies, the women and children scampering closely behind them, until soon all of the horses and buggies and white folk were gone except for Janelle and her father.

So thankful for this opportunity, and wanting to take advantage of it, Virgil Coolidge turned toward the Lakota people who were now slowly moving closer to him and the meteorite.

He smiled at them, making eye contact with some,

and quickly shifting his gaze elsewhere when he found resentment in others.

As Janelle stepped back and stood with Fire Cloud and Black Eagle, her father became the professor he knew so well how to be, meticulously explaining what had occurred tonight to those who seemed eager to listen.

Pride for her father swelled inside Janelle as she, too, listened. She had to fight against reaching for Fire Cloud's hand, for thus far, her father believed that her presence at the village was by coincidence.

Janelle also wanted to introduce him to Fire Cloud, but knew this was not the right moment. Noon would come quickly, and she wanted her father to have all of the time that he could before having to leave as the others had.

Fire Cloud listened to Janelle's father, wanting to learn about the strange ball of fire. But as he listened, he kept looking over his shoulder at the forest. He truly did not know where else to look for his brother or Bright Smile. It seemed that they both had vanished into thin air, and he did not believe now that he would ever see either of them again.

He scanned the faces of the crowd to find both Tall Night and Red Dawn Wolf.

When he saw neither, he knew why they were not there. Tall Night's mysterious, withdrawn attitude had surely kept him inside his lodge.

And Red Dawn Wolf's sadness over the loss of not only a wife, but also a newborn babe, was keeping him from the wonders of this morning as well.

Fire Cloud decided then that when Janelle's father

was gone, another search would occur for both Moon Shadow and Bright Smile.

But Fire Cloud was beginning to believe that he would have no choice but to accept the loss of his brother.

When he did, he would mourn him deeply.

Out of respect for his brother, even his marriage to Janelle would have to be postponed. That thought only added to the sadness that he was carrying in his heart.

For this woman was the only brightness in his life now. To have her with him day and night would be the only way he could accept losing his brother.

Fire Cloud pushed his tormented thoughts from his mind until it was time to leave again for the search.

He felt Janelle move closer, yet understood why she could not touch him as she listened to her father. Virgil seemed to have entered into a state of euphoria as he explained about meteorites. The strange phenomenon would stay with the Lakota—passed down to their children and their children's children.

He focused on listening so that he would be able to discuss the event logically with Janelle when they were alone having small talk around the fire, or after making love at night when the moon cast its magical light through the smoke hole above them.

Virgil looked at the Lakota and his daughter. "A meteorite is any particle of matter, known as a meteoroid, that survives its fall to Earth," he said. "Although several thousand meteoroids enter the atmosphere each year, only a few actually reach the ground before vaporizing."

He turned and looked at the glowing object. "A meteorite like this enters the earth's atmosphere at a velocity of at least six miles per second," he said. "The friction produces the bright fireball, which is often accompanied by the boom that I heard even back at my home."

Suddenly Virgil took a quick step toward Chief Black Eagle. "When the meteorite is cool enough to move, I would like to take it to my museum to study it more extensively," he said. "I also wish to study the crater in which it now rests."

Janelle's breath caught in her throat, and the color drained from her face when Chief Black Eagle did not even consider the suggestion.

He squared his jaw, his eyes flashing angrily as he took a step closer to her father and said a flat *"Gah-ween,"* which he as quickly interpreted to her father as "No."

"But what good will it do your people?" Virgil said, his own eyes glaring into the chief's. He gestured with a flung-out hand. "You say this is your land? Well, I will give it back to you by taking away this object which sits upon it."

"What has happened tonight has happened to my people for a purpose," Chief Black Eagle argued. "It is an omen. Good *or* bad. The Lakota pay heed to such omens."

"An omen?" Virgil said, flailing frustrated hands into the air. "Hogwash! There are no such things as omens! There is fact. Only fact. And this meteorite is more fact than you will ever probably see again in your lifetime. It is something that needs to be *studied*. It needs to be put on display for everyone to see. You ran off all of the white people tonight. That has to mean that as long as the meteorite is on your property, you won't allow white people to return to see or study it. So I must be able to take it with me when it is cool enough for removal. Keeping it to yourself is wrong. Everyone should have an opportunity to see the meteorite if they wish. You do not want people coming here. So let me take it with me."

"You scorn our beliefs when you laugh at our omens, so I scorn you, white man, and tell you to leave," Chief Black Eagle said, angrily folding his arms across his chest. "Now! You have just cut short your time among my people with your unwise words."

Janelle was in a state of shock over what had transpired between her father and the chief. It had happened so quickly, her head seemed to be spinning from it.

And her immediate concern was for her father. She could see how his face had flushed from anger. His eyes were narrowed as he glared at the chief. She was afraid that he might have a heart attack at any moment, and she had no choice but to intervene.

"Father," Janelle said, rushing to him. She stepped between the chief and her father. "Please don't be so angry. This isn't that important. Please leave. When you are settled down, then perhaps you can come back and talk to the chief again more calmly. But for now, *please* go home and rest?"

"You, of all people, should understand the importance of what has happened here tonight," Virgil said. "Janelle, how many times does one get the chance to see and study a meteorite? How can you expect me to just walk away?"

"You can walk away tonight, then return tomorrow," Janelle encouraged him. She cast a questioning look over her shoulder at Fire Cloud, then looked at her father again. "Fire Cloud will talk with Chief Black Eagle. He will convince him to change his mind."

"Who in the hell is Fire Cloud and why would he be in favor of what *I* want, not his chief?" Virgil yelled. "Step aside, Janelle. I have a score to settle here. I will not give up the meteorite that easily."

Chief Black Eagle stepped closer to Virgil. "You will leave now of your own volition, or I will have you escorted by armed warriors," he said, then shrugged. "It matters not to me which way you choose, but do know this—you are no longer welcome among my people."

Janelle gasped at this threat. She turned pleadingly to Fire Cloud.

When he did not make any gesture in her father's behalf, she knew that it was not his place to. The chief had the final word.

She ached for her father when she saw the instant frustration in his eyes.

Knowing just how important this discovery was to him, Janelle could not help but speak in his behalf. She had no choice but to try to help him in this matter. The arrival of the meteorite tonight was extraordinary, and it might never happen again in her father's lifetime.

She went to Chief Black Eagle. She made certain not to speak in a tone which might be misconstrued as disrespectful by the chief, even as she did speak in behalf of her father.

"Please don't send my father away," she asked softly. "At least not yet. You had said earlier that he could stay until noon. Please allow him this much more time with the meteorite. It is such an opportunity for him. I hate to see it denied him."

Janelle felt angry eyes on her.

She turned to Fire Cloud and flinched when she saw how disappointed he was in her. His eyes seemed to bore right through her with an anger that she knew he was purposely controlling.

She knew why he felt this way. She was going against the Lakota in favor of her father!

When the chief again denied her father special privileges, Janelle could not help but grow angry over the chief's inability to see reason. She truly believed that he was wrong!

"All right, if you don't give my father the privilege of staying on your land to study the meteorite more extensively, at least allow him to remove it later to the museum," she said, hoping that her voice did not reveal her anger. "He *must* be able to study it. Everyone, even your people, would learn from it."

"My people see this fallen object from the sky as holy," Chief Black Eagle said tightly. "And it is on Indian land. No whites can ever touch it or study it more than your father has been able to study it today."

Although she could still feel Fire Cloud's eyes on her, now possibly pleading with her to let this argument go, that it might be ruining the possibility of her ever living among the Lakota, Janelle had to say her piece. Then she would step back and allow whatever happened to happen and say no more about it.

But for her father, she had to try to make the chief see logic.

"Chief Black Eagle, I understand my father's needs, yet I now also understand the Lakota's," she said softly. She gestured toward the meteorite as she continued speaking. "There is something on your land that whites want. For so long whites took from the Lakota. You see no reason to give any white man anything now, especially something that seemed to be sent from the heavens for a purpose . . . something that you deem is holy."

After realizing that her words had fallen on deaf ears, she inhaled a quivering breath, then continued, "But although this object that fell from the sky may be holy, it is still a rare thing. Can you not see the importance of studying it?"

"*Ay-uh*, I see the importance," Chief Black Eagle finally said. "And it will be studied. But only by my people. Not yours."

Janelle suddenly realized how drained she felt. Her exhaustion had begun with Moon Shadow's disappearance and the lengthy search for him.

And now? She had to argue on her father's behalf?

She felt dispirited and at her wit's end.

FIRE CLOUD

She was torn. She wanted to help her father, she wanted to find Moon Shadow, and she didn't want to go against the Indians either by having to take her father's side in this argument that she knew they had lost.

Janelle swallowed back a sob of despair for her father when he turned and walked toward his horse and buggy, his shoulders slumped, his eyes to the ground.

Then he stopped and turned suddenly toward her, holding a hand out for her. She knew that he wanted her to leave with him.

She felt pulled in two directions when Fire Cloud then stepped to her side and gave her a look that told her that if she left, he would believe she had chosen her father over him and his people.

She gazed into his eyes and saw a silent pleading. She knew then where her place was, and with whom.

If she didn't stay *now* with Fire Cloud, she might lose him forever.

She had found him again after fifteen years. And until then, she now knew, she had felt like only half a person . . . only half alive.

Fire Cloud was her heart.

And there was another reason why she must stay. She still felt guilty over Moon Shadow. She must do everything possible to help find him!

"Father, go on without me," she said, her voice drawn. "I came on my own horse."

Seeming to take that at face value, and not doubting that she would soon return to the convent,

Virgil nodded, then went to his horse and buggy and rode away.

Feeling guilty for misleading her father, Janelle turned to Fire Cloud and gave him a sad, downhearted look. "I must leave," she said softly. "I should at least make an appearance at the convent before returning again to search for Moon Shadow and Bright Smile. My aunt deserves no less from me."

"I understand," Fire Cloud said. Out of the corner of his eye he saw Chief Black Eagle walk away toward his lodge, his wife alongside him.

Fire Cloud then looked into Janelle's eyes and gently framed her face between his hands. "I do regret what happened here tonight between your father and my chief," he said. "But it was for them to settle. It was not our place to interfere, but what you did is understandable. You love your father. Do you understand why I did not speak up in your father's behalf and, in a sense, in yours?"

"I hope I do," Janelle said, smiling awkwardly up at him. She eased into his arms. "I'm just sorry that any of this happened, that I felt pressed to speak up for my father, which made it look as though I did not consider your people's feelings at all."

Fire Cloud and Janelle drew quickly apart and turned with a start when they heard people shouting Moon Shadow's name.

Janelle grabbed Fire Cloud's hand and gasped with him when they both saw Moon Shadow at the edge of the village, stumbling toward the meteorite.

Chapter 22

"Moon Shadow . . ." Janelle whispered, then broke into a run toward him. Everyone's shouts turned to gasps as Moon Shadow kept walking toward the meteorite. In a matter of seconds he would run directly into the fiery object!

When they reached Moon Shadow, Fire Cloud grabbed him by one arm, and Janelle his other, just as he was close enough to the meteorite to feel its heat.

Tears filled Janelle's eyes when Fire Cloud pulled his brother into his arms and hugged him tightly. The others surrounded them in a wide circle, relieved that the lost warrior had somehow found his way home.

Glad that Moon Shadow was safe, Janelle took his hand and held it as Fire Cloud still hugged him and talked to him in Chippewa, even though his brother could not hear him.

When Fire Cloud stepped away from Moon Shadow, tears shining in his eyes, he still held his brother's hand in the palm of his own while he spoke to his brother in their language.

He asked Moon Shadow why he had left and where he had gone, and told him about the lengthy search for him. Fire Cloud then waited for his brother to respond.

But instead, Moon Shadow stepped away from him, and Fire Cloud was stunned to see that there was life in his brother's eyes.

Janelle's heart raced when she, too, saw how Moon Shadow's eyes were no longer blank—there was activity there, and movement . . . and recognition.

This was proven when Moon Shadow smiled broadly and excitedly at his brother, then began trying to form words on his lips for the very first time in his life.

A strange silence fell over everyone as they listened to Moon Shadow trying to communicate. His eyes danced with an eager excitement as he smiled and touched his ears, showing that he could hear.

Moon Shadow's smile faded, and frustration replaced it as he realized that only garbled nonsense was coming from his mouth which no one could understand. He reached for Fire Cloud's hand and hurriedly told him in the only way he knew how that he had been far, far back in Meramec Cavern when he felt the floor shake hard beneath his moccasined feet.

He became afraid that it might have been caused by an explosion in his village. He feared that white people might have come and attacked and killed, and he had to see if his brother was all right.

He told Fire Cloud of his experience so quickly that Fire Cloud was finding it hard to follow. Yet the more he understood, the more joy filled his soul.

Moon Shadow said that as he approached the village and saw the bright glow, he realized that he could see! He was uncertain why . . . whether his fear for his brother or the brightness of the burning rock had awakened life in those parts of him that had, until now, lain dormant inside him.

As he continued with his silent message on his brother's hand, Moon Shadow tried again to speak what he was writing. But only jumbled grunts came from within him. Yet the fact that he could utter sounds at all, not to mention hear and see, were cause for celebration!

His world now was full of sight and sound, and soon words. He could hardly wait to experience it all, and no longer be looked at with pity.

Fire Cloud could not stop smiling. It was nothing less than a miracle that his brother was alive, and could now hear and see.

Fire Cloud looked at the meteorite. He knew that the fiery object was somehow the cause of his brother's recovery. He could not help but believe that it had been sent from the heavens for the very purpose of restoring his brother's sight and hearing.

Janelle saw Fire Cloud staring at the meteorite and could almost tell what he was thinking, for the Lakota shaman had spoken of the meteorite as holy. She could see how the Lakota, even Fire Cloud, might believe that the meteorite had a connection with Moon Shadow's sudden recovery.

Even she wondered why Moon Shadow would suddenly regain all of his senses. Yet she knew that surely this miracle had happened today for another reason.

She watched as Moon Shadow again grabbed his brother's hand and began telling him more of his experience.

She had to believe that fear for his brother was the true cause of Moon Shadow's recovery. When he had felt the meteorite's crash vibrate the cave floor beneath his feet, he thought that his brother was in danger and had left to go to him. He became aware of the light from the meteorite, and even by then was slowly regaining his sight. The brightness of the meteorite had only confirmed it.

But it really did not matter what had caused this miraculous change. Janelle sighed with joy as she watched Moon Shadow's eyes meet with his brother's as he again tried to talk. Fire Cloud told him that patience was required now, that soon Moon Shadow would be able to talk as easily as he blinked his eyes!

"*Ay-uh.* In time, Moon Shadow, after I teach you, you will speak as fluently as everyone else," Fire Cloud said aloud, yet still translating the same words into their shared special language. Soon, Moon Shadow would learn the words and their meanings as they were spoken aloud. For now, they were only silent movements on his hand.

"Why did you leave your home and go to the cavern?" Fire Cloud asked, his voice drawn. "And where were you in the cave that no one could find you?"

Moon Shadow responded that he had given up on life and felt that he had been an interference in his brother's life long enough. He said that he had moved to the deepest, farthest recesses of the cave to die amidst the wonders of Meramec Cavern.

He said that he had gone where he was sure no one had been before, until . . .

When Moon Shadow paused and seemed reluctant to continue his explanation, Fire Cloud quickly asked what else Moon Shadow was trying to say.

Moon Shadow then said that he had not been alone in the cavern. Someone else came. Someone was there with him most of the time. She cared for him. She cooked wild game and fed him. She held and rocked him. And he knew who she was by feeling her face. It was Bright Smile! It was the wife of Red Dawn Wolf.

He also told Fire Cloud that he would tell by the desperate way Bright Smile had held him that she had come there to die as well. They would die together.

When he feared for the life of his brother, Bright Smile understood his need to leave the cavern. She led him to the cave entrance, but refused to come further with him.

She had made up her mind.

It was time for her to die. And she told him that no one, not even her friend Moon Shadow, would change her mind.

Stunned, Fire Cloud turned quickly and found that Red Dawn Wolf had come from his lodge to join everyone else as they marveled over the changes in Moon Shadow.

Fire Cloud went to Red Dawn Wolf and placed a hand on his shoulder.

"Red Dawn Wolf, my brother has just told me news of your wife," he said. He proceeded then to tell Red Dawn Wolf the complete details, which was followed by shocked silence.

Distraught, with tears rolling down his cheeks, Red Dawn Wolf asked if Bright Smile had had the baby yet.

Moon Shadow responded, telling Fire Cloud that when Bright Smile had held Moon Shadow in her arms, he had felt no largeness to her belly. That had to mean that she had given birth, but he then also said that there had been no baby with her. Knowing that if the baby had died, she would not want to discuss it, he had left his question unasked.

Fire Cloud, in turn, told Red Dawn Wolf the sad news.

Red Dawn Wolf lowered his face in his hands and tried to control the tremors that shook his body. Then he raised his head, wiped his eyes, then asked a question that pained him deeply.

"Knowing this about the child means only one thing to me," he said, trying to keep his voice steady as was expected of a warrior of his stature. "My wife gave birth to a stillborn. She became so forlorn over the loss of the baby, she did not want to live herself. Why else would she want to die?"

Moon Shadow reached out for his brother and took one of his hands, drawing Fire Cloud around to face him. "I am exhausted," he said. "I will go to my lodge now while everyone else leaves to search for Bright Smile in the cave. I cannot lead you to her, for I was not sure where we were in the cavern. I do

FIRE CLOUD

know that I ventured much farther than I have ever gone with you, my brother."

Fire Cloud drew Moon Shadow into his arms and gave him a long hug, then stepped away so that Janelle could hug him as well.

Janelle wanted to tell Fire Cloud how sorry she was for everything, that she felt responsible for Moon Shadow's desperate flight and need to remove himself from everyone's lives.

Yet part of her saw reason and realized that if he had not gone to the cavern when he had and become so afraid over his brother's welfare, he would still not hear, see, or soon be able to converse.

No, she didn't feel that apologies were needed. Except for one person, it had all worked out for the best. Bright Smile. Now if only she could be found and brought home, the village would have true cause to celebrate.

"We must leave now," Fire Cloud said, gently placing a hand on Janelle's arm. "Do you want to go with me? Or should you return to the convent to assure your aunt that you are all right?"

Fearing what might be found in the cavern—that this woman who had gone there to die might by now have taken her own life—Janelle shook her head. "No, I don't want to go with you this time," she said. "I will go on to the convent. But when you can, please come and let me know how things are."

She noticed that Tall Night had come from his lodge. His eyes held a strange sort of anxiousness as he stood beside Fire Cloud, waiting to leave with him and the others to search for Bright Smile.

Again she wondered if Tall Night's strange behavior these past days had something to do with Bright Smile.

And had he not stayed behind while everyone else had gone to search for Moon Shadow?

Now it was strange that he seemed eager to join *this* search.

Pushing aside such suspicions about a man whom she did not know well, and surely had no right to be judging one way or the other, Janelle gave Fire Cloud a hug, then stood with Moon Shadow and watched the warriors leave again for another hunt.

Janelle felt eyes on her, then turned and found Moon Shadow smiling.

She drew him into her arms and gave him a long, loving hug, then walked him to his lodge.

After he was lying in his pelts and blankets and already drifting off to sleep, Janelle left his lodge and gazed into the distance.

A chill ran up and down her spine as she thought of what Fire Cloud and the others, especially Bright Smile's husband, might find in Meramec Cavern.

Janelle was glad that she would not be there to witness what might be a terrible tragedy.

She hoped that she was wrong, and that Bright Smile was found in time so that she could, as Moon Shadow had, right things in her life.

But something told Janelle that it was never to be.

Chapter 23

As Janelle walked into the convent, she stopped and glanced quickly toward the library, which was only a few footsteps away. She heard a familiar voice and then another. Her father's and her aunt's.

Janelle had seen Virgil's horse and buggy outside. Why he had come to the convent instead of going on to his home? she wondered. Was he so distraught that he needed his sister's love, which she gave so well to those who were downhearted?

She needed to know, and also wanted to tell her aunt that she was all right. Janelle flipped her hair back from her shoulders and drew in a quavering breath for courage, for she was not sure what to expect from her father. He had been immensely disappointed to have been sent away from the Indian village as though he were no more than a child.

She knew how important it was to him to study the meteorite up close; she even saw the wisdom of taking it to the museum. But she had seen Chief Black Eagle's determination, as had her father. The chief would never change his mind about something he and his people saw as holy to the Lakota.

Before she had left the village, Fire Cloud had told

her what the Lakota were saying among themselves about the meteorite.

"*Tomanoas*," she whispered to herself.

They had named it *Tomanoas* and saw the meteorite as embodying three heavenly realms—sky, earth, and water.

They believed that it was sent from the spirit world, and was linked, somehow, to Moon Shadow's quick recovery.

It was a holy tribal object, which would never be allowed to leave their village.

Just before entering the library, Janelle stopped. She found herself torn about whether to tell Sister Mary Ann about Moon Shadow and the miracle that had occurred today. Janelle knew that her aunt would be thrilled to hear this.

Yet she also felt that it would perhaps be stealing something special from Fire Cloud and Moon Shadow if she told her aunt before they had the chance to do it themselves.

She could even now imagine the joy her aunt would feel hearing this about the young warrior she adored.

Yes, she should wait and let Fire Cloud and Moon Shadow do the telling. It was their miracle, which her aunt would see came from the hands of the Lord, not from a piece of fiery rock that fell on land that just happened to belong to the red man, not the white.

That decision made, Janelle hurried into the library.

She stopped dead in her tracks when she found

FIRE CLOUD

her aunt and father sitting on the floor with opened books spread out all around them, bringing one and then another onto their laps to read more carefully.

Janelle also noticed an open journal at her father's side, and a pen and bottle of ink sitting next to it.

She saw several written entries on one page and a drawing of the meteorite she had just left behind at the village.

She could see figures covering the page, with lines drawn to the meteorite, which she deciphered as measurements.

Her father's head suddenly shot up and found Janelle standing there.

Her aunt's gaze soon followed.

"Come here, Janelle," her father said eagerly, as he beckoned for her. "Mary Ann and I have searched through these books and have found many references to meteorites. I am recording everything that I can find, and then will go to our library at the college to compare what I find there."

"Isn't it exciting, Janelle?" Sister Mary Ann said, looking like a child of ten as she sat with the black skirt of her robe on the floor around her, her knees folded beneath it. She had removed her head covering and revealed the short locks of golden hair that framed her pretty, petite face.

Seeing the cropped hair reminded Janelle that if she had chosen to live the life of a nun, she would be wearing her hair that short, perhaps even today.

When she thought of how Fire Cloud loved her hair, and the wonderful bliss it caused her when he ran his fingers through it and slowly brought her lips to his for a wondrous kiss, she knew that she had made the right choice for her life.

Yet as she gazed at her father, who had seemed so boyishly eager as he pored over the pages of the books and now looked up at her without any of the hurt that she had seen back at the Lakota village, she felt guilty. Soon she would ruin the happiness that he had found on the floor of the convent with his sister today.

When he discovered what Janelle's future truly did hold for her, he would surely sink again into despair.

That was why she couldn't tell him.

Not yet, anyway.

He must put his resentment for the Lakota behind him first.

And he did seem on the right track now by studying meteorites without having to be near the object itself.

"See what we have found," Virgil said, again motioning for Janelle with a hand. "Sit with us. In fact, you can write in the journal as I dictate to you."

He smiled again up at her. "It will be like old times, won't it, honey?" he said. "Working together on a project like this might even make you want to return home. You don't have to teach. Be my assistant at the museum, instead."

He lowered his hand, and his eyes begged her. "What do you say, Janelle?" he said softly. "Do you think you might consider being my assistant at the museum? We've much to discover together now that we know of the meteorite that lies on Indian land as we speak."

FIRE CLOUD

Janelle was very aware of how her father actually grimaced at the word "Indian."

She wondered just how much worse his expression would look when he discovered the truth of her feelings for Fire Cloud.

She again felt pulled in two directions, as she had so much of her life since her mother's death. She knew her father needed her, yet knew that she needed her own life as well.

Janelle slowly walked into the room. She was very aware of her aunt's eyes on her as she sat down beside the open journal and lifted it onto her lap.

Her aunt knew what Janelle could not yet say to her father, and she hated pulling her into this momentary deceit.

But this was a very poor time to tell her father the truth—that her life no longer revolved around him.

He would feel left out after she married Fire Cloud and would never accept it. She might not even see him again, which pained her to even think about.

"Now, let's see here," her father murmured, as again he focused on the books. "Meteorites like this are . . ."

He continued to talk and read out loud, and Janelle entered passages in the journal he would want to read later in the privacy of his home. Yet Janelle could not focus on perhaps these last moments with her father. She had trouble concentrating on anything except Fire Cloud and whether he and the others had found Bright Smile.

She wondered when Fire Cloud would come to the convent with his brother to reveal to everyone, especially Sister Mary Ann, that Moon Shadow was at last able to teach the children about his rocks, shells, and anything else he wished to share with them. Soon he would be able to do more than speak with his hands.

"Janelle, your heart isn't in what you are doing," Virgil said, bringing Janelle quickly from her thoughts.

"I'm sorry," Janelle murmured, blushing as she found both sets of eyes on her, her aunt's and her father's.

"You look tired," Sister Mary Ann said, reaching over to gently smooth a fallen lock of hair back from Janelle's face. "Was the Indian ceremony stressful? Are you sorry you stayed the night at the Lakota village?" Then she smiled. "But of course, had you not been there, you would not have witnessed the meteorite."

Janelle's heart sank when she realized what her aunt had said. Her father was now gazing at Janelle with a gaping jaw, and his confusion was quickly turning to anger.

Without thinking of the consequences, her aunt had revealed to Janelle's father that she had not been at the village because of the meteorite.

He knew now that she had been there long before then.

She had to find a way to tell him why without making him too angry.

Her aunt covered her mouth with a hand, then moved slowly to her feet.

Janelle stood as well, as did her father.

"What is this about a ceremony, and staying the

night with the Indians?" Virgil asked, his voice sounding hollow as his narrowed eyes peered intently at Janelle. "You did not go there only after you saw the meteorite fall?"

"Father, I can explain," Janelle said, though not knowing how without enraging him.

"Janelle, I don't want to hear it," Virgil shouted. "This is what happens when I let you come to the convent. You—you've always been infatuated with Indians. Now you go to the Indian village and observe their ceremonies?"

He turned to Sister Mary Ann. "And that you would allow it is unbelievable," Virgil grumbled. "Mary Ann, long ago, when you allowed that first Indian into this convent, I told you that you were wrong in doing it. Now you can see where it has led. My own daughter is involved with the very Indians who a short while ago treated me like dirt beneath their feet."

Janelle gasped and stiffened when her father grabbed her by an arm. "You're coming with me," he said, half dragging her toward the door. "I've had enough of this. You're coming home, Janelle, where you belong."

Janelle gave her aunt a frantic look over her shoulder.

Her aunt sternly spoke Virgil's name, causing him to flinch, then turn slowly to face her. His hand stayed just as firmly on Janelle's arm.

"Virgil Coolidge, you are treating your daughter as though she has no mind of her own, and as though she were a child," Sister Mary Ann said.

"Unhand her this minute, Virgil. And she is *not* going home with you if she doesn't want to."

Janelle scarcely breathed as her father and her aunt faced each other with glares and stiffened jaws.

Then suddenly her aunt won the battle, and Janelle felt her father's grip loosening on her arm. Then he released her, turned, and stomped from the room.

Janelle stood with trembling knees and tearful eyes as she stared at the door where her father had made his exit.

She then turned to her aunt and flew into her arms.

"Thank you," she sobbed. "But then, what of Father?"

"Your father might be fifty-five years of age, but he still has a lot of growing up to do," Sister Mary Ann murmured.

"I hate hurting him," Janelle said as she eased from her aunt's arms.

She went to the window just in time to see her father riding away in a cloud of flying dust down the long lane that led from the convent.

She hated seeing him this angry with her and Sister Mary Ann, yet it was good to see her father's spirits returning.

He no longer looked like a beaten man.

"Perhaps I should go after him," Janelle said, still watching him.

"No, that would just complicate things," Sister Mary Ann said, going to stand beside Janelle at the window. "If living apart from your father is what you want, let it be, Janelle. Your father will calm down. Then we must pray that he will think all of this through and know that the best thing is to allow you your life, instead of trying to run it for you."

Janelle's eyes moved in the direction of the Indian village. She wanted to be there so badly, yet she knew now that it was best to wait until Fire Cloud came for her.

And surely, when he did, he would bring Moon Shadow and share his good news with everyone.

"I'm going to have a tub and hot bathwater taken to your room," Sister Mary Ann said as she walked briskly toward the door. "You can soak yourself for a while, then tell me everything that happened at the village. And I mean before the meteorite fell, for I'm sure you have much to share with your old auntie about a few things . . . such as perhaps Fire Cloud and how you two are getting on with your relationship?"

Janelle turned and gave her a gentle smile.

"Yes, we are truly getting on with our relationship," Janelle said, glad to think about something wonderful after those trying moments she had just experienced with her father.

She now knew that it would be very hard to tell her father about her plans to marry Fire Cloud, now . . . or ever!

Chapter 24

They did not even have to light torches this time. Just as Fire Cloud stepped inside Meramec Cavern, he saw something that filled his heart with immediate despair.

"Bright Smile," he gasped, as his eyes fixed on the still, prone figure. The once vibrant woman, who had spent the last hours of her life with Fire Cloud's brother—who had even saved his life by safely leading him out of the cave—was now dead.

The knife protruded from her flat belly, where her life's blood had flowed from the wound and spread out across the buckskin fabric of her dress. Immersed in his sorrow that such a woman would feel the need to take her own life, Fire Cloud did not hear the crunch of rock behind him. Under normal circumstances he would realize that someone else would also soon see Bright Smile lying there, so beautiful and peaceful in her sleep of death.

If he had not been so distracted himself, he might even have known that her husband would be the next person to see her. His despair would be so great that the heavens would mourn with him.

Fire Cloud was finally shaken from his stupor

when a loud wail did erupt from Red Dawn Wolf, who fell to his knees and gazed through tears at the woman he had loved since they both were children.

Feeling helpless at such a loss, Fire Cloud stood immobile for a moment longer. The warriors came and stood around him, their breathing sharp and filled with pain as they, too, saw the woman they all loved lying dead.

Red Dawn Wolf was still too shocked to even see the knife. His eyes stayed only on his wife's face, his hand moving gently over her pretty features after slowly closing her eyes. Before his friend could notice, Fire Cloud knelt beside him and slowly pulled the knife free of Bright Smile's belly.

As though it were a hot coal against his fingers, Fire Cloud winced and dropped the knife to the cave floor.

Then, shuddering at the blood on the blade, he kicked the knife far into the depths of the cavern.

Still wailing, Red Dawn Wolf lifted his wife's lifeless body into his arms and started carrying her from the cave. Fire Cloud turned and watched, then was aware of someone's hand in his, clutching it so tightly that he felt the bones of his fingers might crack.

Fire Cloud's eyebrows rose when he found Tall Night there, seeming desperate as he watched Red Dawn Wolf carrying Bright Smile.

Fire Cloud was stunned to see the pain in his friend's tear-filled eyes, his hand still grasping hard to Fire Cloud's. He knew that something was very wrong with his friend, who seemed far too distraught even in these terrible circumstances.

After everyone had left the cavern, Tall Night still stood beside Fire Cloud, his hand trembling as he slowly released Fire Cloud's. Fire Cloud grabbed this opportunity to question his friend about his strange behavior.

"Tall Night, is there something that you have not confided in me about when perhaps you should have?" Fire Cloud asked guardedly. "Or should I not even *want* to know?"

Tall Night's eyes wavered. He hung his head for a moment, then slowly looked up again. "I should have not held it inside for so long," he said, his voice breaking. "Had I talked it over with you, and got answers that might have helped my and Bright Smile's situation, she might not be dead in her husband's arms now."

"You and Bright Smile's situation?" Fire Cloud asked, knowing what this must mean, yet hoping that he was wrong.

Tall Night went to the cave opening and watched the procession of warriors as they walked toward the canoes waiting in the river. He could no longer see Red Dawn Wolf or Bright Smile, for the mourning warrior was in the lead, the others following closely behind him.

Fire Cloud went up to Tall Night and placed a hand on his arm. "Come," he encouraged his friend. "We will follow later. Right now, let us go somewhere private to talk. I am your best friend, to whom you can tell all things."

FIRE CLOUD

Tall Night placed his hand on Fire Cloud's and nodded. "Yes, we are best friends, and I was so wrong not to trust you with even my most private sins," he said, swallowing hard. "And, yes, my friend. I *have* sinned."

He lowered his hand, gazed again at the warriors who were now almost at the river, then turned back to Fire Cloud. "Let us go now and talk beneath the autumn leaves," he said. "I do have much to confess to you."

Fire Cloud walked with Tall Night to where the view of the river was blocked by tall forsythia bushes, and Tall Night could not see his beloved's body being taken away by someone else.

Yes, Red Dawn Wolf was her husband. But Tall Night knew that Bright Smile had loved him far more than she had ever loved her husband.

He now opened up and told Fire Cloud everything. Bright Smile had been good friends with Red Dawn Wolf too long for them to truly be the sort of lovers that made a wife content.

She had told Tall Night that when she was in the blankets with Red Dawn Wolf, nothing stirred sensually within her. It was just something she did out of duty.

But one day she found sudden joy in Tall Night's arms. He had caught her and stopped her from a bad fall off a cliff, and then kissed her. That kiss had started something that neither could stop. Their relationship had blossomed into more than friendship.

She had discovered what true love felt like, and had since then had trysts with Tall Night.

When Bright Smile discovered that she was pregnant, she knew that it was Tall Night's child, conceived when her husband had been on a lengthy hunt with several of his closest friends. The hunt had lasted more than fourteen sunrises and sunsets.

He had returned with an injury, which made it too painful for him to make love.

When she had discovered that she was pregnant, she knew the time was wrong for it to be her husband's baby. But Red Dawn Wolf trusted her so much that he did not stop to count on his fingers just when the child could have been conceived.

"So you see, my friend, I have committed the worst sin against my people. I slept with, and loved, another man's wife," Tall Night said. He held his face in his hands as tears spilled from his eyes. "I had a long affair with Bright Smile. It was *my* child that she carried . . . not her husband's. These past days have been heart-wrenching and so strained, for Bright Smile knew that it was time to give birth."

He looked quickly over at Fire Cloud. "Surely this is why she went into hiding," he said, wiping tears from his eyes. "She was ashamed for anyone to see, to know, that the child was not her husband's. For she, too, was feeling the guilt of our sinning. She was afraid that somehow people would know, if they saw the child, that it was not Red Dawn Wolf's."

He swallowed hard and rubbed his brow. "She feared most of all that Red Dawn Wolf would know that it was not his," he said, his voice breaking.

Again Tall Night held his face in his hands. "I am so ashamed of what I have done, and so sad over losing not only the only woman I will ever love, but also our child, for surely it died during birth," he sobbed. "The child died as a punishment for its mother and father's sins."

Stunned at his best friend's confession, Fire Cloud could not yet find words to help take away some of his friend's pain.

And he was reminded of another time, another woman who had been big with another man's child.

His mother!

He remembered the hate he had carried for the man whose child his mother bore. To have slept with another man's wife, and created a baby in his image, not the woman's husband's, made him the worst of men.

But now? Fire Cloud had heard his best friend confess to having done something as shamefully wrong, but he could not think of Tall Night as a bad person, for Fire Cloud knew the goodness in his friend's heart!

Ay-uh, Fire Cloud felt confused, for he could not help wondering if he had been wrong through the years to hate the other man in his mother's life.

Had he been wrong to judge him?

Did one wrongful act make a man totally dishonorable?

And if his mother loved the man, surely he had a good heart, because no one had been as good and sweet as his mother.

She would not have been with anyone whose character was in question.

Suddenly Fire Cloud saw the wrong in hating Gray Wind so much. Fire Cloud's friend was guilty of the same crime, and he did not see him as evil, for he knew that Tall Night was good, through and through. If needed, Tall Night would even give his life to save a friend!

Then something else came to Fire Cloud. He looked quickly over at Tall Night, silent now in his guilt and grieving. Fire Cloud was afraid for his friend's life. If anyone knew about their affair, especially now that Bright Smile had killed herself, Tall Night might die as Fire Cloud's father had died—in a duel of knives.

"Tall Night, we have advised each other often, and today I feel strongly that you should let this go in your heart and mind," Fire Cloud said. "Do not tell anyone else besides me, your best friend, what you have confided today. It will serve no true purpose. You are paying enough for your sin by losing Bright Smile in such a way, a well as the child."

Tall Night stifled a sob behind a hand as he gazed with teary eyes at Fire Cloud.

"Tall Night, I encourage you to spend many days and nights in prayer," Fire Cloud said softly. "After your prayers, you will be a better man. Then you must concentrate only on your people, for one day you will be their leader. By council, you are already the chosen one to follow as chief when your father decides to give the title over to you. You would be letting your people down by not following through with your training and becoming chief when it is asked of you."

"I do not deserve the honor of being chief," Tall Night choked out. "A warrior is chosen to be chief because he is a man of *honor*. I am far less than honorable at this moment."

Tall Night turned to Fire Cloud and placed a hand on his shoulder. "You should take my place and be chief, for you know how you are loved and admired by the people of our village."

"But I am not truly Lakota," Fire Cloud said. "Although your blood and mine have mixed as blood brothers, at heart I am Chippewa. I long for my people. I feel the call of my Saint Croix band of Chippewa. I hope to go there some day, hopefully before my hair is gray and dragging the ground and I amble along in the slow gait of an old man."

"You are Lakota in the eyes of our village," Tall Night said. "Your blood has Lakota blood. It would be sad if you left to return to Minnesota. I would feel only half a warrior without you at my side on the hunt and during council."

"I would feel the same, yet the time will come when we must say our good-byes," Fire Cloud said. He drew Tall Night into his arms and gave him a brotherly hug. "And as for you not feeling noble and honorable at this time, that feeling will pass. Everyone knows that you are a good man. You just happened to fall in love with the wrong woman."

"My brother, thank you for always being so understanding," Tall Night said, returning the hug. "Thank you."

They embraced for a moment longer, then went to the river and boarded Fire Cloud's canoe.

Far ahead, the procession of canoes was taking the fallen Lakota woman home for mourning and burial rites.

As they paddled home, Fire Cloud was anxious to go to his brother. He had to tell him. He had been wrong to carry such hate in his heart for Moon Shadow's father. He would tell him that he had been wrong to wear his hate so visibly.

Hate was a terrible thing, which festered like a wound if one kept such feelings inside for too long.

And then Fire Cloud wanted to go with Moon Shadow to the convent!

What joy they would see in not only Sister Mary Ann, but also the children, to know that Moon Shadow's world was no longer one of silence and blindness.

And what joy it would bring to his brother's heart to see the innocence and beauty of the children!

Fire Cloud was glad to have these things to look forward to, for these next days at his village would be heartbreaking as one of their women was prepared to take her long walk into the hereafter.

Chapter 25

Radiantly happy, Janelle clutched her aunt's hand as she stood between her and Fire Cloud. The children of the convent were all crowding around Moon Shadow, laughing joyously over how their special friend could see and hear them.

"This is not the work of a meteorite," Sister Mary Ann said, beaming as she continued watching Moon Shadow lovingly. "It is the answer to all of our prayers. It is the miracle of prayer that gives us such blessings, not something that happens to fall from the sky."

"Moon Shadow, I will help teach you the alphabet!" one ten-year-old boy named Sam said excitedly to Moon Shadow, even though he knew that Moon Shadow could not yet understand his words.

Cassandra, a small sweet twelve-year-old girl with long red hair crowded Sam out of the way and took Moon Shadow's hand, speaking to him in the way she knew he would understand. She told him that she would delight in teaching him every word that she knew he would enjoy speaking.

She giggled and blushed when she said that she would be careful not to teach him how to speak in her Kentucky drawl that drew so much teasing from the boys of the orphanage.

She told him that she hoped to learn his language one day as well—not only Lakota, but Chippewa.

Fire Cloud stepped closer to Janelle. He bent close to her ear as he watched his brother's eyes take on a special glow. Cassandra continued telling him things, her own green eyes proving just how much she adored Moon Shadow.

"My brother, whose years add up now to fifteen, is smitten with the lovely girl with hair the color of a brilliant sunset," Fire Cloud said, smiling.

Tears of happiness filled Janelle's eyes as she watched Moon Shadow reach up and gently touch Cassandra's face, his eyes absorbing each of her beautiful features. His fingers had been right in telling him how lovely she was when he had first made her acquaintance. That was only six months ago, after she had been dropped off at the orphanage by uncaring parents.

"Yes, I do believe they were stars in the heavens waiting to be born, brought together, and love one another," Janelle murmured. "It is all so wonderful, Fire Cloud."

Her smile waned as she glanced over at him and saw a haunted expression in his eyes. She knew without asking him who he was thinking about.

Bright Smile.

When he arrived at the convent with Moon Shadow, he had told Janelle that the wonders of his brother's recovery had been overshadowed by finding Bright Smile dead by her own hand in the cave. Janelle's heart had sank.

Even now the Lakota village would be mourning the fallen woman.

Janelle could hardly believe it when Fire Cloud told her in confidence that Tall Night had a role in this tragedy, loving the woman and fathering the child who had died.

Everyone at the village thought that Bright Smile had killed herself over losing the child.

Only a few knew the truth.

Guilt. Shame. Despair.

Surely all of these emotions had become too much for the woman to live with.

A sudden hush fell across the room as the huge oak door that led into the convent closed with a bang.

Janelle started toward the door.

"I shall see who it is," Janelle said to Sister Mary Ann. She turned and smiled at everyone. "Please continue visiting with Moon Shadow. He can't stay for much longer. Both he and Fire Cloud must return home soon, for they are needed."

She didn't want to tell the children that they would be leaving to help see to Bright Smile's burial. It was to be a quick ceremony, without the usual days of rituals. Because she had taken her own life, which was a disgrace and an insult to the Lakota, her burial would be brief and without the normal lengthy mourning period. Once she was in her burial place, her name would be mentioned no more. It would be as though she had not existed at all.

"I shall go with you," Fire Cloud said, starting toward her.

"No, please, Fire Cloud, stay and enjoy these precious moments with you brother," Janelle said, watching her aunt go to Moon Shadow and kneel beside him and the children. "Look at my aunt. How happy she is over Moon Shadow's newfound blessings in life."

Fire Cloud smiled as he saw for himself this happiness, then turned back to Janelle. "*Ay-uh*, I will stay, for soon we *must* leave," he said softly. "When we do, would you come with us? You are a part of my people's lives now. It would lift my burden of sadness if you were with me as I say my final good-bye to Bright Smile."

"Yes, I shall go with you," Janelle said softly.

She hurried out into the corridor, then stopped with surprise when she found her father there, hanging his hat and coat on the pegs along the wall.

He had heard her footsteps and turned toward her.

"Father?" Janelle said, eyeing him with amazement. "Father, why are you here?"

Without answering her, he swept her into his arms and gave her a tight hug. "Daughter, daughter," he said, his voice breaking. "I've come to beg your forgiveness. I . . . I was too hasty in condemning you for a curiosity that you were born with and that I even encouraged. It is only natural that you would be interested in the Indians and their ways. It was wrong of me to discourage your desire to know more about them. It is something that even I, were I a young man your age, would want to explore more myself."

FIRE CLOUD 229

Janelle clung to him. She found it hard to believe that this was her father actually begging her forgiveness.

She wanted so badly to believe that he finally understood her, and was not using this scheme to get her to return home and become a part of the lengthier study of the meteorite.

He might even be trying to win her back so that she would speak to the Lakota in his behalf about the meteorite. He no doubt wanted them to allow him to move it to the museum.

No. She had to believe that he was there now because he did feel badly over how he had treated her earlier.

She returned his hug happily, for only a short time ago she had thought that she had lost his love and respect forever.

No matter why he had came back to the convent, she was enjoying this moment with him, for lately, there had been too few hugs from her father.

Virgil stepped away from her, yet he still held her hands. "Daughter, come home with me," he said. "Work with me on the meteorite project and then you can come back to the convent. I promise not to interfere again in your curiosity over the Lakota." He laughed. "Tell you the truth, sweetheart, I would be disappointed in you if you didn't want to learn their customs. You have always wanted to know everything about everything. How could you not show interest in this?"

He dropped his hands from hers and gave her a quizzical look. "But there is one thing, Janelle," he said softly. "Why were you so accepted into their village, even allowed to witness one of their ceremonies, when I'm not even permitted to stand there and study the meteorite?"

Janelle was suddenly at a loss for words. Then her father's gaze moved past her and his mouth opened in a silent gasp. He took an unsteady step away from her.

She was almost certain what he was seeing, for she had heard footsteps coming from the large meeting room, among them the soft-padded sound of moccasins. Fire Cloud, her aunt, and Moon Shadow entered the corridor and stopped beside Janelle.

Janelle turned slowly back to her father and saw an instant rage in his eyes. His jaw tightened, and his hands circled into fists at his sides.

She awaited his explosion, for although he had just promised that he understood her curiosity about the Indians, he had not expected to see them at the convent.

"What is the meaning of this?" Virgil asked, his voice low and drawn. He turned accusingly to his sister. "Mary Ann, can you explain this? Why are these two Indians here?"

He watched the orphans move slowly out into the corridor, then flinched when two children flanked Moon Shadow, each clinging to one of his hands.

"Virgil, now just hold your temper," Sister Mary Ann softly admonished him. "Fire Cloud and Moon Shadow—"

"You speak their names so fondly," Virgil said, interrupting her. He narrowed his eyes at Janelle. "And what is your role in this?"

FIRE CLOUD

Fire Cloud looked at Janelle. Her lips were trembling. At this moment he hated a father who would make his daughter feel trapped. For that was exactly how it looked to Fire Cloud—as though his Janelle was caught beneath the scornful, accusing eyes of her father.

Knowing that the truth had to come out eventually, Fire Cloud stepped up beside Janelle and possessively slid an arm around her waist, drawing her closely to him.

Janelle glanced questioningly up at Fire Cloud, for she knew that what he had just done proved that she was more than only intrigued with the Indians.

Her father had groaned as though he were in pain when Fire Cloud put his arm around her waist.

She watched Fire Cloud proudly address her father, stunned that he would choose now to say the words.

"Your daughter is no longer any of your concern," Fire Cloud said. "She is soon to become my wife."

Her father took a stumbling step away from them, his breathing coming in short, raspy jerks. He struggled to loosen his shirt collar from around his throat with clawing fingers. He seemed to fight for each breath.

The part of Janelle who had always loved her father, and cared for him since the loss of her mother, made her want to go to him and deny everything that was causing him such stress.

When her father choked out her name, Janelle broke free of Fire Cloud's grip and started toward him, but stopped as he placed a hand in the air between them.

"Don't," he said, gasping for breath. "I'll be all right."

Tears burning in her eyes, Janelle stood her ground. She was relieved that Fire Cloud was there to give her moral support as he again placed an arm around her.

Sister Mary Ann hurried to her brother. She took his hands. "Are you certain you do not need help?" she asked.

"Fine as a father can be whose daughter has just said she's marrying an enemy," Virgil said, his eyes steady now with Janelle's. "Yes, an enemy. You saw how I was ordered from the Lakota village, Janelle. How could . . . you even let a man with red skin touch you, much less trick you into marrying him so that . . . that . . . he can brag about having won the heart of a white woman . . . who will brag also about how a white woman performs with him in his blankets."

Janelle went pale and gasped.

"Virgil, that's enough of that kind of talk," Sister Mary Ann snapped.

She gave Fire Cloud and Moon Shadow a quick look of apology over her shoulder as she grabbed Virgil by an arm and quickly ushered him from the convent with his hat and coat.

Virgil stood on the porch with his sister. He yanked himself away from her arm, slapped on his hat, and slid into his long black coat.

"Mary Ann, I warned you long ago about the foolishness of involving yourself with Indians," he said, his eyes flashing angrily. "Now you see why. I have lost a daughter to one of the savages. And as far as I'm concerned, she isn't my daughter any longer."

Sister Mary Ann followed him desperately down the steps. "You can't mean that," she cried. "Janelle has done nothing to deserve such wrath."

He turned and glared at her. "Sister, not only has she, but you have as well," he said, reaching for the reins and swinging himself into his saddle. "I'll be cutting off all monetary support to this convent. Let the orphans go to hell as far as I'm concerned." He brought his face closer to hers. "As for you, you can join them."

Stunned speechless by her bother's coldness, Sister Mary Ann could only gape at him. Then she looked him square in the eye.

"Virgil, you are nothing but a bigot," she said. "Where is the compassion I have seen through your years of giving to the orphanage and convent? Surely it wasn't all pretense. Surely you felt something."

He laughed joylessly.

Sister Mary Ann stifled a gasp behind a hand as her brother rode off in a cloud of dust.

Her eyes lowered, she turned back toward the convent. She could not believe what had just transpired. Was her brother going to cut all financial ties to this convent? Had he actually said that he cared nothing for the orphans . . . or for *her?*

Slowly shaking her head, she went inside the convent. She was not sure how she would explain these latest rantings to her niece.

Chapter 26

Virgil Coolidge rode hard alongside the Meramec River, a twisted grin on his lips. His eyes had the look of a scheming madman as he went over the plan he had conjured up before coming to the convent.

He had visited today only as a ploy; secretly he was planning to find a way to remove the meteorite to his museum. And once he lured Janelle back home to work with him, he would never allow her to leave again—even if he had to keep her under lock and key to ensure it.

He felt such deep resentment, even jealousy, of the Lakota, especially Fire Cloud. Fire Cloud had lured both Sister Mary Ann and Janelle into his clutches.

Most certainly Virgil would never allow his daughter to marry Fire Cloud. He hadn't raised a daughter, sent her to the most expensive schools as if she were a son, for her to waste it all on an Indian. He knew all along that she would get over the notion of being a nun. Well, she would get over the Indian.

Virgil would *not* have half-breed grandchildren in his house. He was a respectable, notable citizen of Saint Louis. His daughter was not going to taint his reputation with redskin blood in his grandchildren's veins.

He chuckled devilishly, thinking how he had already devised a way to make Janelle come to her senses . . . or else.

"Jonathan Drake," Virgil whispered, his eyes gleaming. "Yes, Jonathan will help me. He'll do anything for me because he knows that if he doesn't, all will be lost to him."

Chapter 27

Everything at the Lakota village was quiet. Bright Smile had been laid to rest and was among the stars again, as she had been before finding life in her mother's womb.

Moon Shadow was in his tepee, tired from his time at the convent and the sorrow of the burial services.

Janelle snuggled more closely to Fire Cloud as they sat beside his lodge fire. After her aunt told her what her father had said, how he was no longer going to help with the finances at the convent and the orphanage, Janelle again felt the weight of guilt on her shoulders.

She knew that had she not disappointed her father, he would have no reason to be upset with his sister.

Tears streamed down her cheeks as she thought of the children at the orphanage. If they were neglected in any way, yes, she would feel responsible. She wanted to go to her father and beg, if she must, for him to reconsider.

But she knew for certain that she could not return to live with him, or even help him, for no matter how concerned she was over his welfare, he did not deserve the loyalty she had given to him these past years.

Her loyalty was now to someone else.

To the man she loved, to Moon Shadow, and to her aunt.

Janelle had to find a way to bring in money for her aunt so that things could go on as usual at the convent.

"You have not spoken two words since the burial rites were completed," Fire Cloud said. He lifted Janelle's chin so that their eyes could meet.

"It is my father," Janelle murmured, fighting back another urge to cry. "How could I have so misjudged him? How could I not have seen the tyrant that my aunt saw today? I can hardly believe that he has turned his back on all those he loves . . . or loved. My aunt and I are all that he has in the world. Without us, he will be such a lonely man!"

"He threatened your aunt in anger because he knows he has lost his only daughter to another man," Fire Cloud said, his eyes searching hers. "And not any man. You have fallen in love and will soon marry a man whose skin is red. To your father that is a forbidden act. Because you are going to be my wife, he sees no choice but to turn his back on you."

"But also on his sister?" Janelle said, her voice breaking. "My aunt is everything good on this earth. Her whole purpose in life is to do good for someone else, not herself. When she awakens it is with enthusiasm, for she knows she will be spending the day with those she loves. The children. The nuns. And we three—me, you, and Moon Shadow. She is eagerly anticipating our marriage, Fire Cloud. But even that has been clouded by my father's sudden behavior."

"We must marry soon so that he cannot find a way to interfere," Fire Cloud said. He placed his hands at Janelle's waist and lifted her onto his lap facing him. "Do you agree that we should not wait, that we should give your father no chance to stop us?"

"There is no way on this earth that my father can stop us from marrying," Janelle said, her voice tight. "Just let him try."

"*Gah-ween*, we do not want to give him even the chance to try," Fire Cloud said. He framed her face between his hands and looked lovingly into her eyes. "Tomorrow, my woman. We should get married tomorrow."

"Tomorrow?" Janelle said, her eyes suddenly filled with awe and excitement.

"*Ay-uh*," Fire Cloud said. "As soon as the sun breaks along the horizon, we should become husband and *gee-wee-oo*—which means 'wife' in Chippewa."

"So early in the morning?" Janelle said softly.

"Your father would never suspect that you will marry this Indian as soon as tomorrow, much less at dawn," Fire Cloud said. "Tomorrow, my love, we shall become man and wife. Then let your father try to dictate to you what you can or cannot do."

"But Fire Cloud, I truly don't believe you have to worry about that, ever again," Janelle said, her tears returning at the memory of her father turning his back on her as though she were a stranger, not his daughter. "He said as much—"

"A father who loved you as much as yours has could not quit loving you for any reason," Fire Cloud said, interrupting Janelle.

"He did love me so very much, as I still love and admire him," Janelle said, her voice breaking.

"And he will prove to you again one day that his love for you is as strong as before," Fire Cloud said. "But we must not take a chance that he will use that love to stop you from marrying this Chippewa warrior."

"I am not certain about your people's marriage customs," Janelle said softly. "I am not sure whether I would truly feel married in the eyes of my Lord. Would you understand if I ask that we go to the convent and be married first by a priest there? Then we would be married in your tradition later."

"If that is what you wish, that is how we shall do it," Fire Cloud said. He lifted her into his arms as he moved to his feet. He held her close and carried her to his bed of blankets and pelts, then laid her there as gently as if she might break.

"I want Moon Shadow to be a part of our wonderful day," Janelle said. She trembled with anticipation when Fire Cloud began unbuttoning her white cotton blouse, spreading it open so that her breasts were bare for feasting upon by his tongue and lips.

"Moon Shadow, your aunt, and everyone at the convent who wishes to will be a witness to one of the most beautiful moments between a man and woman in love," Fire Cloud said tenderly as Janelle drew his fringed buckskin shirt over his head, and then pushed his breeches down his legs.

When he was totally nude and waiting, she hurried out of her own clothes. "My husband," she said, her cheeks flushed with the excitement of becoming his wife. "I shall be able to call you 'husband' tomorrow and forevermore. As you shall call me wife."

Fire Cloud leaned his full body down over hers.

He grazed her mouth with his, then consumed her lips in a long, fiery kiss. He nudged her legs apart and sank his body down into her softly yielding folds.

As he entered her, they moaned against each other's lips.

He moved rhythmically against her.

He nuzzled her neck, then brought his lips down over a breast, his teeth gently nibbling on the erect, rosy nipple.

Caught up in wondrous rapture, Janelle laced her arms around his neck and clung to his rock-hard shoulders.

Wanting him even more deeply inside her, his thrusts making her wanton, she opened her thighs more widely. His body responded, the urgency building between them.

His fingers ran through her hair, and he brought her mouth to his in a hot, deep kiss.

Between those kisses Janelle pleaded for more.

They cuddled, caressed, showered each other with kisses, tangled, sighed, and moaned.

Then Fire Cloud stopped long enough to get his breath.

FIRE CLOUD

He rested his cheek against her chest.

Janelle reached down and caressed his tight buttocks, then pressed him even more strongly against her as he again began moving in wild yet even strokes within her.

Soon ultimate pleasure claimed them both and left them breathless and smiling.

They lay beside each other, looking up through the smoke hole, which revealed a moon half hidden behind clouds. In the distance someone beat a sad song on a lone drum. Elsewhere someone wailed softly, so low that hardly anyone could hear him.

Fire Cloud knew who was crying out in torment. It was Tall Night. He had left earlier, immediately after the burial rites, to pray alone in the deepest recesses of the forest.

But Red Dawn Wolf mourned openly and loudly for all to see and hear, to prove his love for a wife who was no longer with him.

"I have never heard anything as sad as a husband's mourning the loss of a wife," Fire Cloud said. He sat up and flipped his long black hair back from his shoulders. He could not help but think that Red Dawn Wolf was mourning the wrong thing! He should have been mourning, instead, how he had lost this woman long ago to another man!

"Mothers and fathers yearn for their children who pass on before them," he said. "But a husband's emptiness after a wife's death goes far beyond what one can comprehend."

"Do not die before me, my love," Janelle said, visibly shuddering at the thought of being without him.

She sat up and drew a blanket around both their shoulders.

She leaned against him. "We must take care of each other to make certain we have a long time together on this earth."

"I will guard you with my life," Fire Cloud said, turning her to face him, then lowering her back down onto the blankets. "Tomorrow. Tomorrow we begin, truly begin, the rest of our lives."

"The rest of our lives," Janelle whispered against his lips as he swept the blanket aside and became, himself, the blanket that covered her.

Again they made love, softly and sweetly, and the tepee seemed filled with the scent of jasmine.

Chapter 28

With all of the children, nuns, and Moon Shadow as witnesses, a priest brought Fire Cloud and Janelle together as man and wife.

Janelle felt as though everything was a dream as the morning sun cast a shadowy orange glow upon her through the windows above.

She was now married to Fire Cloud.

Her aunt had stood watching, her eyes brimming with tears of joy for her niece, for no man could be finer than Fire Cloud.

The ceremony just now over, the excited children came squealing in a mad dash to hug both Janelle and Fire Cloud. Janelle's face felt as though it was frozen in a smile as she went from child to child, and then nun to nun as they came and offered their own quiet congratulations to the new bride and groom.

And Moon Shadow had not been left out. After everyone greeted Fire Cloud and Janelle, they mingled in a wide circle around him, for his ability to see and hear was still too new to be ignored by those who adored him.

Moon Shadow's eyes gleamed as children came

and offered their suggestions on how to say one word or another. But Cassandra stood beside Moon Shadow through it all, and his eyes returned to her more often than not.

Moon Shadow could not look enough at her. Their bond had been formed before he could see and would endure even more devotedly now that their eyes could meet and hold, sometimes more bashfully than not.

Fire Cloud enjoyed seeing the love blossoming between his brother and this girl. So beautiful already at her young age, Cassandra would grow up to be as lovely as Janelle had been at her age.

His brother would wait for her to grow up, and then surely there would be another wedding in the family.

"Fire Cloud, Janelle, can you please come with me?" Sister Mary Ann said, interrupting Fire Cloud's pleasant thoughts.

Janelle turned to Fire Cloud, reveling in the way he placed the arm of a husband, not a lover, around her waist as they walked together down the long corridor until they came to a room at the far end.

"In here," Sister Mary Ann said, motioning with a hand toward a room at the far end of the hall. She stepped aside so that Janelle and Fire Cloud could enter.

Upon first glance, Janelle saw only the semidarkness of the room, the dark green shades at the windows drawn almost to the bottom.

But there was a slight beam of sunshine that crept

FIRE CLOUD

beneath the shades, giving off enough light for Janelle to see a lone cradle sitting along one wall.

Janelle had been in this room before, for it housed various books which were stored away from the library.

She had never seen a cradle there before.

She turned questioningly to Sister Mary Ann, just as Moon Shadow crept into the room and stood beside Fire Cloud.

"Come and take a look," Sister Mary Ann said, nodding toward the cradle. "The child is asleep now, but he will not care if he has an audience. He is beautiful. So tiny and sweet." She looked up at Fire Cloud. "Sweet, beautiful, and *abandoned*."

"Abandoned?" Fire Cloud said, arching an eyebrow. His eyes narrowed as Sister Mary Ann kept gazing at him. "Sister Mary Ann, why is this child singled out? You brought it here, alone, in this spare library, while before you always took the babies to the nursery where the others are."

"Yes, Auntie, why did you bring the child here, and why did you ask us to come and see it?" Janelle asked, hesitating before leaning over to take a look at the baby. Her aunt was acting peculiarly. It made no sense yet.

"When you see the child, you will understand," Sister Mary Ann said, going now to bend over the cradle. Gently she swept the blanket-wrapped baby into her arms, then went and stood between Fire Cloud and Janelle as Moon Shadow came closer.

Everyone watched curiously as Sister Mary Ann slowly drew a corner of the blanket away from the child's face, then gasped with wonder when they saw the baby's skin color. It was like Fire Cloud's and Moon Shadow's—a smooth, lovely copper color.

"Why, Auntie, it is an Indian child," Janelle said. "I don't recall you speaking of any Indian children being brought to the convent."

"Because this is the first," Sister Mary Ann said, unfolding more of the blanket to reveal the child's shoulders, arms, hands, and tiny fingers. "Yes, this is the first."

"When was the child left here?" Fire Cloud asked guardedly, wondering who of his village could be so callous in the treatment of their child. The Lakota and the Chippewa looked to their children as something almost holy, for they were the future of their people. If one was given away, it would lessen the strength of the tribe by one.

"Just recently the child, wrapped in these blankets, was sent through the tiny door," Sister Mary Ann said.

She smiled at Moon Shadow as he moved in closer and reached inside the blanket. The baby curled his tiny fingers around one of Moon Shadow's, even though the child was still deeply asleep and not aware of doing so.

Moon Shadow cast a pleased smile over his shoulder at Fire Cloud, then bent low and brushed a soft kiss across the tiny tot's brow.

Moon Shadow then moved back again as he tried to make out what was being said, though still finding everything garbled.

But for now, it was enough that he could hear!

FIRE CLOUD

Soon he would understand everything being said, for he listened well as everyone took turns teaching him.

"Usually I don't see who brings the children," Sister Mary Ann softly explained. "I even make a special effort *not* to see, for this is something done privately by the one who has chosen to give the child up for adoption. But when I saw that the child was Indian, I hurried to the window and looked to see who was fleeing the convent grounds, in case relatives became enraged over what she had done and came to the convent, demanding the child."

"And who did you see?" Fire Cloud asked, his jaw tightening.

"It was someone whom I had seen before," Sister Mary Ann said.

Pausing for a moment, she slowly rocked the baby back and forth in her arms as the child made sounds of awakening.

"She had come with her husband to bring blankets she made for the orphans," Sister Mary Ann then said. "Bright Smile only started doing this after she began showing in her own pregnancy."

When she heard what sounded like a quiet gasp coming from Fire Cloud at the mention of Bright Smile's name, Sister Mary Ann looked curiously at him.

"Now I believe I understand why Bright Smile did this," she said, still gazing at Fire Cloud, for his reaction was somewhat peculiar. "From the beginning of Bright Smile's pregnancy she must have considered bringing her child to the orphanage, and she wanted to see how the children were treated."

Sister Mary Ann noticed the wary, even shocked, looks that Janelle and Fire Cloud exchanged. "What puzzles me is why the woman would give up her own child, a son especially, when her husband was so devoted to her and would surely be as devoted to the child," she said, now with a guardedness caused by her niece and Fire Cloud's reaction.

Fire Cloud sighed heavily, for he knew that this child abandoned by Bright Smile was not her husband's at all.

It was Tall Night's.

He was totally speechless over why Bright Smile would do this and not let Tall Night know. It was Tall Night's child as well as Bright Smile's.

And it was a son, which all warriors enjoyed boasting about once one was born to them.

Fire Cloud glanced over at Janelle and realized that she had concluded the same thing. Tall Night's child lay there in Sister Mary Ann's arms!

He walked slowly to a window and gazed in the direction of his village. Never had he felt as torn as now. If he told Tall Night about the child, Tall Night would want to claim him, and if he did, he would reveal to everyone the sin that he so desperately needed to hide—a sin that would cost Tall Night not only his right to be chief, but also in the end his whole people.

For such a truth as this, Tall Night would be sentenced to something even worse than death. He would be banished from his tribe, to wander forever without a life with his people, without a tribe he could call his own.

Yet Fire Cloud knew that he could not just leave the baby at the orphanage, especially with the skin color proving its heritage. Because the child was Indian, he would never be adopted. Whites would turn the other way when they came to see the babies. And most redskins had children of their own. There was no need to adopt.

Janelle saw how troubled and silent Fire Cloud had become. She turned to her aunt. "Auntie, I need to have a private moment with Fire Cloud," she murmured. "We shall not be long."

She turned to Moon Shadow, gave him an uncertain look, then led Fire Cloud from the room.

They went and stood on the back porch, where the air was brisk as another autumn day showed its loveliness.

"Please tell me what you're thinking," Janelle rushed out, her hands in Fire Cloud's as he turned and stood gazing down at her.

He explained the fears and doubts that lay heavy on his shoulders.

"What should I do?" he said, looking over as Moon Shadow came and stood beside him.

Moon Shadow reached for his brother's hand and used their special language to ask him what was troubling him. He said that he was adult enough to know about babies and who fathered and mothered them.

Had he not been around enough babies at the orphanage and their village?

Having always shared almost everything with his brother, Fire Cloud saw it best to explain to him about this child, and the mother who had brought him to the orphanage.

It was surely shortly after she went to the convent that Bright Smile had come to the cave. She had gone there to die. She delayed long enough to help Moon Shadow during his own moments of weakness and unhappiness.

Fire Cloud explained everything to his brother and said that he could not leave the baby at the orphanage. Then he made his brother proud by asking him if he had any suggestions as to what to do.

Beaming proudly that his brother showed enough confidence in him to actually ask for help, Moon Shadow wrote back to him on his hand a response that left Fire Cloud in awe, for it did seem such a logical thing to do.

Then Fire Cloud wrote his brother a response, saying to Moon Shadow that if he and Janelle went to Minnesota with the child, as Moon Shadow had suggested, to help protect its identity, and raised him as their own, what of Moon Shadow? Would he go to Minnesota with them?

He reminded Moon Shadow of their long talks about this subject, how people might make Moon Shadow feel uncomfortable over how he was conceived.

Moon Shadow's chest swelled with pride as he told his brother that he would never shy away from such attention, for he was proud of his parentage.

But it did not matter, for Moon Shadow did not

FIRE CLOUD

want to accompany Fire Cloud and Janelle on the long voyage to Minnesota. He wished to stay among the Lakota, who had become his true people.

Yes, he would miss Fire Cloud terribly, as well as Janelle, but he said that he no longer needed someone to see to his needs, as he had in the past. Moon Shadow was able now to fend for himself in all ways!

He still had so much to teach the children at the orphanage, especially since soon he would be able to talk aloud to them.

Moon Shadow encouraged his brother to return to his true people, to his home, for had it not been Fire Cloud's dream to be there again with his grandfather?

Touched deeply by his brother's love, wisdom, and especially his understanding of Fire Cloud's deep desire to be among his Chippewa people again, Fire Cloud drew Moon Shadow into an embrace.

Then he turned to Janelle. "My brother has just released me of my duties to him," he said, his voice breaking with emotion. "I am now free to return to my true home."

"By home, you mean Minnesota?" Janelle asked.

"*Ay-uh*, Minnesota, the land of lakes and wild rice, where I learned the hunt, where I grew to love riding both in a canoe and on a horse, and the joy of being Chippewa," he said. "I have so missed my grandfather! I have so missed my people."

He drew her quickly into his arms and hugged her tenderly. "My brother suggests that you and I take the child to my homeland of Minnesota," he said.

"He thinks we should raise the child there as our own. No one will ever be the wiser."

"We can adopt the child?" Janelle murmured, easing from his arms and gazing into his dark eyes. "The child will truly be raised as ours?"

"*Ay-uh*, the child will be ours, for always," Fire Cloud said, that thought filling him with a wondrous joy.

Then his smile faded. He knit his brow and looked at the floor. "I do not know how I can take such joy from having this child as ours, when my friend Tall Night ends up with nothing."

"He will soon be chief," Janelle reassured him. She gently lifted her face so that they could look into each other's eyes again.

"My darling husband, is not that a great thing?" she asked. "Is that not enough for a man who should feel blessed for not having been discovered in his deceit?"

Moon Shadow gazed at Fire Cloud, for he realized why his brother was torn. He reached for his hand and told him that no friend could be any more devoted to Tall Night. Tall Night, on the other hand, had kept much from Fire Cloud. He had slept with another man's wife and had even got her with child.

So he did not see how anything Fire Cloud did now was near the deceit that Tall Night was guilty of.

Fire Cloud responded that it did not seem right to keep this child's birth from him. Tall Night believed the child was stillborn.

Then Fire Cloud turned to Janelle and told her

what he had explained to his brother, his eyes filled with emotion as he awaited her response.

"The final decision about whether or not to tell Tall Night is yours," Janelle said. "You know that I will agree to whatever you choose to do."

"Thank you for giving me that," Fire Cloud said softly. He took one of Janelle's hands and one of Moon Shadow's, and together they went inside again. The child was back in the cradle, and Sister Mary Ann was sitting nearby on a chair, slowly rocking it.

When Sister Mary Ann saw them enter the room, she moved to her feet.

Her eyes went slowly from one to the other, as Fire Cloud explained that Tall Night was the father of this child, and that everyone, even Red Dawn Wolf, believed it was dead.

He went on to tell Sister Mary Ann that he and Janelle wanted to adopt the child and asked her to keep silent about who had brought the child to the convent should anyone ever discover the truth behind Bright Smile's death.

"And, Auntie, can you please continue caring for the baby until Fire Cloud and I get things ready for our journey to Minnesota?" Janelle asked. "I'm not certain when that will be. And . . . and I have someone to see. Father. Oh, how am I going to find the courage to tell my father about my marriage to Fire Cloud, and that we are moving to Minnesota?"

"Minnesota?" Sister Mary Ann said, her voice drawn. "You are moving so far away?"

"Auntie, we *must*," Janelle said. "It has been Fire

Cloud's dream for so long to be reunited with his Chippewa people. Now is the time."

Janelle sighed nervously. "But my father," she said, her voice breaking. "How can I tell him all of this? It's so much . . ."

"You have always found courage when you needed it, and so will you soon—enough to tell my brother about your marriage," Sister Mary Ann said, placing a gentle hand on Janelle's cheek. "Don't rush into it if you don't wish to. You will know when the time is right."

"As I must tell Tall Night about the baby," Fire Cloud blurted out. The decision to do so, so suddenly obvious, was alarming not only to him, but to Janelle.

"Are you certain?" Janelle asked.

"All I know is that had I fathered a child and my best friend knew that it lived and did not tell me, I would see him as my enemy once I discovered the truth," Fire Cloud said, his voice drawn. "Yes, I must tell him."

"Again, do not rush into something that troubles you this much," Sister Mary Ann suggested, this time to Fire Cloud. "For now, go home. Janelle, Fire Cloud, is this not your wedding day?"

She turned to Moon Shadow. Knowing how to write messages on the palm of his hand, she told him to take the newlyweds home and make certain no one disturbed them on their first night as man and wife.

Moon Shadow gave Fire Cloud and Janelle a playful smile, then nodded to Sister Mary Ann that, yes, he would escort his brother and his bride home.

He could make certain that no one interrupted their love nest for the rest of the day, and the entire night.

They all went and stood over the baby's cradle. Janelle already felt a bond that would grow through the years. She looked forward to holding him and nurturing him. She would happily give the child what Bright Smile couldn't.

Chapter 29

The fire in the firepit burned low and sweet from the chips of cedar that Fire Cloud had dropped across the logs earlier.

Janelle had gone down to the river to pluck some of the remaining flowers of fall to enjoy during these last days in Missouri. Meanwhile, Fire Cloud had busied himself preparing a surprise for his wife before she returned to their lodge. He had placed lighted candles all around the inside of the tepee.

Fire Cloud and Janelle lay now beside the fire facing one another on their bed of plush pelts. The candles' glow cast dancing images on the buckskin walls of the dwelling.

"This is so romantic," Janelle said. "You are so clever to think of candles."

She snuggled closer to him. "Thank you," she murmured. "It is so beautiful tonight in the lodge. I feel so beautiful." She giggled and gazed into his eyes. "*You* are so beautiful."

"Men are not beautiful," Fire Cloud said, chuckling.

"You are, my darling husband," Janelle said,

moving closer to him so that their naked bodies could press together.

She would have never imagined a love as pure, or as wonderfully sweet, as her and Fire Cloud's love for each other.

Just being with him made her feel at peace with all that had recently happened in her life. He was like a delicious elixir, and the headiness of her feelings for him never faded.

The thought of a lifetime with him made her heart soar. He had given her not only his love, but a steadiness in her life that she had never felt before.

She felt so blessed, and thanked God each night as she gazed at the stars. She would never stop saying a thank-you to the heavens for this man who was now her very soul.

Fire Cloud reached up and swept back Janelle's golden hair from her face, then leaned low and pressed his lips against her. She felt as though she was floating, the sensations inside her were so rapturous.

Wrapping her arms around his neck, she drew him closer, her breasts pressed against his muscled, bronzed chest, his manhood delving amidst the curls between her thighs. Soon he would take her to a place so blissful, so joyous, she swooned at the mere thought of their bodies interlocking again.

"My woman, I love you more than words can say," Fire Cloud said as he looked into her eyes.

"As I love you, my husband," Janelle murmured. Then her breath was stolen away with hot passion when he swept his arms around her and turned her so that she was beneath him, one of his knees spreading her legs so that he could push his throbbing hardness inside her.

He began his rhythmic thrusts, taking her mouth by storm, kissing her wildly.

His hands cupped her breasts, pressing urgently into her warm flesh.

Her hands moved over his back as she reveled in the feel of his smooth copper skin.

She wove her fingers through his thick black hair and kissed him with even more heat, their bodies rocking together.

Fire Cloud moaned deeply as he felt the feverish pleasure rise within him almost to the breaking point.

Yet he held himself at bay to be sure that she felt the same excitement.

"Do you feel it?" Janelle whispered against his lips. "Do you feel the passion? The joy of our bodies being together?"

"I feel it all, and more," Fire Cloud whispered back. "You have filled my soul with wonder."

"I am yours, forever," Janelle said.

She gasped with utter bliss as the trembling began deeply within her and she felt that magical splendor sweep through her, making her cling and strain against him. She felt his body jolt suddenly, then quiver and quake against hers as he, too, found that moment of rapture.

Afterwards, Fire Cloud held Janelle in his arms.

She swept kisses across his brow.

Then they moved apart and lay on their sides facing each other, smiling.

"How many children do you wish to have?" Janelle suddenly blurted out, causing Fire Cloud's eyes to widen.

And then he smiled and placed a gentle hand on her cheek. "As many as *Kitchi-Manitou*, and your God, will bless us with," he said.

"Then you wish for a whole tepee full of children?" Janelle said, giggling softly.

"If that is what we are blessed with, *ay-uh*, I would enjoy many children, but *only* . . ." he said, pausing.

She saw a glint of teasing in his eyes. "But only *what*?" she asked, her own eyes dancing now.

"Only if they are in your image, my wife," Fire Cloud said.

"Even our sons?" Janelle said, her heart bursting with love and adoration for her husband.

"Well, perhaps it would not be best if our sons took on the features of a woman," Fire Cloud bantered back at her. "But our daughters must have your nose, your beautiful eyes, your—"

"Shh," Janelle said, placing a hand over his lips. "Let's not talk, for will it not take much lovemaking to make all of those children that we both wish for?"

His lips formed a teasing smile. "*Ay-uh*, much," he said, chuckling. "And children cannot be made by merely talking about them, can they?"

"*Gah-ween*," she said, proud of knowing many of

his Chippewa words now, and seeing such joy in her husband's eyes when she used them.

"Then let our bodies do the talking, my wife," Fire Cloud said.

He swept her fully into his arms and gave her an all-consuming kiss, as their bodies came together in that magical dance of love that they now knew so well.

Chapter 30

Fire Cloud was still unsure of how the news about his child would affect Tall Night, but decided not to put off telling him any longer. He and Janelle sat on blankets before Tall Night's lodge fire. Their presence was accepted even though Tall Night was still sadly withdrawn.

"It is good that you came today," Tall Night said. He offered Janelle a bowl of stew from the pot that hung over his lodge fire. His mother had brought the stew a short while ago.

Janelle nodded a silent thank-you to Tall Night as she rested the bowl on her knee.

"It is hard to bear, keeping this silence about the woman I loved," Tall Night then said. "Her shame in killing herself is known by everyone, and speaking her name is now forbidden in our village. It is as though her own people are trying to pretend she never existed."

He ladled stew onto another wooden bowl and handed it to Fire Cloud. "She *did* exist, and she always will," he said quietly. "In my heart she will always be with me. But what of the child? How can I see the child as a part of me when I did not even know if it was a boy or a girl? How can one imagine a child if he did not know its . . ."

Fire Cloud reached out and placed a gentle hand on Tall Night's shoulder.

"My friend, my wife and I have come to tell you something that we were at first hesitant about, yet feel it is only fair that you know," Fire Cloud said, his voice drawn. "Tall Night, we have news of the child . . . of *your* child."

Tall Night was taken aback by this, so much that he dropped his half-filled bowl of stew, splashing it all over his bare legs.

"What are you saying?" Tall Night gasped, ignoring the heat of the stew on his skin. "What about my child? How *could* you know anything about it?"

"Tall Night, as you know, Janelle and I went to the convent yesterday and exchanged vows in the tradition of her people, as we will one day soon exchange the same vows in my Chippewa tradition," Fire Cloud began, being meticulous in everything he said before finally telling Tall Night that he was a father, that his child, a son, was not dead.

"And?" Tall Night said, his voice tight. "What is it you seemed hesitant to say? You mentioned my child. Why?"

Fire Cloud nervously cleared his throat, then continued. "Tall Night, after we had spoken our vows, Sister Mary Ann took us to a room and showed us something very special," he said. "It was a child, a Lakota boy child. That newborn child was brought to the convent by his mother before she went to Meramec Cavern to die because of her shame at bearing a son to a man other than her husband, and her shame of loving you instead of Red Dawn Wolf."

Tall Night's breath was stolen away. "You are saying that I have a son?" he gasped. "He was not stillborn? He was taken to the convent by his mother and given away, before she . . ."

"*Ay-uh*, all of that is so," Fire Cloud said softly. "Tall Night, this child is your *son*. What are you going to do about him?"

"I must see him," Tall Night said, scrambling quickly to his feet.

"Think clearly, Tall Night, before doing something that you might regret later," Fire Cloud encouraged him as he rose to his feet and placed both hands on his friend's shoulders.

"You are saying that you do not think it is best that I see my son, that I claim him?" Tall Night stammered. In frustration, he wove his fingers through his thick hair and lifted it back from his shoulders. Suddenly he grinned. "A son. I have a son. He did not die!"

"A son that I—that my wife and I—offer to raise for you. Your doing so might start a series of events which could end in your banishment or death," Fire Cloud said, his eyes searching Tall Night's. "Think. Do what, deep inside your heart, you know is best, not so much for you and your son, but for your people. They expect you to be chief. Do you understand what I am trying to say?"

"I am so torn," Tall Night said, his teeth

clenched. He began pacing. "I *do* know what is expected of me. I am to be chief. Yet I still feel very dishonorable. Maybe I am not fit to fill my father's moccasins in the capacity of chief."

"Tall Night, do not think so badly of yourself," Fire Cloud advised. "Everyone makes mistakes. Yours was to love a woman too much. When you become your people's chief, you will prove over and over again your worth, not only to them, but also to yourself, by centering your whole life around your duties to your people."

"I have always lived for the time when I would be chief," Tall Night said, his voice breaking. "I will fight for that right now, and I will prove that I am worthy of being my people's leader."

Fire Cloud embraced Tall Night, then stiffened when his friend said what he hoped he would not say.

Tall Night stepped away from Fire Cloud. "I must go see my son and hold him at least one time," he said. "My brother, will you take me to him?"

Fire Cloud's eyes wavered as he and Janelle exchanged quick glances.

Then Fire Cloud looked intently at Tall Night. "Is seeing the child wise?" he asked. "What if holding your son makes you want to not give him up for someone else to raise?"

"I am not giving my son up for just anyone to raise," he said, smiling. "My best friend, my *gee-gee-kee-wayn-zee*—brother—is going to be my son's *gee-dah-dah*—father. No one could be better suited than you, Fire Cloud. No one is as decent, wholesome, and noble and caring."

Tall Night turned to Janelle. He took her hands. "And no woman could be any better suited to be a mother than you," he said warmly. "I willingly hand my son over to your care."

There were more emotional embraces.

Then they stepped outside.

Janelle took Fire Cloud's hands. "I have someone to see, also," she said, her voice drawn. "Husband, as you take Tall Night to see the child, I shall go see my father and talk with him. I would rather get this behind me so that I can stop thinking about the horrors of it."

"Then you go and get this done," Fire Cloud said. He drew her into his embrace, then walked with her and Tall Night to the river where she took one canoe in the direction of her father's home, and Fire Cloud took his in the direction of the convent.

He and Tall Night each manned a paddle as they sat quietly with their own thoughts.

Fire Cloud was proud that he had chosen to tell his friend about his son. Had he not, he would always have felt that he had done his friend a grievous disserve.

And now he could hardly wait to see Tall Night with the child, if only for a few moments. Tall Night would carry his memory with him into each of his future councils. He would see the child in his memory forever.

And Tall Night would know that he would be

able to travel north to Minnesota country and see his son at any age he wished to.

Ay-uh, things would work out best this way.

Then he remembered having not told Tall Night everything. He and Janelle would be leaving the area for Minnesota soon. Tall Night's son would go with them.

He wondered whether, if Tall Night knew that his son was going to be taken so far away, he would change his mind about giving him up. Minnesota was many nights' travel from Missouri!

Fire Cloud would tell him, he quickly decided, but not now. His friend already had too much to absorb without knowing that when he gave his son up for Janelle and Fire Cloud to adopt, the child would soon be far, far away.

Hopefully, Tall Night would see that this was only right, for were his son there, so close, might not he be tempted to see him too often and draw suspicion as to why?

Yes, Fire Cloud would tell Tall Night.

But later.

Chapter 31

Thick maroon-velveteen drapes hung at the windows in Virgil Coolidge's private office at Coolidge College.

Sunlight was bright and warm as it filtered through the sparkling-clean glass panes onto the walls lined with expensively bound books at one end, and a fireplace at the other. A slow fire burned on the hearth.

A massive oak desk sat in the very center of the room on a plush Oriental rug. Virgil sat behind it, a half-smoked cigar hanging from a corner of his mouth.

"I came as soon as I received word that you wanted me," Jonathan Drake said, standing stiffly opposite the desk from where Virgil sat with his brow furrowed. He seemed deep in thought as he stared down at a closed journal on the desk.

Then Virgil yanked the cigar from his mouth, rested it in an ashtray on his desk, and turned slow, glinting eyes up at Jonathan. "Sit," he said. It was more a command than a request.

Virgil waited for Jonathan to ease down onto an oak chair, then sighed heavily. "Jonathan, I've brought you here for a purpose," he said, resting his elbows on the desk and placing his fingertips together before him. "I've something for you to do for me, Jonathan. Are you game?"

"Don't I usually do what you ask of me?" Jonathan said, his voice drawn.

"Well, not always," Virgil said, placing his hands palm side down on the desk. He pushed himself up and held his face closer to Jonathan's. "If you did, you'd be married to my daughter now, wouldn't you? You wouldn't have allowed that sonofabitch savage to get near her, much less plan now to marry her."

"Marry . . . ?" Jonathan gasped. "She's going to marry an Injun?"

Virgil laughed sardonically. "Well, not if I can help it," he said, sitting abruptly.

Virgil slid the cigar between his lips. He struck a match and placed the flame to the cigar, inhaling deeply once it was again aflame and sending its smoke down the back of Virgil's throat.

"What do you mean?" Jonathan asked, leaning forward. "You do have a plan, don't you? You aren't going to let her marry a savage?"

"It's up to you whether or not it happens," Virgil said, his eyes narrowing.

"What do you mean, it's up to me?" Jonathan asked, nervously running a finger between his stiffly starched white collar and his long neck.

"I wouldn't be doing this to my daughter were I not at my wit's end with her," Virgil said angrily. He inhaled two more quick puffs, then again rested the cigar on the edge of the ashtray.

He opened the journal and idly turned the pages without even looking at the entries. He still stared at Jonathan.

"I just can't believe that Janelle could be planning to marry that Indian called Fire Cloud," Jonathan said, his voice strained. "I can't believe she is turning her back on everything she has known, especially her father and her wealth, to live among savages. She'll live in a tepee, cooking, cleaning, sewing, and whatever god-awful else a squaw is forced to do for her savage husband."

Virgil shuddered at the thought of his beautiful daughter wrestling around in the Indian's blankets, actually allowing him to fondle her and make love to her. Eventually they would have children.

Half-breeds!

Virgil's blood ran cold at the thought.

"I just can't let her do it," Virgil said, slamming a fist on the top of the desk. "My heart won't take knowing my daughter has lowered herself to marrying a redskin."

Again he slammed his fist on the desk, then rose quickly from the chair and went to the window. He glared toward the river, where down a mile or so stood the convent that he had built with his own fortune. Through the years he had financially supported his sister and the nun's life she had chosen. Mary Ann was perhaps the most intelligent person he had ever known.

He had thought that Janelle came second to his sister in intelligence, but not anymore. Anyone with an ounce of a brain would not choose the pitiful, poor life of an Indian squaw over the riches that Virgil had to offer his daughter.

When he died, his wealth would be Janelle's, and in the will he had stated that it was up to Janelle how much she wished to share with her Aunt Mary Ann.

Virgil had almost called in a lawyer to change the will to make certain his sister got nothing when he died, because of how she had encouraged Janelle's relationship with the redskin.

He had hesitated to do that, for he knew that if things didn't change quickly between Janelle and the Indian, he would be forced to take even her out of his will. He would make sure his money went to the betterment of his college and the museum, not to his daughter.

He especially did not want his sister to have any of it. He had just told her as much!

In his estimation, Mary Ann had betrayed him by allowing redskins to come to the convent—whether for a visit or to bring their fancy blankets, it was surely done to eventually get something back.

Had his sister never allowed it, Janelle would never have seen Fire Cloud that first time those many years ago.

Now she was a grown woman. He was a mighty warrior.

And it was up to Virgil Coolidge, with the help of Jonathan Drake, to change his daughter's life back to what it should have been before she ever knew Fire Cloud.

He turned and glared at Jonathan, clasping his hands together behind him.

"Jonathan, what I am going to ask of you could be considered dirty and underhanded, even mean-spirited, by those who do not understand that my life has been centered around my daughter," Virgil said. "Jonathan, tell me. Are you ready to help your old, loyal friend one more time?" He pointed to the door. "If you aren't willing to help me in my time of trouble walk away now, but never show you face again at Coolidge College."

He stepped up behind his desk, placed his hands flat on the top, then leaned low so that his face was inches away from Jonathan's. "But know this, Jonathan, if you *don't* help me, damn it all to hell, I won't only fire you from Coolidge College, I will make certain you do not get another decent job anywhere. You will not teach another day in any other school."

Jonathan was taken aback by the threats which he knew Virgil was capable of seeing through. That Virgil could forget the loyalty Jonathan had given him throughout their years as colleagues made Jonathan afraid. He knew how powerful Virgil had become in Saint Louis, as had he back in Boston. Those who looked up to Virgil, who admired him not only for his riches, but also for his intelligence and generosity toward charities, would do anything he asked.

Even if it looked as though he had a vendetta against someone, they would still help him, for they knew that whoever did not do things on his terms would be out the monies he gave them.

Jonathan knew that Virgil was not all that well-liked, but his money and influence were.

Jonathan was wealthy in his own right and didn't

even need employment, but he didn't want to be without a job. Working and teaching people, mainly college students, was his life. Without it, he would feel dead inside, especially now that he would not have Janelle as his wife. She could have taken away any bitterness put there by this tyrant of a man . . . Virgil Coolidge.

At this moment Jonathan despised Virgil more than he hated Janelle for making him look like a fool.

The old saying was "Like father, like son."

Well, he saw it now as "Like father, like daughter."

He loathed them both, yet would do whatever he must to stay on the better side of Virgil.

"What do you want me to do?" Jonathan asked, his voice strained. Again he nervously pulled at his shirt collar as perspiration formed on his skin.

"Here's what I want you to do," Virgil said, launching into his plan. He smiled devilishly as he saw how pale Jonathan had become.

But when Jonathan's lips quivered into a slow smile, Virgil knew that his old friend understood his reasoning.

"I'll do it," Jonathan said, pushing himself up from the chair.

"*Now*, Jonathan, not later," Virgil said. He put his cigar between his lips, clasped an arm around Jonathan's shoulder, and escorted him to the door.

"Don't waste any time, Jonathan," Virgil said. "Go now. You know the old adage that haste makes waste? Well, that isn't true here."

"Don't you worry about a thing," Jonathan said,

reaching for his tall hat, which hung on a peg from the wall. He shoved it onto his head.

Jonathan walked out into the corridor with Virgil and faced him. "It's as good as done," he said, then walked away through the crowded hall.

Virgil sucked on his cigar and leisurely rocked back on his heels, watching until Jonathan had pushed through the huge glass entry doors and was gone from the building.

Then Virgil's eyes widened as he grabbed his chest. A sudden pain there seemed to be ripping him open. The cigar fell from his mouth as he gasped out the words "Help me!" He found his knees buckling, the pain was so severe. At last he found relief in a dark void of unconsciousness.

The young women and men, their arms burdened with books, crowded around Virgil as he lay in a heap on the floor, his eyes closed, a small stream of saliva leaking from the corner of his mouth.

"Is he . . . dead?" one of the girls asked softly.

Chapter 32

Fire Cloud was caught up in his memories of the first time Tall Night had taken his son into his arms. Tall Night's tears of pride had shone in his eyes as he gazed down at the tiny face that mirrored Bright Smile's. Lost in his thoughts, Fire Cloud had not noticed the passage of time.

Until now.

Seeing that the sun was past its noontime position, Fire Cloud realized how long his wife had been gone.

He had not expected her to stay with her father long, especially after giving him news that Virgil Coolidge would not have taken easily.

Her duty to her father had required her to be truthful to him in every respect. But duty would not have made her stay to listen to his abusive rantings.

"If she told her father that we are traveling soon to Minnesota, that might have truly sent him into a fit of rage," Fire Cloud whispered to himself.

He stooped to slide another log onto his fire to ward off the chill that deepened each day as autumn took a stronger hold on the land. Then he went outside and gazed down the river, hoping to see Janelle in her canoe, her dreaded deed finally behind her.

But he saw only a few warriors pushing their canoes out into the river, on their way to Saint Louis to trade the thick pelts of the animals they had trapped on their most recent hunts.

Fire Cloud's own hunt had been delayed until he arrived at his homeland, where he would proudly walk the forests his forefathers had before him.

He was keenly aware of a tugging at his heart remembering the hunts when his father had taught him the art of shooting a larger bow, saying that soon he would have one of his own, which his father would make for him.

That bow had never been made, for his father's life had been snuffed out too soon.

Recalling the pain of losing a father made Fire Cloud glad that Tall Night had chosen to keep his relationship with his son a secret.

Had Tall Night openly claimed his son, Red Dawn Wolf would have had no choice but to challenge him.

"*Ay-uh*, it is right that the child now belongs to Tall Night's best friend and his wife," Fire Cloud whispered, again watching the river for signs of Janelle returning to him.

Still she did not come!

He was not sure how to interpret her absence, whether she had been delayed out of her own choosing, or because her father had forbidden her to return to her husband, perhaps even physically stopped her.

"It has been too long now," Fire Cloud whispered. "She should be home with her husband!"

Not wanting to think she might have been harmed

by her angry father, he went back inside his lodge and paced.

He made himself think of other things.

His mind wandered to his brother. Moon Shadow had asked to stay at the convent today to be with the children a while longer.

"It was not for the children he stayed," Fire Cloud said to himself, feeling a slow smile play along his lips. "But instead, for a beautiful young lady."

His brother would wait for Cassandra to be the marrying age that whites deemed right. But had Cassandra been born Lakota, she would be old enough to marry now.

Moon Shadow did not want to do anything to arouse the ire of whites, such as asking for a young white woman's hand in marriage before they even saw her as a woman.

"Janelle . . ." Fire Cloud said aloud. "Wife, where are you? Your husband is counting out moments until we will be in each other's arms again."

Fire Cloud was tired of waiting and afraid that something was wrong. He knew how anxious Janelle was to put this visit with her father behind her and return home. Fire Cloud yanked on the sheath that held his long, heavy knife, grabbed up his rifle, and ran from his lodge.

He yelled to the first person he saw that he was headed for Saint Louis and would return soon. But he did not say why he was going there, for he did not want anyone to know his concern.

He hoped that he was overly eager for his wife's

arms and not correct in his terrible suspicions about her absence.

"If her father has harmed her . . ." Fire Cloud hissed from between clenched teeth as he ran toward the river.

Soon he was traveling down the river, his eyes alert for any movement ahead of him.

The river was empty at this particular place, except for Fire Cloud desperately drawing the paddle through the water. Finally he saw the first signs of the city up ahead, but it was not Saint Louis he was headed for.

It was Coolidge College!

When the college loomed large on its hill overlooking the Mississippi, his eyes searched for Janelle's canoe beached on the riverbank, but he did not see it.

Still, he had to see if she had been there, and when she had left. Perhaps she was at the mansion?

But Fire Cloud knew that he would have to be careful how he handled the situation, for to most whites he was nothing but a savage.

If he caused any commotion, he could be arrested and put in a cell.

No matter how many of his people came to speak in his behalf, even his own wife, he knew that if the authorities wished to hold him in jail, or even sentence him to death, they could. Yet he would take any chance necessary to have his wife with him again.

Fire Cloud beached his canoe. He started to reach down and grab his rifle, then thought better of entering the white man's teaching establishment with a firearm.

Sighing, he covered his rifle with a blanket, then held his head high and hurried up the concrete steps that led him into the building.

Once inside, he stopped, scarcely breathing as he looked around him. This place, built from Janelle's father's money, was grand. The walls were paneled in oak. The floors, also oak, gleamed as though someone had just waxed them with bear's grease.

Rooms reached out on all sides from a long corridor that ran from one end of the building to the other.

Young people he knew were students came and went, their arms filled with books. Though they saw him standing there, no one stopped to offer him assistance. They only stared, some with resentment, others with distaste or a keen curiosity.

Still, no one stopped so that he might ask whether or not his wife had been there.

Suddenly a large, tall woman came and stood eye to eye with Fire Cloud. Her gray hair was bound in a tight bun atop her head, and she sported strange-looking eyeglasses which seemed to make her eyes look larger than normal.

"What do you want here?" she asked, in her voice a sound of cool loathing. She placed her hands on her hips. "Well? Do I have to speak to you in Lakota to get answers from you? I know how, mind you. So what is it? Lakota or English? Speak up. Then be on your way. This is a place of higher education. I am certain you have no knowledge of such things."

Forcing himself to shrug off her insults, Fire Cloud's jaw tightened. "Do you know where I might find Virgil Coolidge?" he asked in English, his voice as unfriendly as this woman's steady stare.

He purposely did not ask for Janelle. He did not want to prompt more insults from this woman by letting her know that he was seeking Janelle.

He smiled to himself thinking about her reaction if he told her that Janelle was his wife.

But he was not there for games. He was there for his woman.

"What on earth would you want with Professor Coolidge?" the woman said mockingly.

Another woman, without as severe a face or hairdo, had heard Fire Cloud mention Virgil Coolidge's name as she stepped from her classroom.

"Virgil Coolidge was taken away only moments ago," she said in a kind voice. "He had a heart attack. He has been rushed to the hospital."

Fire Cloud stiffened. He could only conclude that Janelle's news had caused Virgil Coolidge's heart attack.

He did not ask whether she went to the hospital with her father, for surely she had. Now he understood why her return home was delayed.

"Where is this hospital? Which one? There are three," Fire Cloud blurted out. The women looked guardedly at each other.

"Why do you want to know?" the tall, gray-haired woman asked.

When Fire Cloud didn't respond, for he still felt it was best not to mention Janelle's name, even the nicer of the two women would not reveal where Virgil Coolidge had been taken.

Angry and frustrated, Fire Cloud left the building. Not knowing which hospital to go to, he ran in the direction of the one he knew was closest. If he did not find Janelle there, he would go to the next, and the next. He would not stop until he had Janelle with him again!

Chapter 33

After going to two of the city's hospitals, Fire Cloud at last came to the third, a four-story brick building that looked out over the river. Fire Cloud drew gasps of alarm and disbelief as he entered through the double doors.

Just inside the door, a woman dressed all in white scurried toward Fire Cloud and stopped before him. When she gazed quizzically up at Fire Cloud from her very short height, he was glad to see no scorn, fear, or bigotry in her violet eyes.

"Sir, may I inquire why you are here?" she asked, trying to hide her nervousness by sliding her hands into the front pockets of her nurse's uniform.

Fire Cloud smiled at her use of the word "sir," knowing that most whites would never refer to any Indian with such a polite term.

Then he reminded himself that he was not there to smile at anything. He was searching for his wife and he expected to find her with her father.

Briefly he regretted not questioning the woman at the college about Janelle. That quickly he could have had answers as to her whereabouts.

Yet he still knew that his decision had been right.

He wanted to protect her from insults from people like that woman back at the college.

"I am here to ask about Virgil Coolidge," he said cautiously. "I was at Coolidge College and was told that he had a heart attack. Was he brought here?"

"Yes, Mr. Coolidge is here, but he is very ill," the nurse said, now even more nervous since she knew who this Indian was inquiring about—one of the most affluent, respected gentlemen in the city.

What connection could this Indian have to Mr. Coolidge?

She could only assume that Mr. Coolidge, out of the goodness of his heart, had helped this poor soul in some way. He did hand out his money in many charitable ways.

Surely that included Indians whose lives had been torn apart by white people.

"Sir, Mr. Coolidge is gravely ill. He is unconscious," the nurse then revealed. "He isn't allowed any visitors. Of course, should his daughter arrive, I will most certainly take her to her father's room. While unconscious, he has been saying her name."

"Then you are saying that Janelle Coolidge is not here?" Fire Cloud said, his voice drawn. "She has not been here?"

"No, sir, Mr. Coolidge was brought in alone," she said. "Janelle should be here. It is the doctor's opinion that Virgil Coolidge might not last even another hour."

Her face became flushed, and she lowered her eyes. "I have said too much," she murmured, then lifted her eyes and glanced to her side as someone came out of the shadows with a quick step.

"I'm Jonathan Drake," the man said hurriedly, his concern for Virgil Coolidge quite evident. "I am Virgil Coolidge's friend . . . an associate. Did I hear correctly? Virgil Coolidge is going to die?"

"A man who has suffered such a severe attack as this rarely lives much longer than a few hours, Mr. Drake," the nurse said, recognizing his name, for Virgil Coolidge had faintly whispered it during his moments of rambling. "Can I take you to him? He has said your name more than once while unconscious."

"He has?" Jonathan said, grabbing his hat from his head. He clutched its brim hard, then looked over at Fire Cloud.

He saw Fire Cloud's dark eyes suddenly narrow with hate. His hands hung in tight fists at his sides and his jaw was tight.

Feeling guilt clench at his gut, Jonathan feared this Indian's wrath once he told him what he had done only moments ago to Janelle.

He had succeeded with at least that part of Virgil's plan and had gone to the college to tell him that the deed was done. There he had discovered that Virgil had been taken to the hospital.

And when he heard the gentle-voiced nurse say that Virgil might die, he had forgotten his concerns about Fire Cloud and rushed out to ask about his friend's condition.

And now he felt as though he was shrinking under Fire Cloud's steady glare.

But Jonathan knew that he had no choice but to tell Fire Cloud the truth. Even though the Indian could get so angry, he might slit Jonathan's throat in the very presence of this nurse.

He would rather tell him, though, than face the authorities.

Perhaps Fire Cloud would be so anxious to set Janelle free, he would forget Jonathan's role in her imprisonment.

Perhaps Fire Cloud would even be so grateful to Jonathan for taking him to Janelle, he would forgive him for following orders from a man half out of his mind.

Jonathan had to set Janelle free and explain to her why he had taken her captive, or she might blame him for everything. Kidnapping was a major crime, the punishment either hanging or life imprisonment.

With that in mind, and hoping that Fire Cloud would realize that he must not harm him if he wanted to find Janelle, Jonathan said, "Fire Cloud, will you please step aside with me?"

Jonathan's strained voice proved his uneasiness. "I've something to tell you," he added.

Jonathan gave the nurse a sideways glance, then again looked intently at Fire Cloud. "What I want to tell you must be said in private," he said, his voice now sounding somewhat choked.

Fire Cloud glared at Jonathan, but this man knew something about Janelle, so he went with him into the shadows of the corridor. Then Jonathan told him a plot that Fire Cloud found incredible in its viciousness. He could not believe that a father would do something so fiendish to his own daughter.

"You know where my wife is?" Fire Cloud said, grabbing Jonathan by his throat with his large hand. "Tell me. Tell me now."

"Unhand me and I . . . will . . . tell you," Jonathan choked out as he pulled at Fire Cloud's fingers in an effort to release them from his aching throat. "I will even take you to her."

"She had better not be harmed," Fire Cloud said as he eased his hand from the man's throat.

"She isn't—at least not in the way you might think," Jonathan said, wincing at Fire Cloud's anger.

"Take me to her," Fire Cloud ground out.

"Follow me," Jonathan said, walking shakily toward the front double doors.

Fire Cloud followed Jonathan around to the side of the building, where Jonathan grabbed the reins of his horse from a hitching rail. He gave Fire Cloud a questioning look. "How did you arrive here?" he asked guardedly.

"I came in my canoe then continued the rest of the way on foot," Fire Cloud said impatiently.

Jonathan thought for a moment. Then he gave Fire Cloud his horse's reins, and stole a nearby horse for himself. Soon they were riding in the direction of Coolidge College.

Fire Cloud knew that Janelle had been mistreated in some way and was in dire trouble. Yet he still did not question Jonathan, for soon he would see firsthand what this evil man had done.

If she was harmed, Fire Cloud would not think

twice before yanking his knife from its sheath and stabbing it into the white man's belly.

He would flee with his wife before anyone found out.

He fought against such thoughts, for he couldn't see how Janelle's father, or this man who had planned to marry her, could truly harm her.

Frighten her, perhaps, into forgetting him.

But actually do her bodily harm?

Gah-ween, he did not think so.

That was the only thing that was keeping him sane until he finally had her in his arms again. From that moment on, he would be certain that she never traveled this land alone.

When they arrived at his homeland, only then would he feel that she was safe.

Jonathan turned down the lane that led to Coolidge College. Fire Cloud followed him to the very back of the college, where they left their horses.

Jonathan then brought him to a door which opened to reveal steps leading beneath the tall building. They were entering a place he knew was called a cellar. He became instantly wary of his wife's welfare. It was dark and dank and reeked of all sorts of smells, with tiny windows on each side allowing little light to see by.

And although the building was not very old, numerous cobwebs crisscrossed the low beams above Fire Cloud's head.

He brushed away the cobwebs as Jonathan led him onward. Both men had to bend to avoid hitting their heads on the beams.

Suddenly Jonathan stopped and turned to face Fire Cloud. "I want to clear something up right now," he blurted out. "When I last left Virgil, he was upstairs in his office, very capable of scheming against his daughter. I only discovered that he had been taken to the hospital later when I went to tell him that I had done as he had asked."

Jonathan swallowed hard. "I wasn't thinking straight at that time, or I would have set things right with Janelle then," he stammered. "I wish to do so now, though, and hope that you will consider that when you realize what I have done. I just want to be allowed to leave the area, Fire Cloud. Please allow it."

The more Jonathan said, the more Fire Cloud was certain that this man had terribly wronged Janelle. He had to control himself against harming him, for first he had to be taken to Janelle.

She was down in this hellhole of a place, a captive.

"We're almost there," Jonathan said, again moving forward.

Fire Cloud was soon aware of a brighter light up ahead, and recognized it as the flickering flame of a lantern. When they reached that light, he knew they would reach Janelle.

Fire Cloud could no longer just follow Jonathan. He stepped up beside him, grabbed him by an arm, and slung him to the earthen floor.

Jonathan groaned with pain, his foot having twisted beneath him when he fell. Fire Cloud ignored his moans and broke into a run, not stopping until he came to Janelle.

The lantern on the floor revealed Janelle, tied with rope to the back of the chair and bound at her ankles.

So furious that he could have killed those two men in one blow, Fire Cloud slid his knife from its sheath and soon had cut all of the ropes from Janelle.

Crying, trembling, Janelle flew from the chair and clung to Fire Cloud.

In a rush of words she explained how Jonathan had abducted her. She was still in her canoe on her way to speak with her father when she saw Jonathan on the riverbank waving her down. He lured her to shore by telling her the only thing that would alarm her enough to make her come to him—that her father was ill.

Jonathan then told her that her father refused to go to the hospital, and Janelle must talk him into it.

Janelle continued telling Fire Cloud between sobs how Jonathan had pleaded with her, telling her that she needed to talk her father into going to the hospital or he might die.

Panic-stricken and certain that she was responsible for her father's sudden illness, Janelle had believed Jonathan. She had stupidly, trustingly, gone with him to the college.

When they arrived and went to the back of the college instead of the front, she had become puzzled. Jonathan quickly told her then how her father had been in the cellar searching for supplies when he had taken ill. Jonathan left her father there.

She asked why he had not gone for help, and he reminded her that her father was an independent man. He did not want anyone to know that he had been stricken again by anything, in case he looked sickly in the eyes of his associates.

"When I went into the cellar with Jonathan, he manhandled me and tied me to the chair," Janelle cried.

"It was all a ploy to abduct you," Fire Cloud said angrily, finding it hard to believe that her father had never been in the cellar at all, but upstairs waiting for his daughter to be taken there and tied to a chair.

"He wanted me to have time to think through what I had decided to do with my life. He was going to keep me there until I promised to forget you," Janelle said, wiping tears from her eyes.

When she turned and saw the ropes dangling loosely from the chair, she shuddered. "I have no idea how long he was going to keep me here."

"If Jonathan had not brought me to you, you might never have been set free," Fire Cloud said as he gently took her by the shoulders and turned her to face him. "You see, my wife, your father is no longer able to do anything. He *is* in the hospital now. His condition is poor. He had a heart attack, probably shortly after sending Jonathan to abduct you. Perhaps thinking through the fiendishness of his plan was too much for him."

Janelle's eyes widened. "My father is in the hospital?" she said.

"He is . . . not expected to live," Fire Cloud said, seeing that this came as a blow to her, even though she had every reason to hate the man.

"I must go to him," Janelle said urgently.

He took her by a hand and they made their way through the tiny, dark cellar. Fire Cloud stopped when he came to where he had left Jonathan on the floor.

He was gone.

Chapter 34

As clouds billowed across the sky, gray and heavy, Janelle stood at her father's bedside. She clutched Fire Cloud's hand, not caring who saw their open affection.

She needed Fire Cloud's comfort now as never before, for when they arrived at the hospital she had discovered that her father was barely alive.

She gazed down at him now as he lay in a white hospital gown, a blanket drawn up just beneath his armpits. She saw him as an old, tired man, his closed eyes sunken into his face, his lips drawn tightly over his teeth.

It was strange that she had never noticed his teeth were bucked.

But now, while he lay in his deep sleep of unconsciousness, many things about him seemed changed.

There was a strange pallor to his skin. His nostrils flared with each of his short gasps of breath. His eyes sometimes moved beneath his closed lids, as though somewhere deep within him he was reliving his past, perhaps seeing Janelle as a small daughter who climbed adoringly on her father's lap so that he could read to her.

It was easy to recall these moments now with such fondness, for they helped her forget what he had done to her only a short time ago.

At this moment when she knew that she was losing him forever, she realized that she could forgive him everything.

She even felt somewhat responsible for how he now lay there so still, perhaps feeling unloved.

But she made herself remember that she deserved to have a life of her own, and her father had tried everything within his power to keep her from the happiness she had found with Fire Cloud.

That he would go as far as to . . .

Her thoughts were stilled and she covered her mouth with her free hand when she saw sudden life in her father's eyelids. They were fluttering slowly open.

When Virgil finally gained consciousness and saw Janelle standing there, he knew that he had only a few moments left to make amends with her.

"Daughter," Virgil said in a shallow whisper.

Janelle could tell that he was fighting to say every word.

"Janelle? Sweetheart, do you forgive me?" Virgil gasped out. "Can I die knowing that you forgive me for what I had Jonathan do?"

Janelle fell to her knees beside her father's bed. She took his hand. "Shh," she whispered. "Don't worry about me. Oh, Father, I do, I do forgive you."

She was trying hard not to cry, for she knew these were probably her last moments with her father. She might be hearing his voice and looking into his eyes

FIRE CLOUD

for the last time. It tore at her heart to know that he would soon be taken from her.

Her father's death would leave a strange void, a void that she knew well from when her mother had passed away.

"Daughter, I . . . only . . . did what I did because I love you," Virgil whispered. His eyes grew wild and he began choking; then his body was suddenly still, his eyes locked in a stare.

"Papa," Janelle cried, calling him the name she had used when she was only a girl.

Janelle hugged her father as sobs tore at her.

Fire Cloud felt her pain, for had he not lost both a mother and father when he was but a young brave? Losing parents left a child feeling an aloneness that was hard to explain.

Having his baby brother to fill his empty heart had been Fire Cloud's reprieve.

And Fire Cloud would be there to help Janelle with her loss, for even though her father had turned into a tyrant these past months, he knew that Janelle loved him no less now than before.

He put an arm around her waist and drew her up into his arms. He held her close as she cried against him.

When the doctor entered the room and discovered that Virgil was dead, he took Janelle by an elbow and ushered her into the corridor. Fire Cloud went with them.

"I know it's hard to let go, Janelle," Doctor Jamieson said, only occasionally glancing at Fire Cloud as he talked. "But your father had been living on borrowed time for two years now. He was actually told in Boston that he might not live six months. Your father brought you back to Missouri and established the college in your name to leave you something when he died. He only became the curator at the museum when his heart held on longer than everyone had thought possible. Your father told me only a few days ago that he had only one regret—that he had been so hard on you, for all he truly wanted was your happiness."

Almost sobbing, Janelle tried to understand how her father could regret being so hard on her, yet still have her abducted and taken prisoner.

"Only a while ago, shortly before you arrived, your father became conscious long enough to say something to me. He told me that he had spoiled your happiness by doing something foolish," Doctor Jamieson said. He rubbed his brow thoughtfully. "He didn't tell me what he had done. He just said that he hoped he had time to apologize to you and wipe the slate clean before dying. He knew that your happiness now centered on the man you planned to marry, and that he so badly wanted to understand and give you his blessing."

Doctor Jamieson leaned lower and looked into Janelle's eyes. "Did he get that chance, Janelle, to apologize?" he asked softly. "Did he give you and your chosen man his blessing?"

"He apologized, but . . . he . . . was gone before he was able to say anything about Fire Cloud," Janelle said. She reached over and took Fire Cloud's hand. "I didn't get the chance to tell him that Fire Cloud and I are already married."

She noticed how this made the doctor straighten his back and stare almost dumbfoundedly at Fire Cloud.

"Doctor Jamieson, this is my husband," Janelle said, proudly lifting her chin.

Doctor Jamieson's jaw tightened as he stared at Fire Cloud, his friendly, warm attitude suddenly gone.

"I've business to attend to," Doctor Jamieson said, then went back inside the room where Virgil Coolidge lay, *his* thoughts and prejudices stilled forever.

"Let us go now," Fire Cloud said, his voice drawn. "I will stay at your side as you prepare for your father's burial."

Janelle nodded and started walking down the long corridor with Fire Cloud. She regretted how her father had not, even on his death bed, come to terms with what she wanted out of life. If he had, he would have looked at Fire Cloud and given them his blessing.

She did know that she would never feel guilty over how her father's last days on this earth were spent. It had been his choice to be stubborn where Fire Cloud was concerned.

She did regret, though, that their children would have no grandparents to dote on them.

Yet had her father lived, he would not have been able to put his prejudices aside, especially since his grandchildren would be labeled by the white community as "breeds."

She was anxious now to continue with the rest of her life. Soon she and Fire Cloud would be traveling to Minnesota with the adorable baby boy.

"We've yet to name him," Janelle blurted out just as she stepped out into a blustery day of early October.

Fire Cloud gave her a quizzical look, and she was glad to find that she could laugh softly.

"Darling," she said. "Tall Night's son? The son we will raise as ours? We've yet to name him."

"While we are on the long journey to my homeland, we will have time to go over names," Fire Cloud said, directing her toward the horse he had taken from Jonathan.

He stopped and looked into the distance. "I wonder where Jonathan Drake went?" he asked. "The last I saw of him was in the cellar just before finding you."

"He's probably hightailed it out of the area if he knows what's good for him," Janelle said, shivering at the thought of Jonathan leaving her in the cellar with the cobwebs, mice, and spiders.

"He had *better* be gone, for if I ever come face-to-face with him again, he will wish he had never laid his hands on you," Fire Cloud said sternly.

Janelle glanced up at the window of the room where her father had taken his last breaths.

She still could not see how he could have gone as far as he had.

"Forget it all," Fire Cloud said as he saw where she was looking, and knew why. "Put it behind you."

"I won't be able to until Father is in his grave and I am far, far away from here," Janelle said, hugging Fire Cloud when he lifted her into his arms and held her before placing her in the saddle.

Then he mounted, too, and they rode together toward her mansion, a place she would gladly be rid of as soon as possible. Her father had erased the good memories there with his scheming and vindictive ways.

"Just think of Minnesota land when your thoughts stray to sad things," Fire Cloud said as he held Janelle around the waist. "Think of azure skies, crystal-clear lakes, and the many varieties of birds and animals that I will aquaint you with. Think of wild rice and the excitement of the rice harvest."

"I am so eager to see it all for myself," Janelle said, then gasped and grabbed Fire Cloud's arm. "Lord, Fire Cloud, look in the river. It's . . . Jonathan."

Fire Cloud saw Jonathan's body trapped in debris at the very edge of the river. He also saw something else. A knife in Jonathan's chest.

"He killed himself," Janelle said, looking quickly away from the gruesome sight. "He surely knew I'd turn him in to the law for what he did. He couldn't live knowing that he might spend the rest of his life behind bars, or die with a hangman's noose around his neck."

"Just act as though you did not see him," Fire Cloud said stiffly. "I do not think it is wise of us to tell anyone what we have seen. The white authorities might try to build a case against me, since they take all opportunities they can to arrest men with red skins."

"Yes, let's ride on past," Janelle agreed, though shuddering at the thought of leaving Jonathan there in the water.

"Again, let your thoughts be carried far away from these tragedies," Fire Cloud urged her. "Think of the wigwam that we will build together and the first fire we will share in our lodge."

"We will be home," Janelle said, sighing.

"Tell me about the wigwam," she then said, wanting to envision it when they traveled north.

"The Chippewa dome-shaped wigwam consists of a pole framework covered with birchbark," Fire Cloud said, seeing it himself as he described it. "Beginning at the doorway a mat is unrolled along the base and tied to the first horizontal poles. Mats and furs for sleeping and for storage sit around the sides of the inside of the wigwam. Dyed bulrushes tied over basswood bast make the colorful floor mats. Food is cooked around a central fireplace surrounded by rock, which also supplies warmth. A smoke hole is at the top center. The only other opening is the doorway made of buckskin."

"I want to make our wigwam a home for you," Janelle murmured.

She smiled as he drew her back more closely to him. She felt his breath on her ear as he bent low to nuzzle her neck.

"I love you so," Janelle said, turning her face so that he could give her a sweet, gentle kiss.

Chapter 35

Janelle watched Fire Cloud secure the last of their belongings in his canoe. Soon Fire Cloud would be saying farewell to his life spent with the Lakota and his brother, and would see his true people again. Soon they would live where grandfather pines sang and swayed in the wind!

And Janelle would be leaving behind everything that she had shared with her father. She had already sold the mansion and had given the sole ownership of the college to the stockholders.

She had given a good portion of the money from the sale of her home and expensive furniture and paintings to her aunt, even though Virgil's will had left a good portion of money to his sister so that she could continue her good work at the convent and orphanage.

But the largest portion had been left for Janelle.

She had gone into council with the Lakota and had given them a large sum of her inheritance, keeping an equal amount to take to Minnesota to share with the Chippewa people.

Seeing the good that she could do with her inheritance, she could now feel proud of her father and his accomplishments instead of sad at how he had become, in the end, bitter, resentful, and jealous.

He had not wanted to share her with anyone.

Jonathan had been an exception. He had been hand-picked by her father, but only because Virgil had known that he would not actually lose her to this man. She would have been married in name only. His choice for her husband would ensure that she was still an integral part of Virgil Coolidge's life, for her father could dictate Jonathan's every movement and he would obey like a slave its master.

She hoped that once she was gone from this area, she could leave all bad memories behind and revel in her new life with her husband.

She even thought she might already be with child, for the time for her first monthly period since her marriage had passed and she had not shed one drop of blood.

She was thrilled imagining a child born of their special love.

She would know by the time they reached Minnesota, for the journey would be slow. By the end, another monthly flow would have already been due and passed.

If no blood had come by then, she would be able to tell Fire Cloud that either a son or a daughter was growing inside her womb.

Secretly she wished for a son, for he would be the image of his Chippewa father.

And he would be a brother to Tall Night's son. They would be as true brothers in all things.

But if she had a daughter, would not she become

the light of her brother's life? Would not he become her protector? Her confidante? Her best friend?

Yes, it was so good that Tall Night's son would be a brother to their children. Janelle and Fire Cloud had vowed that no one would ever have the chance to tell him otherwise.

She knew that they must choose a name soon, for she did not like referring to the child as Tall Night's son every time she thought about him. In her heart, he was already hers.

Yes, on their journey north they would give him a name.

"I gave Moon Shadow my horse and my newly made bow, so that he will feel close to me when I am gone," Fire Cloud said, pulling Janelle from her thoughts. He took her hands. "Everything else is packed and in our canoe."

Janelle looked over her shoulder at the canoe that was half beached on the rocky shore. She then gave Fire Cloud a mischievous smile. Fire Cloud's eyebrows arched.

"What thoughts make you give your husband such a playful smile?" he asked, placing a hand to one of her rosy cheeks.

"I will never tell," Janelle said, still smiling.

She quickly corrected herself. "I mean I shall not tell you *yet*," she said.

"And so my wife is going to be a woman who keeps secrets from her husband?" Fire Cloud said, his own lips forming a slow smile. He knew that whatever she was not saying had to be something special.

The word "yet" made him wonder if she might be keeping news of a child from him. What else would make her eyes shine so beautifully today? Why else would her skin take on such a radiance?

He had seen it happen to his mother shortly after she had shared the news that she was pregnant with Moon Shadow.

At that time he did not know that his father was not the child's father, and as he thought back to that day now, he recalled no trace of shame in his mother's eyes or voice.

She had truly been content knowing that the child she carried was her lover's. That proved to him just how much she had adored this man. He had filled his mother's heart with a joy that her own husband could not give her.

"Now it is *you* who seems lost in thought," Janelle said, searching his eyes. "Darling, what were you just thinking about? Or do you wish to keep that a secret from me?"

"*Gah-ween*, I do not want to keep any secrets from you, ever, as I wish you would not keep any from me, even something you have chosen to tell me later," Fire Cloud said, a frown suddenly creasing his brow.

He placed his hands at Janelle's waist and drew her up closer, his eyes gazing intensely into hers. "My *gee-mah-mah*—mother—kept too many secrets from my *gee-dah-dah*—father—and you know the results of her deceits," he said regretfully. "Both my father and mother are now dead."

"I'm so sorry," Janelle said. She flung herself into

his arms. "I truly, truly do not want to keep anything from you. I have only begun to believe that . . ."

Still she did not want to tell him, and not so much because she wanted to wait for a special time, but because she was afraid that saying the words might jinx her and she would not be pregnant at all.

But she did see how he desperately wanted to keep her from being like his mother.

And Janelle knew the importance of not planting doubts in her husband's heart, for he might think that if she would choose to keep one secret, she might choose to keep many.

"I think I might be with child," she blurted out.

She was filled with joy when she saw the wonder in her husband's eyes, and then the happiness that came with realizing that she could be carrying a child . . . their child.

He gently placed his hands at her waist and eased her away from him so that he could get a full view of her. His eyes fell upon her abdomen, and she knew that she would never forget how he looked with such awe at her belly. He surely envisioned a tiny thing curled up inside her womb, a heart already forming and beating out a rhythm that would be there until he was taken from this earth again, hopefully only as an old, old man.

She only now realized that she referred to the child as a "he." She smiled at that, finding every aspect of this newfound joy a thing of awe.

"A child," Fire Cloud said, fighting off tears of joy.

He again remembered his mother and that first

time she laid his hand on her naked belly so that he could feel his brother moving around inside her.

He would never forget his mother's sweet, gentle giggle as Fire Cloud then pressed his ear to her belly in hopes of hearing his brother breathing.

"What are you thinking right now?" Janelle asked.

"About my mother and my brother," he said, his voice breaking.

"You are speaking of your brother?" Moon Shadow said, walking down a slope toward Janelle and Fire Cloud.

They both turned to him, amazed at something besides the fact that she might be with child. It was as though the hand of *Kitchi-Manitou* had touched Moon Shadow and told him to speak clearly and understand all words spoken to him. Overnight, it seemed, Moon Shadow could converse intelligently with everyone.

Sister Mary Ann had told Janelle that such miracles could happen, when by the grace of God, the knowledge of words and their meaning came to someone, almost overnight.

Janelle had heard of a Sister Kathryn from somewhere in France who had been deemed a saint when she performed similar miracles.

Janelle knew that her aunt had been praying a lot these past weeks for Moon Shadow. She was beginning to believe that her aunt was responsible for this miracle and that if it became news, Sister Mary Ann might also be given the wondrous title of saint.

But her aunt backed away from such publicity. She loved her role at the convent and orphanage. Too much attention might ruin things for the nuns and children, so only the Lakota knew of this miracle.

"Moon Shadow, in about eight-and-one-half-months' time, you might become an uncle," Janelle said, as Moon Shadow's eyes moved swiftly to her flat tummy. "I am almost certain that I am with child. And I am wishing hard for it to be a boy."

"I will be an uncle?" Moon Shadow said, beaming first at Janelle and then Fire Cloud. Then his smile faded. "But I will not be with you to see the baby. I will not be able to hold him, for I will be here, and you will be there."

"It does not have to be that way," Fire Cloud said, gently. "We can pack a second canoe. You can follow ours to our homeland."

Moon Shadow sighed heavily. He turned and looked at the Lakota village, at the women doing their daily chores, the men bringing in game they had downed with their arrows, the children romping, playing, and laughing, and the horses in the corrals behind the lodges.

Then he turned in the direction of the convent. He could not even envision a life without those children and the nuns, especially Sister Mary Ann . . . and Cassandra.

Ay-uh, his life now, which included so many special people, was good. He could not see it any other way, even though staying loyal to those who loved him meant he must turn away from his brother and Janelle. It had not been a hard decision, yet he would miss his brother with every beat of his heart, and now Janelle as well.

Moon Shadow turned back to Fire Cloud. "I will always feel blessed for having you as a brother. You have been so devoted, but I am happy with my life with the Lakota and those at the convent. I do not want to leave them. And it is time for me to be independent, my own man. I can only be this if I break the ties that have always bound me to you, my brother. I will always love you, Fire Cloud, and will miss you, but you now have your own family to think about—Janelle, the child she might be carrying, and . . ."

He stopped short of including the baby that awaited Fire Cloud's and Janelle's arrival today. Except for Tall Night, no one at the Lakota village knew of the child, or ever would. It must be kept secret for Tall Night to have the life that had been mapped out for him since he took his first breath. That day a future Lakota chief had been born. Nothing should take away that which Tall Night had lived for!

"We each are getting what we want out of life," Moon Shadow quickly interjected. "Sister Mary Ann has even asked me to become a teacher at the orphanage. It makes me feel important and vital!"

"A teacher?" Fire Cloud said. He grabbed Moon Shadow and gave him a hefty hug. "I am so proud of you. Moon Shadow, I will so miss you, yet when I think of you, I will smile, for I will know that you are happy."

Fire Cloud did not want to lower Moon Shadow's spirits so he did not elaborate on what else he felt at this moment—that he would be leaving half of his heart in Missouri by leaving Moon Shadow.

FIRE CLOUD

Janelle looked past them and saw the Lakota assembling and coming from the village toward the river. Tall Night led the procession, in his eyes a sadness only a few people would understand.

A child.

His child.

His child would soon be on his way to Minnesota, and Tall Night did not expect to ever see him again. He would not torture himself by going to Minnesota. It would hurt too much to have to turn his back on his son to return to Missouri without him.

Ay-uh, Tall Night was paying for his sin by losing both the woman and the child, but thankfully not completely. One was dead, but the other was very much alive, and would have a wonderful mother and father to look after him. Fire Cloud and Janelle would raise this young brave to be a noble warrior!

Tall Night did wonder if his son would resemble him when he grew into adulthood. That way, Fire Cloud might feel as though he was with his old friend when they were both young and full of spirit.

Janelle could see in Tall Night's expression that he might be thinking about his and Fire Cloud's relationship through the years, as well as the son he could not raise as his own. She saw the shine of tears, and even a slight smile as he walked now more briskly into Fire Cloud's arms as they hugged and said their good-byes. Everyone else formed a wide semicircle around them.

Janelle moved among the people, giving hugs and smiles as she said her final farewells. She did not believe that she and Fire Cloud would ever return, for they needed to stay in Minnesota and keep Tall Night's baby as far from Missouri as possible.

They could never risk anyone discovering the truth, for it would ruin too many lives.

After many emotional embraces, Fire Cloud and Janelle had said farewell to everyone. They boarded the canoe and were soon on their way to the convent for more good-byes, and the child.

When even these were done with, they finally began their true journey toward the muddy Mississippi that led to Fire Cloud's homeland. Janelle held the child in her arms, a warm blanket around him to ward off the chill from the spray of water and the breeze which hinted that too soon autumn would turn to winter.

Fire Cloud knew that he wouldn't arrive in time for the wild rice harvest this year.

But he would be there next year. And he and his wife would be a part of it!

His arm muscles corded with each movement of the paddle in the water, and then he paused and lifted the paddle long enough to only float when, at the far side of the river, where there was a clearing, he could see who stood on the river bank. His heart ached, for he was seeing his friend Tall Night perhaps for the very last time in his life.

He lifted his hand in greeting.

Tall Night returned the wave.

Janelle was not sure whether to lower the child so that Tall Night would not be reminded all over again of what he had lost. But she saw his eager gaze and knew that he was there to see his son one last time.

Fire Cloud's jaw tightened as he steered his canoe toward the shore. Although he knew that his decision might change the destiny of a son and father forever, he could not keep his friend from one last moment with his tiny child.

When they came closer to the riverbank, Tall Night stepped out into the water and walked toward them, stopping at the canoe when he was waist-deep in the river.

"One last look," he said, his gaze on the blanket as Janelle drew the corner back for Tall Night to see.

Fire Cloud moved closer to Janelle and watched his friend's eyes fill with pride when he saw the tiny face of his son, a face that did resemble Tall Night's even at his young age.

And when the child opened his eyes and gazed up at Tall Night as though he knew he was looking at his father, Fire Cloud's throat constricted. He felt at that moment that he should shove this child into Tall Night's arms and tell him that it was not right for them to be separated.

But it was Tall Night's decision. Whatever he chose to do now was final. There would be no turning back if Tall Night decided to keep his son. Once the canoe was in deeper water and moving again toward Minnesota, Fire Cloud would remove the child from his thoughts.

So would Janelle, even though he knew that it would be harder for her, the woman, than for him.

For although she had not had the baby with her these past several days, in her heart she was already bonding with him as though she were his mother and he her son.

Even though this was a sad moment for Fire Cloud, seeing his best friend perhaps for the last time, he realized that something good had come out of the awful tragedy. Fire Cloud had learned not to judge people as quickly as he had his mother's lover. All those years' emotions wasted on hate were just that—wasted.

Fire Cloud felt cleansed, through and through, and all because his best friend had proved to him that no man was completely bad.

"Cloud Walker," Tall Night suddenly said, interrupting Fire Cloud's thoughts. "I would like to name my son Cloud Walker, for when I look into the clouds in his absence, I will see him walking there as a proud warrior. When the sun smiles down through the clouds, it will be my son smiling down at me."

"What a lovely name," Janelle said, choking back a sob. "What a beautiful way to think of your son."

"Cloud Walker," Fire Cloud said, gazing down at the child who suddenly smiled up at Tall Night. "Do you see? Your son also thinks the name is beautiful."

"No, not *my* son," Tall Night said, taking a step back so that he and the child could no longer see each other. "From this moment forth, I will think of him as *your* son. Even when I look heavenward, I will see him as your son. I will be proud for Cloud Walker, always."

The breeze lifted a spray of water into the canoe, and Janelle covered the child's face again with the blanket.

She almost cried when Tall Night suddenly splashed closer and flung his arms around Fire Cloud's neck.

"Friends forever?" Tall Night whispered into Fire Cloud's ear.

"Forever," Fire Cloud whispered, their warm embrace continuing.

Then Tall Night returned to shore and Fire Cloud paddled the canoe to the middle of the river again. His strokes were eager, for his homeland awaited his arrival.

As did his grandfather!

He would not allow himself to remember that someone else would be there.

Moon Shadow's father.

No. He would not let thoughts of that man trouble him again. He felt at peace with that part of his past, and knew that he could arrive home and be with his grandfather.

Ay-uh, his grandson was returning home, and not empty-handed. He could hardly wait for his grandfather to meet Janelle and know of her sweet nature.

The child in her arms? Could he truly lie to his grandfather and pretend it was his?

Gah-ween, he would not begin his life there with a lie.

But his grandfather would be the only one who deserved the truth. Everyone else could decide themselves the parentage of this child. Fire Cloud and

Janelle would always call him their son. So who would have cause to doubt that he was?

Fire Cloud looked over his shoulder, to give Tall Night one final wave. When he found him gone, he knew that was best. Their last good-byes were those of hugs and precious words that only true friends would say to one another.

"It is such a beautiful day," Janelle said, sighing. "How I do love autumn in Missouri. I can't deny that I shall miss it."

"Perhaps, but when you live your first autumn in Minnesota, I believe you will no longer miss what you have left behind."

Janelle smiled sweetly at him. "When we arrive at your village and live there for the first night as a family, such a night it will be."

"And it will just be the beginning," Fire Cloud said, filled with utter contentment. When he would begin missing Moon Shadow, he would envision his brother at the orphanage and how he loved being with the children and teaching them.

And when he missed Tall Night, all he would have to do was look at Cloud Walker to see his old friend.

He faced forward, his arms drawing on the paddle even more eagerly.

Home.

He was finally going home!

He could almost taste the lake trout and the chanterelles, the lovely golden mushrooms that grew among the fiddlehead ferns in Minnesota's forests.

Had it truly been all those years ago that he had buried his beloved mother beneath the willow tree?

Time did pass so quickly.

He vowed that he would savor to the fullest each and every moment with his woman and the children they would have. He did not want to reach old age with regrets!

Chapter 36

Minnesota—September 1878—"Moon of Falling Leaves"

A flock of wild turkey gobbled in the thick brush. Eagles soared gracefully over a camp of wigwams set up temporarily near the wild rice field in the Saint Croix River. A herd of white-tailed deer drank in the early mornings from the shore.

Having given birth to her and Fire Cloud's fourth child only a week ago, Janelle was too weak to participate in the wild rice harvest this year. She sat on a comfortable pallet of thick furs and blankets as she watched the Chippewa warriors poling their canoes through the rice fields while women knocked the grains into the canoes with a pair of cedar sticks.

It was with much pride that Janelle watched her ten-year-old son Cloud Walker taking over her duties in the canoe with Fire Cloud.

Every once in a while Fire Cloud would look her way to see if she was all right, for she had had trouble this time with the birthing.

The child had not fared as well as their other three children had during childbirth. Their daughter was frail, so frail that some had not even expected her to live.

She lay asleep in a cradle in a wigwam only a few

feet from where Janelle sat. Janelle's ears were always alert to her child's first cries of awakening, for she was eager to place her tiny daughter to her bosom to feed her.

With each feeding of Janelle's rich milk, the child's condition bettered.

She believed now that her and Fire Cloud's daughter would live, whereas only a few days ago they had watched her every breath, thinking each would be her last.

Janelle was confident now that her Blue Swallow would live to be a grandmother one day!

And not only because of how much milk she could drink, but because Janelle had willed her to live.

Janelle had also prayed to heaven for her daughter's life, as she knew her aunt had, for Fire Cloud had gone to the nearest trading post and sent word to Aunt Mary Ann of the child's condition.

Fire Cloud had also asked her in that wire to inform his people at the Lakota village that he was a father now for the fifth time.

Of course no one at the Lakota village, except for Chief Tall Night, knew that only four of those children were born of Fire Cloud and Janelle's love.

Janelle expected her Aunt Mary Ann, as well as Moon Shadow, his wife, Cassandra, and their one child to arrive within the month, for they had sent word back that they were coming for a family reunion. She could hardly wait to see her aunt, for it had been ten long years now since they had said their good-byes in Missouri.

Moon Shadow had been there two times before

with his wife and was free to come as often as he wished, for his father had died by his own hand only two sleeps after Fire Cloud had left the village with his mother.

Moon Shadow's father had lived a coward's life, and he had died a coward's death.

Moon Shadow was not touched in any way by this knowledge, for he had never even known the man. And that past was behind him.

Moon Shadow was a man in his own right now, a proud warrior who claimed the Lakota tribe as his. He had married Cassandra on the year of her eighteenth birthday. She had given birth to their first child only nine months later. They had named the child White Eagle, for the moment he entered the world, a white eagle had swept down from the trees and flown over them.

Janelle had adapted well to the Chippewa way of life, just as Moon Shadow had to living without his brother.

As a beautiful golden eagle swept down over Fire Cloud's canoe, Janelle felt something mystical happening. Fire Cloud had told her about his connection with eagles and how he felt his father near him whenever an eagle made itself known to him.

He had told her about the day he had buried his mother, when an eagle had stayed high in the weeping willow tree as though to protect her grave when Fire Cloud had to abandon it.

The golden eagle let out an eerie cry, then soared upward and was soon hidden behind a billowy cloud.

Janelle turned her eyes to her husband and found him gazing at her. In his expression she saw a mixture of pride and concern for her and their tiny daughter.

To assure him that things were all right, Janelle gave him a warm smile and a wave.

Satisfied enough, Fire Cloud resumed poling through the wild rice plants that were thicker and heavier in the water this year than in any of the years past.

Even now, much rice lay drying in the sun or was being parched over a fire in deep vats. The outer husks had been removed by tramping them in a skin-lined pit. Then the rice was winnowed with the aid of a birchbark tray.

When this was all done, and the harvest was a great success, the Chippewa people would hold the ceremony of the First Fruit to thank *Kitchi-Manitou*. The wild rice was important to the Chippewa both as a food, which they prized, and as a cash crop, which they sold to whites.

Shrill laughter and squeals behind her caused Janelle to turn and watch the children who were too young to participate in the harvest.

They were playing games. This time it was hide-and-seek.

Janelle watched her children, all sons, scamper into the outer fringes of the forest to hide, while a pretty little girl their same age counted down to the number one and then ran to find those who were hiding.

Janelle sighed as she gazed up at the trees. It was another autumn. The colors this year were even more vibrant than those before. It was as though God had sprinkled paint of various colors through the trees, turning them into a vibrant patchwork.

One by one, leaves would drift down from a limb, occasionally blowing over into the river and settling in it like a miniature colorful canoe.

Squirrels were everywhere, gathering acorns and hickory nuts to hide for when the snows covered the ground in a thick, deep blanket of white.

The sudden tiny whimpering of her daughter quickly drew Janelle's attention.

Easing up from the pallet, she went to the wigwam where a low fire burned in the center of the lodge. Not far from it sat the cradle that Fire Cloud had made for his daughter with his own hands.

Janelle and Fire Cloud's little princess lay on a mattress made of down from cattail plants and a luxurious rabbit-fur blanket woven from long strips of cottontail pelts.

"Sweet child," Janelle murmured as she gently swept the blanket-wrapped baby up from the cradle, her face all that was exposed to Janelle's feasting eyes.

A daughter made partly in her image, and partly in her husband's. She had her father's copper skin but her mother's azure eyes and tiny curls of golden hair.

Her lashes were thick and long and lay closed over her cheek like beautiful veils.

"My tiny, precious child," Janelle whispered as she sat down on pelts close to the fire.

She cradled her daughter against her as she raised

a hand and slowly parted her dress where she had purposely left a slit for easy breast feeding.

Her breast now exposed and ready, Janelle's heart swelled with joy as she placed her daughter's tiny lips to the nipple.

"Feed, my darling," Janelle whispered, her eyes brimming with tears of happiness as she felt her body giving her child nourishment. "One day you will feed your loved one from *your* breast, for, my darling daughter, you will grow up and be the most beautiful wife any warrior could ask for."

Hearing her child's contented suckling sounds, her tiny fingers kneading Janelle's breast as she fed from it, Janelle gazed into the fire and became lost in thought.

She remembered their first day at the Chippewa village, how so many were exuberant to see Fire Cloud again, especially his grandfather, Chief Sitting Fox.

Chief Sitting Fox had recognized Fire Cloud right away. He had said that Fire Cloud was an exact replica of his father.

Janelle would never forget Chief Sitting Fox's joy at seeing his grandson after having missed him for too many years.

But Chief Sitting Fox had said that he had known that Fire Cloud would come home to be with his true people, that he had prayed every night for his return.

Chief Sitting Fox had said that he had kept Fire Cloud alive in everyone's minds and hearts so that when he *did* return home, he could be accepted as the next chief after his grandfather. That was the way it should have been had Fire Cloud not courageously left the village with his banished mother. Chief Sitting Fox had made sure that his courage was never forgotten.

Fire Cloud had been accepted by his people, but not as quickly as his grandfather had hoped. Because of his lengthy absence living with the Chippewa's avowed enemy, the Lakota, some had spoken against Fire Cloud in council.

Others had accepted him.

In time after they grew to know Fire Cloud and met with him in many councils, he was accepted as a true, noble man and a born leader.

He had been chief now for a full year, for Chief Sitting Fox had passed on to the other side at that time. No one had voted against Fire Cloud. He was admired by everyone. He was the true grandson of their beloved fallen chief, a grandson who filled his grandfather's moccasins and walked tall in his shadow.

"My wife, how is our little Blue Swallow?" Fire Cloud asked, drawing Janelle from her thoughts. She saw that he was not alone. All of their children were in the wigwam, just now sitting in a circle around the fire as they watched their tiny sister with pride and happiness.

"She has never been as hungry," Janelle said, laughing softly at the tiny lips still drawing more nourishment from her body.

"It is the wild rice harvest that has made her hungry," Fire Cloud said, moving to his haunches before Janelle, his eyes feasting on his wife's pretty face.

"Do you not smell the rice parching over the fire? We will have much for our meals through the long winter."

"I can see your happiness," Janelle said, reaching with her free hand to smooth some locks of black hair back from Fire Cloud's eyes.

"My woman, it is a time of much rejoicing," Fire Cloud said, now settling down beside Janelle, his eyes moving from child to child.

Cloud Walker, Swift Bear, Bright Arrow, and Little Buffalo.

Standing next to one other, they were almost like stair steps, for they had been born one year apart. The years after that Janelle had tried, and failed, to have the daughter she had craved after four sons.

"*Ay-uh*, we have much to rejoice over," Janelle said, smiling to herself when she recalled that first time she had seen Fire Cloud. When their eyes had met she had known it was for a purpose. It had just taken longer than she would have wished to know what that purpose was.

But that was yesterday.

And this is today, she thought happily to herself.

She was blissfully happy with her husband and children. She loved being a part of the Chippewa people's lives.

She was more Chippewa now than white.

Even from the moment she clung to her own mother's breast, Fire Cloud and his people were her destiny.

She was Fire Cloud's!

"It is now time for ball play!" Cloud Walker said,

bringing Janelle's thoughts back to the present. "*Gee-mah-mah*, can you come out and watch?"

"As soon as your sister is fed and asleep again in her cradle," Janelle said, smiling from child to child as she saw their excitement at the mention of ball play. "But you go on now. Prepare yourselves for the game. But, little ones, be careful. The game can sometimes be too rough."

"Not too rough for the sons of our people's chief!" Cloud Walker boasted as he stood and puffed out his tiny, copper chest above the waistband of his breechclout.

They had asked to wear their breechclouts this one last time before the cooler breezes called for a full set of buckskins. They all felt freer in their breechclouts.

"I shall go out and make certain the ball play does not get out of hand," Fire Cloud said, then leaned over and brushed a kiss across Janelle's lips before rising to his feet.

She smiled into his eyes, then watched him and her sons leave the wigwam.

She listened to their excited voices as they prepared for the game. She knew the game well and could envision what the children would be doing about now—painting their faces. She had been told that the wood of a tree that had been struck by lightning had mysterious properties. In preparing the ball players for the game, the medicine man of their village sometimes burned splinters of this wood to coal. He gave them to the ball players to paint themselves with so that they might be able to strike their opponents with all the force of a thunderbolt.

Upon first learning about this particular ritual, Janelle had quickly thought of something else that could be as useful. She had brought a bag of ash from the meteorite to Minnesota and suggested to her sons that they wear it when they played.

The first time they wore this ash they won the ball game, and had since, time and again.

But worried that their winning might be construed as unfair, she had shared this knowledge with all of the ball players.

Now each boy wore the same meteorite ash. Their competitors were fierce and challenging.

"I knew the meteorite would have to have some use for someone," Janelle whispered, smiling as she placed her daughter back in her cradle.

The meteorite still lay on the very earth it had fallen upon those ten years ago.

Since her father's death, no other white people had shown interest in the meteorite. To them, it was just something for the Lakota to walk around. It was nothing to them now but a lump of fallen rock.

"*Gee-mah-mah*, the game begins!" Cloud Walker shouted from outside the wigwam. "Come, *gee-mah-mah*. See your sons play!"

"Your *gee-mah-mah* is coming," Janelle said back to him.

She stepped outside and found Fire Cloud waiting for her. He took her hand and led her to a pallet of furs.

She sat down with him and watched as the game began, her sons becoming as fierce as they could at their young ages. Their moccasined feet kicked at the ball, some falling and rolling along the ground when another young brave purposely tripped him.

Janelle gasped, then felt the reassurance of her husband's arm as he slid it around her waist. "Let your sons be young braves today, not sons," Fire Cloud suggested softly.

Janelle turned smiling eyes up at him. "Do you know how soon they will be warriors?" she said, hating to think about the quick passage of time. One day she would wake up and realize that she was old and a grandmother!

"*Ay-uh*, and we will be so *me-nah-day-nee-no*—proud," Fire Cloud said.

He rose from the pelts and took her hands in his. "Come," he said softly. "Our sons will not even realize we are gone."

He led her back inside their wigwam and lowered the entrance flat, tying it closed so that they could not be interrupted.

Without words, they undressed each other.

Although it was too soon for her to make love after having her daughter, she could at least feel the wonders of her husband's hands and lips on her naked body.

"Let me shower my love upon you, my *gee-wee-oo*," Fire Cloud said, gently kissing her body as she moved her own hands over his.

Janelle sighed with joyous contentment.

Fire Cloud wrapped his arms around her and brought her body up next to his. His lips came to hers in a soft, sweet kiss, their bodies awaiting the promise of all their tomorrows.

They did have forever, for theirs was a love everlasting.

Ay-uh—the past was past.

Hetchetu-aloh—it was finished!

Dear Reader:

I hope you enjoyed reading *Fire Cloud*. The next book in my Signet Indian Series is *Spirit Warrior* about the Shoshone Indians. This is an exciting, mystical story filled with much emotion, mystery, passion, and devoted love. I hope you will read it and enjoy it.

For those of you who are collecting my Indian books and want to read more about them and my fan club, please send a self-addressed stamped envelope to:

> Cassie Edwards
> 6709 N. Country Club Road
> Mattoon, IL 61938

or check my Web page on the Internet at

> www.cassieedwards.com.

Thank you all for your support of my books. I truly appreciate it.

Always,

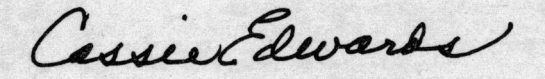

Cassie Edwards

In celebration of the publication of

FIRE CLOUD
by Cassie Edwards

ENTER FOR THE CHANCE TO WIN
a stunning Native American-design jewelry set, hand-picked by author Cassie Edwards!

No Purchase Necessary
Open only to U.S. residents aged 18 and up

One Grand Prize winner will receive a beautiful sterling silver and lapis jewelry set, including a necklace, bracelet, and earrings. And Cassie Edwards herself will call the winner to congratulate them!
Five runners-up will each receive an autographed copy of FIRE CLOUD.

Enter for the chance to win either by visiting the Penguin Putnam Inc. web site at www.penguinputnam.com or by sending a postcard with your name, address, telephone number, e-mail address, and an indication as to whether or not you wish to receive information in the future via e-mail about other great romance books to:

Penguin Putnam Inc.
NAL Advertising/Promo Dept. (EH/Fire Cloud)
375 Hudson Street
New York, NY 10014.

All hard copy entries must be postmarked by December 10, 2001 and received by December 17, 2001. All e-mail entries must be received by December 10, 2001, 12:00 p.m. EST. Limit one entry per person.

Official Rules for the FIRE CLOUD SWEEPSTAKES

NO PURCHASE NECESSARY.
Open only to U.S. residents aged 18 and up.

How to Enter:
    1. To enter online simply indicate your full name, address, phone number, e-mail address (if you have one), and indicate whether or not you wish to receive future e-mails about other romance books. Entries may be sent either online or by regular mail. To enter by regular mail, print or type the required information and send your entry to Penguin Putnam Inc., NAL Advertising/Promo Dept. (EH/Fire Cloud), 375 Hudson Street, New York, NY 10014. All hard copy entries must be
postmarked by December 10, 2001 and received by December 17, 2001. All e-mail entries must be received by December 10, 12:00 p.m. EST. Limit one entry per person.

    2. Entries are void if they are in whole or in part illegible, incomplete

or damaged. No responsibility is assumed for late, lost, damaged, incomplete, illegible, postage due or misdirected mail or entries.

3. Penguin Putnam Inc. ("Sponsor") and its parent and subsidiaries are not responsible for technical, hardware, software or telephone malfunctions of any kind, lost or unavailable network connections, or failed, incorrect, incomplete, inaccurate, garbled or delayed electronic communications caused by the sender, or by any of the equipment or programming associated with or utilized in this Sweepstakes which may limit the ability to play or participate, or by any human error which may occur in the processing of the entries in this Sweepstakes. If for any reason the online portion of the Sweepstakes is not capable of being conducted as described in these rules, Sponsor shall have the right to cancel, terminate, modify or suspend the Sweepstakes. In the event of a dispute over the identity of an online entrant, entry will be deemed submitted by the authorized holder of the e-mail account.

Winners:

1. 1 Grand Prize winner and 5 runner-up winners will be selected from all eligible entries received by the entry date, in a random drawing held on or about January 2, 2002 by Sponsor.

2. Winners will be notified by mail and e-mail (if possible). Grand Prize winner will receive a congratulatory telephone call from author Cassie Edwards. The odds of winning depend on the number of entries received.

Prizes:

1. One Grand Prize winner will receive a sterling silver and lapis jewelry set (earrings, necklace, and bracelet) – Approximate Retail Value ("ARV") $139.00 for the set of all three items. Five runner-up winners will each receive an autographed copy of FIRE CLOUD – Approximate Retail Value ("ARV") $10.00 each.

2. There is a limit of one prize per person.

3. In the event that there is an insufficient number of entries Sponsor reserves the right not to award the prizes.

Eligibility:

This Sweepstakes is open to residents of the U.S. aged 18 or older. Employees and members of their immediate families living in the same household of Sponsor, its parent, and subsidiaries are not eligible to enter. Void where prohibited by law.

General:

1. No cash substitution, transfers or assignments of prizes allowed. In event of unavailability, sponsor may substitute a prize of equal or greater value.

2. All expenses, including taxes, (if any) on receipt and use of prizes are the sole responsibility of the winners.

3. Winners may be required to execute an affidavit of eligibility and release and, if so, the affidavit must be returned within fourteen days of notification or another winner will be selected.

4. By accepting a prize the winner grants to the Sponsor the right to use his/her name, likeness, hometown and biographical information in advertising and promotion materials, including posting on the Sponsor's web site, without further compensation or permission, except where prohibited by law.

5. By accepting a prize, winner releases Sponsor, its parent and subsidiaries from any and all liability for any loss, harm, injuries, damages, cost or expense arising out of participation in this Sweepstakes or the acceptance, use or misuse the prize.

Winners' List:

For a list of prize winners, send a self-addressed, stamped envelope by January 15, 2002 to: Penguin Putnam Inc., NAL Advertising/Promo Dept. (EH/Fire Cloud), 375 Hudson Street, New York, NY 10014.